FARM GIRL
by Linda Shertzer

D1711354

Farm Girl

Linda Shertzer

JOVE BOOKS, NEW YORK

FARM GIRL

A Jove Book / published by arrangement with
the author

PRINTING HISTORY
Jove edition / July 1997

The Putnam Berkley World Wide Web site address is
http://www.berkley.com

ISBN: 0-515-12106-1

A JOVE BOOK®
Jove Books are published by The Berkley Publishing Group,
200 Madison Avenue, New York, New York 10016.
JOVE and the "J" design are trademarks
belonging to Jove Publications, Inc.

PRINTED IN THE UNITED STATES OF AMERICA

10 9 8 7 6 5 4 3 2 1

1

COTTONWOOD, KANSAS, 1866

"*EXCUSE ME, MA'AM.*"

Callie Jackson wiped away her tears and looked up. The stranger held his battered hat in front of him in a gesture of submission, but there was something about the set of the man's broad shoulders and squared chin that made her doubt he would ever be completely subservient to anyone.

"It appears I've come at an inconvenient time."

"You certainly have!" Olive Luckhardt shot back.

Before Callie could say a thing, the ladies of the Cottonwood Methodist Ladies' Evangelical, Temperance, and Missionary Soul-Saving Spiritual Aid and Comfort Bible Society, who had been hovering protectively around her ever since Aunt Samuela had died, now closed ranks.

Her hands resting on her broad hips, Olive demanded, "Can't you see there's just been a funeral here?"

He surveyed the room.

"A man would have to be blind or very stupid not to

notice that most of the folks here are wearing some amount of black, depending on how close"—he glanced at Olive's stark outfit—"or how much obligation they felt toward the deceased."

Olive gave a haughty snort and crossed her plump arms as much as she could over her ample chest.

The man turned back to Callie. "Please accept my condolences, ma'am. Who passed away?"

"My aunt. She . . . she raised me." Somehow she couldn't bring herself to use the phrase "she was like a mother to me" when her aunt had never, ever made her feel that was so.

"I'm sorry to disturb you, but I just rode into town, so I couldn't have had any idea." He gestured toward the numerous buggies and buckboards assembled outside, visible through the open window. "I only stopped by this house because it looked as if, with so many people here, I'd stand a good chance of somebody offering me a job."

"You should be ashamed of yourself, young man. Have you no respect for the dead or sympathy for the living?" Olive demanded haughtily.

"Imagine! Trying to conduct business at a funeral!" Widow Marsden declared.

"Now show a little respect—and go away," Olive asserted.

"There's no need to bother Miss Jackson now." Mildred Preston, as usual, took charge of the confrontation. The rest of the ladies lined up in battle formation around her. "There'll be plenty of opportunity to bother her tomorrow."

"Yes, indeed. You might stand a better chance of being hired tomorrow if, right now, you just went on your way," Miss Jemima Finchcroft gently suggested, fluttering her thin fingers nervously in front of her ruffled bodice.

Callie reached out to still the little old maiden lady's hands. But Miss Jemima continued to throw curious glances at the stranger.

Callie could hardly blame her. The man certainly was

worth watching, even if he did look awful skinny in his ill-fitting clothes.

He was of about average height. His hands looked callused and sinewy holding his battered hat. Long hours in the sun had burnished the planes of his angular face and bleached the top of his brown hair. His pale blue eyes shone in his tanned face as if they held an inner light of their own.

Callie forcibly pulled herself away from dwelling too long on the details of his appearance. Aunt Samuela had reminded her often enough that being overly concerned with mere outward appearance was vanity and only gave a person leanings to unwarranted frivolity and profligate spending—not to mention a propensity to succumb to the dangerous, forbidden, and sinful temptations of the flesh.

"I wouldn't ordinarily be so rude, Miss Jackson," the stranger continued, "but, well, I'm pretty desperate."

The ladies of the Society closed even tighter ranks about her.

But there was an expression of honesty in the man's eyes that shattered Callie's reserve and made her cast aside her customary caution.

After all, she argued with herself, *what mortal sin or unnecessary expense could come from just listening to him?*

"Who are you then, mister?" she asked. "And what is it that makes you so desperate?"

"My name's Harden Daniels," he pronounced proudly. Then his tanned face broke into a mischievous grin. "I could tell you a sad tale of being the sole support of an invalid widowed mother or a passel of orphaned brothers and sisters."

"I suppose you could."

"But the truth is, ma'am, for some unaccountable reason, I've always been right partial to keeping body and soul together. Lately, I've found myself getting mighty hungry."

Callie decided not to smile, no matter how clever he might be. Whimsy didn't suit a staunch Christian soldier— at least, that's what Aunt Samuela always maintained. But it was awfully difficult not to return this man's contagious grin.

"I need to work so I can eat. That's why I'm desperate."

From the looks of him, she could believe it. But she shook her head. "I'm very sorry. There's really nothing—"

"I'm a sober, honest, God-fearing man. I don't use tobacco or foul language. I'm not prone to gambling. I can read and cipher. I'm a pretty fair farmhand. I'm not averse to tackling any chore. And, if I do say so myself, I'm pretty quick to learn new jobs, too."

She still shook her head. "I'm sure you are, Mr. Daniels. However, we—" With a deep sigh, she corrected herself. "*I* already have four reliable farmhands. Perhaps someone else—"

"With so many men returning from the war, there aren't too many jobs around here," he reminded her with a small grimace. "Or anywhere else, for that matter."

"I understand. And I'm sorry, but there's really nothing I can do for you."

"I don't need to be paid much."

"That's not the point." She didn't see any need to tell him Aunt Samuela hadn't paid the farmhands much, anyway.

"I don't eat much," he persisted.

"That's hardly a problem on a farm."

"I don't take up much room on a bunk."

"I . . . I'm not concerned about that," she replied. She really didn't want to think about Mr. Daniels lying on any bed.

"I'm real reliable. I won't let you down."

"You should add unwavering tenacity to your list of good qualities."

He grinned and reached up to rub the back of his neck. "I would've thought persistence would count in my favor."

"Only up to a point."

Mildred suddenly stepped between them.

"Now, see here, Mr. Daniels. We've had about enough of this nonsense," she scolded. "Miss Jackson—why, we've *all* told you very plainly there's no work for you here. Now, move along before we're forced to call for the sheriff." She surveyed the crowd, as if already searching for the law.

Again, ignoring everyone else, Mr. Daniels addressed only Callie. "Are you going to call the sheriff, ma'am?"

"I hope you won't make that necessary. But there still isn't anything I can do for you."

The man opened his mouth again, no doubt to tell her more of his sterling qualities. But before he could actually say anything, Mildred said forcefully, "Good-bye, Mr. Daniels."

"Miss Jackson—"

Mildred was right. She had to follow her example. "Good-bye, Mr. Daniels," Callie repeated.

"Thanks for your time, anyway, ma'am." He shrugged and turned away.

"That was the proper thing to do, Callie," Olive reassured her with a little pat on the shoulder.

"Your aunt would've approved," Widow Marsden told her.

Yes, Callie thought with unaccountable disappointment. She was very sure her cold, domineering aunt certainly would have sent the tall stranger on his way, empty-handed.

But as she watched Mr. Daniels stride toward the doorway, she couldn't help notice that his shoulders were set with just as much pride and assurance in his rejection as they'd been when he'd still had hopes for a job. A man like him would be a good worker—would be good to have around, no matter what. It really was a shame to send him away, but what else could she do?

All of a sudden, Callie had the most unusual urge to change her mind.

No, she couldn't! She shouldn't!

She supposed she could always blame her confusion on her aunt's sudden passing and on being left on her own for the first time in her life. She knew Aunt Samuela most certainly would *not* have approved of what she was about to do.

But she had to do it anyway.

"Mr. Daniels, wait!"

He stopped and slowly turned around.

All about her, Callie heard the ladies of the Society draw in a collective, surprised gasp. She also realized that just about everyone else had also stopped their conversations, and were apparently waiting with bated breath for her to continue.

"Please don't go away yet."

"Then you do have a job for me?"

"No. But you're certainly welcome to stay for a meal." Feeding this destitute drifter was the least she could do for him.

She gestured toward the dining room, but he made no effort to move.

"Miss Jackson, I'm a proud man who doesn't take handouts. I prefer to work for what I get."

"Another point in your favor?"

"I always thought so. But apparently no one around here does."

Callie tried to hide the little twinge her conscience gave her.

"However, seeing as how times have gotten a bit hard, and seeing as how my ma always taught me not to waste food, I do believe I'll take you up on your offer."

Callie felt a little wave of relief eddy around her.

"Just hang your hat by the door and help yourself."

"Thank you, Miss Jackson."

Quickly fluttering to his side, Miss Jemima eagerly offered, "I'd be happy to show you where everything is."

Harden turned to the little lady. "Thank you, too, Miss . . . ?"

"Miss Finchcroft," she replied with a little giggle. "But all my friends call me Jemima."

Harden noted that everyone resumed their own meals and

conversations, obviously having lost interest in a solved problem. Miss Jemima slipped her hand into the crook of his arm and began guiding him toward the generous spread offered on the dining room table.

"Well, Miss Jemima, I certainly appreciate your kind hospitality to a poor, hungry man."

"Oh, pshaw. 'Tweren't nothing. There's plenty here to share." She handed him a plate.

It felt smooth and cool in his hands. How long had it been, he thought with regret, since he'd eaten from real china instead of from a tin plate or even a tin can?

He examined the white plate. It was perfectly plain. Just like this house with its bare wooden floors, stark furnishings, and plain muslin curtains. Just like Miss Jackson herself.

He glanced back to where she was sitting in a cushionless straight-backed chair placed against the wall, surrounded by a Praetorian guard of stern-faced matrons and spinsters.

She wore a baggy black dress that was so rusty and out of fashion, it had probably been her late aunt's when she was just a girl. Why would she pin her auburn hair back from her face in such a severe bun? Everything around her, everything she did, made her look as plain as dirt and dull as dishwater.

What was her late aunt like, Harden wondered, to have lived such a spartan life and to have forced it on her niece? Or did this lusterless lady also live this life by choice?

"Squirrel stew," Miss Jemima explained as she piled a spoonful onto his plate.

"Sounds . . . tasty."

He didn't feel all that hungry anymore, but eating something—or maybe just pretending to eat some of these concoctions—would at least give him an excuse to hang around here a little longer. Do a little reconnoitering, he figured.

If only he could manage to convince Miss Jackson to hire

him. His sources had told him the Jackson farm was the nearest neighbor to Otis Fielding's.

Of course, they'd also told him the place was run by a spinster and her niece. His sources were usually pretty reliable, even if they hadn't been able to warn him about the ladies' ages or stern personalities, or the fact that one of them would up and die.

It didn't matter. He *had* to get a job here. None of the other farms suited his purpose.

"Gopher goulash," Miss Jemima described, putting a tiny serving onto his plate. Leaning closer, she whispered, "Some of them foreigners who settled a bit north of town brought it. I'm not so sure about their heathen cooking."

As they moved along the heavily laden table, Harden could feel the curious gazes of the townspeople studying him. Did they regard him as a foreigner and a heathen? he wondered.

Fielding ought to be here today, too, since he was their nearest neighbor. Harden looked around but so far hadn't been able to spot anyone who fit the description his sources had supplied him with. Right now, maybe that was just as well. He didn't want to show his hand too soon and spoil the plan.

"Pigeon pie. Roasted venison haunch. Corn bread. Coleslaw. Apple cobbler. Huckleberry pie," Miss Jemima urged as she spooned individual helpings onto his plate. "And let's not forget the possum casserole."

"Did . . . did you make it?" he asked and managed to refrain from retching. That was about the only polite thing he could think to say about possum casserole in the presence of a lady of Miss Jemima's delicate sensibilities.

"Oh, pshaw, no."

"Was it made by another one of those heathen foreigners?" he asked her with a little wink.

"Oh, no, no," she replied with a giggle. Then she drew her lips into a tight knot. "But it might as well be. It's the

Widow Marsden's. I swear, I think that's the only thing that woman knows how to cook. That's mainly because Deke—that's her good-for-nothing son—is too lazy to raise their own food, so he just hunts. Why, that woman wouldn't know what to do with a piece of civilized meat."

"But what did you contribute to this feast, Miss Jemima?"

"I made the potato salad—in the bowl with the red and yellow flowers." Her birdlike fingers fluttered outward to indicate the correct bowl. Then she leaned a little closer to him and whispered confidentially, "It's much better than Miss Silesky's—that stuff in the blue bowl." Her thin lip curled in disdain.

"Another heathen foreigner?" he asked with a grin.

"Oh, no. She's a nice Christian lady—just not a very good cook."

"I think I'd rather trust you. Give me two helpings of yours, please." He leaned even closer and whispered, "I'm sure, if a lady as sweet as you made it, it'll be the best I ever tasted."

Miss Jemima held her hand in front of her face, blushed and giggled, and did just about everything but faint dead away on the spot.

"I think my plate's pretty full. Why don't we move along to a place by a window," Harden suggested, "and give everyone else a chance to get at all this wonderful food?"

"Oh, yes, indeed," Miss Jemima agreed, fanning herself vigorously with her hand.

Harden wasn't familiar with the layout of the rest of the house, but he could easily see how to get back to where Miss Jackson was sitting. Her auburn hair acted like a bright beacon in the sea of black that surrounded her. It was important that he get near her. It was very important that he convince her to hire him.

Slowly but inexorably, he continued to move through the crowd, with Miss Jemima trailing faithfully behind him.

"Where are you heading, Mr. Daniels?" Miss Jemima asked.

"I figure we ought to be able to catch a good breeze by that window." He casually indicated the one right next to where Miss Jackson was sitting, surrounded by her bodyguard of staunch church ladies.

"No, no." Miss Jemima giggled. "I mean, what's your final destination?"

"Oh, out West . . . here and there . . . around and about. I guess I don't have a real destination." That was probably what most people would expect to hear from a drifter.

He stopped at the window. He was relieved that none of them gave any sign that they noted his presence. Apparently, they believed gentle Miss Jemima was a competent enough guard to keep him out of trouble and out of their hair.

"Where are you from, Mr. Daniels?" Miss Jemima asked.

"I was born in Virginia," he replied.

He took a forkful of potato salad. "My goodness, this *is* the best I've ever tasted!"

After several more ravenously swallowed forkfuls, accompanied by expressions of delight, Harden turned back to Miss Jemima.

"But enough about my uneventful life. My ma always taught me it was extremely ungentlemanly to bore a lovely lady such as yourself with dull personal details."

"Oh, a gentleman like you could *never* be boring, Mr. Daniels!" Miss Jemima protested, fluttering her hands in front of her again.

"Oh, you're just being polite. Why don't you tell me about yourself instead? Have you lived in Cottonwood long? I do believe I detect a lovely Southern drawl," he teased with a bold wink.

"Do you?"

Miss Jemima's pale blue eyes were misty with her

immediate infatuation. Harden figured he should be grateful that, if nature hadn't been able to bless him with fame and fortune, she'd at least been able to endow him with some charm. In his line of work, that probably served him better, anyway.

"Oh, my, yes. Yes, I guess you do. My family and I left our farm on the outskirts of Atlanta, Georgia, and came to Kansas in the summer of 1843."

Harden pretended intense interest in Miss Jemima's giggling chatter, all the while picking over the contents of his plate. The little lady might be a bit scatterbrained, but he had to admit her potato salad was the best-tasting thing on his plate.

However, his true attention was devoted to what the ladies of the Society were saying to Miss Jackson, and to what she replied to them.

"Giving that poor drifter a handout was certainly a kind thing to do, Callie," the lady who seemed to be in charge told her.

So her given name was Callie, Harden noted. Not that it made any difference. Oh the job, of course, he'd be sure always to call her Miss Jackson.

"On the other hand," the lady in charge continued, "I really can't say as I completely approve of your gesture, no matter how well-intentioned." She crossed her arms tightly over her chest.

"Mildred," Callie chided. "I could hardly send the poor man away hungry."

"But do you really think that was wise?" The plump lady who had scolded him looked to the lady in charge for corroboration. Her thick eyebrows were drawn into a frown. "I mean, he might steal—"

"Steal what, Olive?" Callie asked with a bitter little laugh. "The heirloom silver tea service? The diamond tiara? Aunt Samuela never had any use for such vain, foolish ornamentations."

"Well, still . . . I mean . . . Your aunt wouldn't have been none too pleased to see the likes of him in this house," Olive reminded her.

"Aunt Samuela never allowed any of the farmhands in the house, anyway," Callie commented.

"Of course not—and with good reason. He's just a solitary, irresponsible drifter," Olive said. "A man who only stops in one place just long enough to make enough money to move on to someplace else."

"That may be," Callie agreed, "but we shouldn't judge him ill just because he hasn't been as blessed in his circumstances as we have."

He heard the ladies grudgingly grumble and grunt their agreement.

"Remember, 'Be not forgetful to entertain strangers,'" Callie quoted, "'for thereby some have entertained angels unawares.'"

Olive snorted. "He doesn't look like much of an angel to me."

Another lady leaned closer and murmured, "He does look sort of tarnished."

"Downright fallen, if you ask me," a pinch-faced woman remarked.

"No, no. Callie's right, you know," Mildred conceded reluctantly. "A little Christian charity and plain, old-fashioned hospitality never hurt anyone."

Olive heaved a deep sigh. "Well, I suppose, if you say so."

"We should be grateful to Callie for reminding us of our duty," Mildred said.

"Oh, yes, indeed," all the other ladies agreed.

"Callie, sometimes you show a wisdom beyond your years," Mildred said. "However, I know your aunt was very concerned about you. Why, only last week, at the monthly meeting of the Society, she had a very serious discussion with all of us"—she nodded her head, indicating the assembled membership—"regarding your future."

"My future?"

"Samuela knew that this world is no place for a young lady alone," Mildred continued. "She also knew she'd raised you very sheltered from the ways of the world. Therefore, she made certain stipulations to your inheritance."

Harden's interest in this conversation sharpened. This could have some bearing on his obtaining work here.

"What are those . . . stipulations?" Callie asked.

Harden could hear a definite quaver in her soft voice. It didn't have the expected sound of grief, but held the unmistakable ring of fear and uncertainty.

"As you know, your aunt was the greatly esteemed founder and president emeritus of the Cottonwood Methodist Ladies' Evangelical, Temperance, and Missionary Soul-Saving Spiritual Aid and Comfort Bible Society," Mildred told her.

"Yes, I know."

"And you also know that your aunt placed a great deal of trust and confidence in the membership."

"I'm sure she did," Callie said quietly.

The ladies nodded, confirming Mildred's assertions.

"And, even though you're twenty-two years old, Samuela felt that your youth and inexperience might prevent you from seeing your choices with clarity and from making your decisions with a certain perspective granted only by the advance of years."

"I . . . I still have a place to live, don't I?" Callie asked cautiously.

"Of course, my dear."

"I now own the farm, don't I?"

"Of course—on one condition."

Harden stopped chewing—he almost stopped breathing—so that nothing would interfere with his being able to hear what the lady had to say. Even Miss Jemima had stopped recounting her own life story and was shamelessly eavesdropping.

Very slowly Callie asked, "What's the condition?"

From the corner of his eye, Harden watched Mildred strike an imposing stance, as if preparing to make a momentous announcement. He almost expected some of the other ladies to give out with a loud drum roll and trumpet fanfare.

"As president of the Cottonwood Methodist Ladies' Evangelical, Temperance, and Missionary Soul-Saving Spiritual Aid and Comfort Bible Society," Mildred proclaimed, "it is my duty to inform you that, in accordance with Samuela Lucretia Jackson's last will and testament, you will be able to keep the farm *only* if you continue to live a moral, upright, sober, and prudent life, just as your aunt did."

Callie appeared to give a little sigh of relief. "That's not a problem. I've *always* tried to be moral, upright, sober, and prudent."

"Under your aunt's firm and watchful guidance," Mildred reminded her.

Harden watched Callie try to give her chin a proud lift. But he recognized very well the drooping resignation in her shoulders that came with perpetual, strict supervision, and a constant reminder of one's shortcomings.

"You know how she kept a real eagle eye on everything you did," Olive added.

"How she watched everything *everybody* did," another amended.

"Therefore," Mildred announced, "your aunt appointed the Society the sole arbiter of your behavior."

Callie gave an audible gulp. "Arbiter? Of my behavior?"

Harden watched Mildred nod.

"But I don't have any behavior!" Callie protested. "I work on the farm and go to church. There's very little chance for wrongdoing at either location."

Mildred shrugged. "Be that as it may, we've made a solemn promise to Samuela that we can't just simply ignore."

Callie drew in an audible breath. Harden waited for her reply.

At last, very slowly and very quietly, she asked, "What happens if you all decide I'm not living up to my aunt's—or your—expectations?"

2

"*You'll be disinherited*," Mildred responded without a blink of hesitation or even a hint of sympathy.

None of the other ladies of the Society seemed to be the least bit sympathetic, either.

Was it something in the water around here, Harden wondered, that made all the women so hard and plain? What a shame Miss Jackson appeared to have been drinking far too much of it.

"The farm will be sold," Mildred continued her dismal threat, "and the proceeds distributed to a worthy missionary charity under the supervision of the ladies of the Society."

This Aunt Samuela must have been hard as nails and tough as old jerky, Harden decided, right down to the bottom of her soul, to do something like this to her own niece.

Callie was silent again, apparently thinking over this shocking news. Finally, in a very small voice, she asked,

"How long will you be keeping account of my behavior? Forever?"

"Apparently."

Callie hung her head in resignation.

Mildred gave a deep sigh and seemed to drop her authoritative stance.

"Well, quite frankly, Callie," she admitted, "when we ladies of the Society promised Samuela we would look after you, this is not exactly what we had in mind."

"It's not?"

"Of course not!"

Callie looked up again. Harden thought he detected just a bit more hope in her bright green eyes.

The vibrant color gave him a little jolt. *How could any woman with eyes and hair those colors look so abysmally plain otherwise?* he marveled. Then he returned his attention to what the ladies were saying. He was only here because he had a job to do. It didn't matter one bit what his boss looked like, just as long as the job got done.

"In the first place, we never expected Samuela would die so soon," Mildred told Callie.

Harden had the feeling it had come as a bit of a surprise to Aunt Samuela, too.

"We never supposed we'd have to be responsible for you for so long a time," Mildred continued. "In the second place, we can't devote all of our time to monitoring your behavior. After all, we ladies of the Society have homes of our own, families and friends—and other interests besides you."

Harden could imagine that just about everything in town was a matter of interest to these ladies, with or without a promise or a last will and testament from someone obligating them to do it.

"Then why don't you just let me be?" Callie pleaded.

"Because a promise is a promise. And because . . . well, we *can't* just leave you on your own. Things are changing around here. There are more people moving into town and more strangers coming and going all the time. More chances for you to meet a man we don't know."

Mildred shot Harden a deep frown. He jammed another forkful of potato salad into his mouth and grinned back at her.

"A man who has no morals, no scruples!" She leaned forward and murmured ominously, "There'll be more opportunities for temptation."

"Oh, yes, indeed," the ladies agreed with varying degrees of dread and enthusiasm. "Lots and lots of temptations."

"We all know there's only one certain way to protect you from such temptations," Mildred said. She paused ominously, then pronounced, "We've decided you have to get married."

"Oh, no!" Callie protested.

"Oh, yes, indeed," the ladies agreed.

"Only by being married to a man who is as sober, thrifty, and hardworking as your late aunt was can we be assured that you'll live the exemplary life Samuela intended you to live," Mildred told her. "And that you'll get to keep your farm."

"Oh, no! Oh, no!"

Harden noted Callie's hands in her lap, twisting her handkerchief into a tight bundle.

"This is ridiculous!" she protested. "I won't get married just to keep a farm that's rightfully mine anyway—and to release you all from some silly promise you made without my knowledge. I don't see any need for any of this. I've been perfectly happy alone—"

"You weren't alone. You lived with your aunt," Mildred reminded her.

"But now you really are alone, dear," Olive pointed out.

Harden was sure Miss Jackson appreciated the reminder.

"Face facts, Callie," Mildred said sternly. "We ladies of the Society have had much more experience in matters like this than you've had. We've all discussed this matter at length and we've decided this is the only sensible solution."

"It's not! It can't be!" Callie protested. "It makes no sense at all."

Mildred reached out and patted Callie's shoulder.

"Trust us, dear. We know what's best for you. We're only doing this for your own good."

Callie hung her head and seemed to sink down into the very wood of the chair on which she sat.

"Then I'm afraid you're going to be watching out for me for a long, long time."

"Don't despair, dear," one of the ladies said sweetly through a forced smile. "You're still young. There's plenty of time to find a husband— even for you."

"But I'm not in love with any man I know. I don't think I could even bring myself to fall in love with one of them, not even to keep my farm."

"Who says you have to love him?" the pockmarked woman asked.

"You wouldn't be the first woman who married a man she didn't love just to keep a roof over her head," a sour-faced woman grumbled.

"Whether I'd fall in love with him or not doesn't matter, anyway. No one will ever marry me." Very quietly Callie finished, "I know very well that no man has ever found me attractive in the least."

Harden grudgingly acknowledged he would have to agree with her on that matter.

"There'll be plenty of men looking to marry you now that you own this farm," Olive remarked wryly.

Harden thought Callie was sinking deeper and deeper into her chair.

"Don't worry, Callie," Mildred comforted her. "We wouldn't allow you to marry just anyone. You're like a daughter to us. We'll find you a husband your aunt would have heartily approved of."

"That's what I'm afraid of," Callie murmured.

Watching the plain, mousy woman, Harden shook his head. *How in tarnation do they ever expect to do that?* he wondered. Even though he'd never met the woman, he couldn't imagine the man stern Aunt Samuela would have approved of. And what man would possibly want Callie Jackson?

In spite of the thin line of dark clouds gathering on the western horizon, the rooster crowed loudly from the top of the henhouse, announcing the new day.

Callie tossed a log into the firebox, heating up the cast-iron stove so she could make coffee and pancakes and warm up the leftover huckleberry pie for the farmhands' breakfast.

In the distance she heard the whistle of the train as it stopped briefly in Cottonwood.

"Well, what do you think, Prudence?" she asked the gray and white cat basking in the early-morning light on the windowsill. "Are they traveling east or west?"

Prudence just stretched and yawned.

"Oh, you never have an opinion," Callie playfully chided. "It doesn't matter, anyway. I know very well I'll never have the chance to ride a train."

With a little sigh, she turned back to work.

"I don't even know as I want to," she observed as she set the heavy cast-iron frying pan on top of the stove. "I mean, where would I go? I don't know anyone who lives anywhere else."

She paused as she reached for the heavy ceramic mixing bowl and a wooden spoon. No sense in pondering that now. She shook such useless thoughts from her head. More quickly, she started taking flour and baking powder out of the cupboard.

"I'm being silly, Prudence. How could I ever leave this farm? This is my home."

The whistle sounded again, then faded into the distance as the train pulled away from Cottonwood.

Callie heard the cows in the barn lowing their familiar

call to be milked. But this time they sounded very urgent. She frowned.

"Now what are they complaining about?"

She pulled aside the muslin curtain and glanced out the side window of the kitchen. The field was empty.

"My goodness, they must still be in the barn," she realized. "Why hasn't one of the farmhands let them out already?"

Wiping her hands on her apron, she hurried out the back door.

A big black dog and a little brown-and-white-spotted dog slipped out from under the porch and started jumping up and down and barking joyously.

"Hush, Frugal. Hush, Refrain. It's too late now," she scolded. "If something *is* wrong, you two should've been barking a lot sooner."

The two dogs whined an apology and trotted over to lie in the shade of the big oak in the backyard.

Prudence, obviously unconcerned with the constrictions of time, eventually joined Callie on the porch.

The pigs grunted and wallowed in their pens. The reddish brown hens with their little yellow chicks were already scratching in the run. The farmhands should have been in the yard outside the barn, hitching the mules to the plow. But no one was anywhere in sight, and there wasn't another human sound to be heard.

"My first real day trying to run this farm without Aunt Samuela, and already I'm having problems," she lamented.

Prudence flicked her white-tipped gray tail in obvious disdain of human foibles.

"What if they've gone to town—to a saloon—and gotten drunk?" Callie worried, pacing back and forth across the porch. "What if they're still there? How do I get them to come back?"

Prudence didn't have any suggestions or even a word to comfort.

"What if they're back, but they're just still sleeping?" she asked with a little more hope. "What if they're already awake and suffering from bad hangovers? What can I do except fill them up with hot, black coffee and send them back to work?"

Prudence meowed an apparent agreement with that solution.

Callie headed toward the bunkhouse. As she crossed the yard, she kept looking around, but still couldn't find a sign of the missing farmhands.

"Mack! Josh!" she called.

No answer.

"Pete! Willy!" she called as she knocked on the door.

Still there was no answer.

She yanked open the door. All the men were gone. Only a mouse scurried across the bare floor and back into its hole in the wall.

Callie looked around. There wasn't any shaving gear sitting by the washbasin. There weren't any shoes stuck under the bunks. There weren't any clothes hanging on the pegs by the door or lying around. The place was so empty, it looked as if they had even taken the trash with them.

Only the empty bunks and the inspirational samplers hanging on the walls that Aunt Samuela had made her stitch when she was very young, remained.

"Oh, it can't be!"

She dashed to the other side of the room.

"How can you be such a fool?" she chided herself. "Do you think when you get to the other side they'll all suddenly jump out and yell 'surprise'?"

She turned around. The room was still empty, and deathly quiet.

"They're gone for good," she told herself, "and you know it."

She could feel her shoulders gradually lowering with each step. She made her way to the center of the room and slumped into one of the hard, wooden chairs.

"They've left me all alone. But why?"

Then she noticed the unevenly folded piece of paper, held in place by a rock, lying on the table.

"They left me a note?" she murmured as she reached out a shaking hand and moved the rock.

A dire foreboding about what the note was going to say sent a cold shiver up her spine. She wasn't sure she wanted to read it after all, but she *had* to know what had happened to her farmhands—and why.

The thunk the rock made when she replaced it on the table echoed hollowly through the empty bunkhouse.

With shaking fingers, she smoothed as many wrinkles out of the paper as she could. Dark rings left by a coffee cup smudged the faint pencil markings and made the childish scrawl even more difficult to read.

"Dere Miss Callee . . ."

She sighed. They couldn't even spell her name right—or anything else for that matter. Well, she thought with small consolation, at least they'd had the courtesy to leave her a note.

She read further.

"It ain't yore fawlt. We bin planning this for a long time, but we wuz to frade of yore ant, so we all just wated till she wuz ded. We just can't stomik this place no moor. We gone west to make our forchoons. Bless you, Miss Callee."

"Bless me?" she repeated angrily. "If this is a blessing, I'd hate to see a curse!"

It was signed Mack, Josh, Willy, and Pete, but Callie knew Pete was the one who had written it because the other three couldn't read or write at all.

"How could they do this to me? What in heaven's name am I going to do now?" she demanded angrily as she crumpled the paper into a tiny ball. "Thunderation!" she shouted, and heaved it across the room.

She held her head in her hands, pressing hard against her forehead as if that could take away some of the pain pounding there. It did very little good. With each throb of her head, she could feel the tears welling in her eyes.

What did it matter whether she led a moral life or not? If she couldn't work the farm, it wouldn't be worth anything, and if the farm wasn't worth anything, she wouldn't be able to pay her bills and she'd lose it anyway. Then what would she do?

Sympathetic clucking noises from the doorway roused her. She looked up, blinking hard to clear away the tears.

"Bob!"

Bob in Pieces stood in the doorway, shaking his head.

"Good old reliable Bob!"

Now she wanted to weep with relief. If she hadn't felt so shaky and weak with shock and worry, she'd have run and embraced him.

Bob bent down and picked up the piece of paper Callie had tossed away. He smoothed it out with the thumb, index, and middle fingers remaining on his hand, and glanced over it. He shook his head, forlorn.

"Oh me, oh my, I knew this was coming."

"What? Did you know they were leaving? Why didn't you warn me?" Callie wailed.

"No, no, no," Bob protested as he limped into the bunkhouse. "I only knew those slimy polecats hated the ol' battle-ax."

"Battle-ax!" she repeated with shock. "Is that what they called her?"

He nodded as he eased himself into one of the chairs. "That and a few other choice words I can't repeat for your delicate ears."

"But I never heard them complain."

He laughed. "Course not. Your aunt kept you sheltered from the farmhands—just like she kept you from everythin' else. Yep, they hated her, all right."

"But why?"

Bob shrugged. "Them darn rules of hers. No t'baccy. No likker—not even for medicinal purposes. Not bein' able to cut loose with a good 'gol-durn it to Hades'—even when a man dropped an axle on his toe."

In spite of her predicament, Callie had to grin.

"Always havin' to keep their vests on and their shirts buttoned all the way up to the neck," Bob continued. "Havin' to go to church twice on Sundays, and Monday and Wednesday nights, too. Even on the other nights, when a man might think he had some time to himself, she made 'em sit and listen to her drone on and on readin' them borin' sermons."

"They were very . . . uplifting," Callie offered, feeling she ought to show some sort of loyalty to her late aunt.

"They were borin'!" Bob asserted.

She really couldn't argue. Even loyalty didn't seem to win out against the plain truth.

"Not bein' able to go into town to see the ladies at Hawkins Saloon whenever a man felt the need—if you'll pardon me for bringin' up a subject like that to a real lady," he continued. "That's not strict. That's just plain *inhuman!*"

He shook his head in puzzlement.

"But you never did anything to them. I never expected they'd do anythin' like this to *you.*"

"I didn't either," she said sadly.

"When I saw them scabby varmints early this morning, sneakin' through town with all their paraphernalia, headin' for the train station, I suspected this might be what they had in mind. That's why I stopped by to see if you was all right."

She sprang to her feet. "Do you think I might still be able to catch them at the station and talk them into staying?"

"No, no," he called. "The train's been and gone—and they're all long gone with it."

She collapsed back into the chair. "I thought having the ladies of the Society monitoring my behavior so I could keep my home was my worst problem."

"Is that what those ol' busybodies told you?"

She nodded. "It wasn't just them. It was Aunt Samuela's idea."

"Figures, but I don't think they gave her much argument." He gave a humorless chuckle. "Yeah, they'd be mighty

quick to point out your shortcomin's. But I bet you won't
see any o' them doin' somethin' that might actually help you
keep your farm—like some real work."

She gave him a sad little grin.

"Nope," he continued. "I sure can't picture Miss Jemima
hitchin' up a team o' mules to the plow, or Wider Marsden
sloppin' the hogs. I certainly can't picture Mrs. Preston or
Miss Olive tossin' a pitchfork o' manure. Course, I don't
know about the other ones, but maybe if Mrs. Preston had
had a couple o' kids to keep her busy, she might not be
pokin' her nose in where it don't belong."

She grimaced. "Their idea of help is to find me a husband
just like Aunt Samuela."

Bob shuddered with foreboding. Then he snorted and
waved away the idea.

"I'm surprised they didn't try to do that years ago. They
seem to enjoy fixin' up other folks, even though most of 'em
couldn't catch a man for herself with a bear trap! 'Ceptin'
maybe Mrs. Preston. But seein' as how her husband's the
minister, I reckon that don't count."

Callie couldn't help but laugh at Bob's cheerful jokes. But
her relief lasted only a moment. Then stark reality hit her
again. She rested her head in her hands.

"Oh, Bob, I don't know anything about running a farm."

"Oh, fiddlesticks! You know plenty. And you know I'll
help as much as I can."

Bob didn't have a steady job, but he always seemed to be
busy doing something for somebody. She knew he'd be
right there, helping her, when she needed him.

"Come along." He took her by the hand, urging her to
stand. "You can tell me all about it while we give those poor
cows some relief."

"It's a shame Aunt Samuela never hired you, Bob," Callie
said as she rose and followed him.

"She always said she preferred to hire a man with all his
fingers and limbs." He leaned down and tapped on his
wooden leg as he limped along to the barn. He shot her a

wide, toothy grin. "Guess it don't count that I still got all my own teeth."

"It's a shame she didn't set more store by the qualities of trustworthiness and loyalty in her employees than in mere body parts," Callie said glumly as she settled onto the milking stool. "Then I might still have some farmhands."

She sat there quietly for several minutes, taking some small comfort from resting her head against the cow's soft, warm side. The only sounds were the lowing of the cattle and the tinny squirting of the milk into the buckets as she and Bob worked.

Finally, the last bucket was full. Callie straightened her back and sighed. "Well, that's all done. But, oh, Bob, I'm still in such a fix. What am I going to do without my farmhands?"

"Ha! Good riddance!"

"What?"

"Good riddance to 'em, I say," he repeated even more forcefully. "If them odiferous, pustulatin' skunks'd leave you at a time like this, who knows how much you could've trusted 'em ever again? Just pick yourself up and go on into town and try to hire some new hands."

"I can't do that!"

"Why not?"

"I don't know anything about hiring farmhands. I don't know who doesn't already have a job."

She rose and began pacing about, kicking up straw and dust as she went. Suddenly she stopped and turned to Bob.

"How about Zack Keegan?"

"You don't want him," he told her as he dumped the last bucket of milk into the large pail. "The man's slower than molasses in January. By the time he got your corn planted, it'd be time to harvest the pumpkins."

Callie grabbed one handle of the pail while Bob took the other.

"What about hiring Oscar Barrett?" she asked as they began carrying it to the springhouse.

"Nope. You got to keep on him every minute. I swear to Pete, the man would forget to breathe if you didn't remind him."

"Eugene Redmond?"

"Nope, he'll work out just fine till the first pay. Then he'll squander it all at Hawkins Saloon, and you won't see him standin' upright on his own again for a couple o' months. Then he'll have the nerve to come back to you, askin' for his old job back!"

"Jack Norton?"

"Nope, he left for San Francisco 'bout three months ago."

"Oh, dear. Then how about Ben Harper?"

"Land o' Goshen, no!" Bob exclaimed, throwing up his hands. "He died two months ago."

"Oh, my goodness! There, you see," Callie asserted.

She heard her voice crack. She could feel the tears of frustration rising again. Aunt Samuela had sheltered her too well.

"I don't have any idea what kind of men to look for. Tarnation! I don't know who's still in town or even who's still alive anymore! I need someone reliable . . . dependable . . . sober . . . honest . . . hardworking."

She realized that in her confusion she was starting to babble. She also realized, as she paced about, that she was absolutely helpless to do anything about it.

"I need someone who's a good farmhand, and . . . and not averse to tackling any chore."

Suddenly she stopped and smiled to herself. "Someone who's pretty quick to learn new jobs, too."

"That's the spirit!" Bob said encouragingly. "What's got you smilin' again, Miss Callie?"

"I know exactly what I need to do," she told him, heading across the yard for the house. "I just hope I can still find him."

"Him? Who are you talkin' about?" he demanded.

"Oh, tarnation! What was his name again?"

She must really be upset, she decided. How could she

forget the name of a man who looked the way that stranger did?

"Who?" Bob repeated.

"Daniels!" she said, fairly breathless with excitement and with the satisfaction of finally remembering his name. "Harden Daniels."

Saying his name aloud brought not just his face but his entire body vividly back to her memory with unsettling clarity. She had spent her life going to school or church or doing business with the men in town. But none of them sprang to mind so quickly and with such sharpness and completeness as did the image of Harden Daniels.

"Harden Daniels?" Bob repeated. "That's the drifter who shows up lookin' for work after your aunt's funeral."

"That's him."

"You can't hire him! You don't know nothin' about him."

"Now you sound like a member of the Cottonwood Methodist Ladies Evangel—"

"Miss Callie!" Bob declared with pretend horror. "There ain't no need to go insultin' me."

"Sorry. But I need to find Mr. Daniels. Do you have any idea if he's still in town?"

Bob shrugged. "Didn't see him sneakin' onto the train with your aunt's lollygaggin' farmhands. Didn't see him ridin' out o' town on his horse or on the stage. Stands to reason he's still hangin' 'round."

"Where? I don't think he has enough money to stay at Roger's Grand Hotel. I guess I'll have to search out all the people in town who have rooms for rent. I'd hate to think I'd have to search the alleyways for him."

Bob scratched his head and chuckled. "Oh, I don't think you'll have to do that, Miss Callie. Like as not, he's where all the drifters go—Hawkins Saloon."

"Oh, dear."

Everyone in town knew about that place's dubious reputation. In spite of Aunt Samuela's efforts to shelter her, even Callie had heard the tales. For years, the ladies of the

Society had waged a fierce campaign to close down the place. But for some strange reason, the saloon remained open and continued to thrive.

Callie pressed her lips together with more determination than she had ever felt before. "I guess that's where I'll have to go."

"Oh, mercy, Miss Callie! Do you really want this man that bad?"

Did she really want Harden Daniels? she asked herself. What did she really know about him? Nothing, except that his strong arms and broad shoulders made him look as if he could handle a lot of work. That and the look in his blue eyes made her believe she could trust him.

After only a moment's pause, she nodded emphatically. "Yes, I do."

3

CALLIE DECIDED SHE should at least be grateful that the thin dark line of clouds on the horizon hadn't advanced very far. By her reckoning, it might be several hours before the rain began to fall. She would be dry when she arrived in town, and that was good. It would be pretty hard to get new farmhands to take her seriously if she looked as if she didn't even have enough sense to come in out of the rain.

Callie stood, poised on the edge of the sidewalk in front of Hawkins Saloon and stared at the swinging doors, fiddling with the edge of her shawl.

"Miss Callie, you're gettin' as bad as Miss Jemima," Bob pointed out with a chuckle.

The cruel certainty that she would one day be a wizened little old maid just like Miss Jemima Finchcroft was bad enough, but it was horrifying to think that she might turn out to be as big a scatterbrained fidget. She slapped the ends of her shawl down into place and held her hands together, tightly under control, at her waist.

"Suppose the ladies of the Society see me?" she still fretted, glancing about nervously.

"Heck of a time to be thinkin' about that now," he reminded her with a chuckle.

"No, no, seriously! What if they think I'm actually going inside?" she fretted. "Will they think that's bad enough behavior to take my farm away from me?"

"Some of 'em might. One of 'em—mind you, I ain't sayin' who—but one of 'em sure will," he stated ominously.

Callie cringed as she glanced about for Widow Marsden's pinched, disapproving face. If any one of the ladies of the Society would find a reason to have her farm taken away from her, it would be that hard-hearted lady.

"But I'd be real surprised to see any o' them fine ladies hangin' 'round this place."

Several men she didn't know tipped their hats as they passed between her and the swinging doors of the saloon. Callie nodded in response, hoping the brim of her bonnet would hide her face from prying eyes.

"But what if someone else sees me and reports back to them?" she whispered as the men strolled away. "You know how fast gossip   "

Bob shrugged. "Then I reckon you better stop jawin' on the sidewalk and get yourself inside."

"But what if—"

"One thing's for certain," he informed her, all the joking suddenly vanished from his voice, "if you don't get somebody besides me to help you real quick, you *will* lose your farm."

Once again she glanced with apprehension at the swinging doors. "At least come inside with me. Please."

"Nope. You can't look tough like your aunt if you got me trailin' along like some kind o' nanny."

She nodded. "Then I suppose I really do have to do this myself."

With a determination she certainly didn't feel, she pushed open the swinging doors.

She blinked. It took a few seconds for her eyes to adjust to the dimness within. The air was heavy with the odor of stale tobacco, cheap toilet water, and the acrid smell of whiskey. She sniffed and stifled a cough. She didn't want to do anything that would attract anyone's attention. Maybe that way, if things didn't work out with Mr. Daniels, she could just pretend she'd never even been here.

At least the place was almost empty. The bartender was slowly wiping off the top of the bar. In the back, a man was sweeping the floor and setting up knocked-over chairs.

A man lay faceup in the sawdust on the floor, still sleeping where he'd probably fallen over drunk the night before. His half-empty glass still rested in his limp hand.

Some of the tension in Callie's shoulders relaxed with relief. Thank goodness *that* wasn't Mr. Daniels!

A few men lay slumped over the various card tables, snoring loudly. It was hard to identify them from the back. Was one of them Mr. Daniels? Would she have to wake up each one to find out? Would she have to touch them and shake them to wake them up? She knew she wouldn't have the courage to do that. Maybe she could just lean over and shout in their ears.

What if none of these men were Mr. Daniels? Callie thought with a burst of dread. What if he was upstairs . . . in one of *those* rooms . . . with one of *those* ladies? Then how would she get him? Or would she have to wait in this place until he finally came downstairs again?

As she stood there, debating what to do next, she heard to her left the clunk of ceramic on wood. She turned. In the corner, seated at the table by the window, drinking from a thick white mug, sat Harden Daniels.

He was alone, and he was watching her very carefully.

She wasn't used to having any man watch her. Even the few men she knew—Mr. Corrigan at the general store, Doc

Hanford, even the Reverend Preston—usually all but ignored her.

But Mr. Daniels's pale blue eyes swept over her, from the tip of her poke bonnet to the toes of her worn shoes. He seemed to take in her every detail. He seemed to be paying more attention to her appearance than even *she* did.

It felt so bizarre to imagine this stranger noting her hair, her eyes, her figure, actually studying her features and movements. *He must really be bored here,* she decided. What in the world could he find so interesting about her?

Aunt Samuela had warned her about the evil things men thought when they watched a lady. Was that what Mr. Daniels was thinking about her? She refused to allow herself even to consider the possibilities. But she felt a warmth rising up her throat and across her cheeks, anyway.

How long had he been watching her? Had he seen her when she first entered? Had he been watching her even as she stood debating with Bob on the sidewalk?

She hadn't tripped over anything coming through the swinging doors. She'd managed to still her fidgeting hands. Still, she had the awful feeling he could tell just how scared and unsure of herself she was.

Callie noticed that, even as Mr. Daniels continued to watch her, he also seemed to be aware of what little was going on in the saloon, and of the activities out on Main Street as well.

What could anyone find so interesting on the streets of a small, quiet town like Cottonwood? she wondered. Why did it seem to her that this stranger to town was watching and waiting for someone?

It certainly couldn't be her. No one had ever watched or waited for her—not even Aunt Samuela.

Another thing: Callie had shown up here, but Mr. Daniels still seemed to be watching and waiting for someone. Who else could he be looking for?

Without taking his eyes off her, Mr. Daniels lifted his cup and drank. He still hadn't said a word.

Was she supposed to make the first move? She supposed she'd have to so that she could keep her farm, so that she wouldn't have to marry a man she didn't love, especially since he wouldn't love her in return. Especially since Mr. Daniels didn't seem to be doing anything, and she knew she needed him right now more than he'd ever need her.

She drew in a deep breath and walked toward him.

"Good morning, Mr. Daniels," she said very quietly, so as not to attract the attention of the people in the saloon who were awake and not to wake the ones who were still asleep.

"Good morning, Miss Jackson." He rose. "What are you doing here?"

"I . . . I was looking for you."

She wouldn't want him to get the impression that she thought he was special, but she might as well admit the truth from the start. She didn't want to waste any more time in this place with fancy words and distractions than she absolutely had to and risk getting caught by the ladies of the Society.

"Well, it looks as if you found me." He pulled out the chair beside him and brushed the sawdust off the seat. "Please sit down, ma'am."

"I'll stand, thank you."

"There's really no need—"

"If the ladies of the Society see me standing in here, I can at least offer the excuse that I'm just passing through looking for farmhands. But if I'm sitting down, it looks too much as if I'm actually a customer here. There won't be any excusing that!"

"I appreciate your predicament, Miss Jackson. But my ma always taught me never to sit when a lady was standing, and after last night, I'd sure like to sit, so I wish you would." He tapped on the back of the chair.

Last night? she repeated to herself. Her mind leaped ahead to the first logical conclusion.

"I thought you said you don't drink and carouse, Mr. Daniels."

She couldn't let him get away with lying to her even before he'd been hired.

"I don't."

Then what else did he do that kept him awake? she wondered as her mind jumped to the next logical—if embarrassing—conclusion.

Aunt Samuela might have tried to keep her sheltered, but Callie wasn't so ignorant that she didn't know about the very obliging ladies working at Hawkins Saloon. Why should it matter to her what Mr. Daniels did? He wasn't her employee yet.

"When your bed is as hard as a rock, you don't get much sleeping done," he told her.

"I guess not," she admitted. She hoped in the dim light he couldn't see the color that she knew came with the heat she could feel flooding her cheeks.

"It was even more difficult when the folks in the room next door argued very loudly all night," he continued. "Especially since I was tired after riding all day."

"I see." It seemed an innocent enough excuse, and a bit more charitable than the idea she'd come up with.

"Are you still going to make me stand?" His grin widened. There was a soft pleading in his blue eyes and an underlying intensity that made her believe that if she didn't sit down voluntarily, he would pick her up and set her in the chair. The thought of being in Mr. Daniels's arms was even more unsettling than the thought of being caught in a saloon by the stern ladies of the Society.

"No, oh, no. Of course not."

If she must sit, at least she'd sit only on the edge of the chair. If she sat too far back, it might appear as if she had really settled in. She also made certain she kept an appropriate distance between herself and Mr. Daniels. She tried to make very sure that her back was turned to the door and that she was sitting far enough back from the window so that a casual passerby outside, glancing in, couldn't identify her.

Mr. Daniels motioned to get the bartender's attention.

"Another for me. And one for the lady," he ordered, then seated himself.

"It's coffee, isn't it?" she asked anxiously.

"The bartender tells me it is. I'm not so sure. But I told you before—several times—I don't hold with strong drink."

"Yes, you did," she acknowledged sheepishly.

"Then don't you think it's about time you started believing me?"

Callie didn't answer. It was going to take more than a pair of honest blue eyes and a cup of coffee to make her trust this man unconditionally. But taking his word on this was a start.

Giving her a grin, he leaned back in his chair. "So, you say you've come looking for me."

"Yes, I have."

"Now, what could there possibly be about me that would interest a lady like you?"

Callie swallowed hard to suppress the thoughts that came to her mind. Why hadn't Aunt Samuela warned her about the vivid images that could run through a lady's head when she looked at a man? Maybe cold, chaste Aunt Samuela had never had such images in her head. They'd never run through Callie's before. But then, she'd only been having this problem since Mr. Daniels had arrived in town.

"You told me you needed a job, Mr. Daniels."

"Yes, ma'am."

"Do you still need that job?"

She held her breath, hoping and praying he would say yes. But the infuriating man waited until the bartender had set a cup in front of her and poured them both something that looked more like mud and smelled more like kerosene than coffee.

Callie sniffed at the contents of the cup, then put it back down, untasted.

"I see what you mean," she murmured.

"I thought you already had all the farmhands you needed," he finally replied.

Why couldn't he just give her a straight answer and make things a whole lot easier?

"I did, but . . . well, it seems they all left town this morning," she admitted.

"Then I guess it looks like you do have a job available for me after all."

"Right now I have jobs available for several men."

The thought briefly crossed her mind that Mr. Daniels could easily handle all four men's allotment of chores. Now, if he would just pick one of them and get to work . . .

"I think I told you once before, Miss Jackson. I'm a man who has no qualms about taking advantage of a situation."

"I recall."

What was it Mildred had said about strange men coming into town? Callie tried to remember. Men with no scruples? No morals?

In spite of his open cheerfulness, the man did seem to harbor a silent secretiveness about him. She felt reassured that she had decided to deal cautiously with him.

"How do you intend to turn this situation to your advantage, Mr. Daniels? I . . . I can only afford to pay you the same wages," she told him as sternly as she could. "I have to have enough money to go around just in case . . . no, *when* I hire some more men."

"It's good to see you still have hope." He gave her a little grin. "That's all right, ma'am. Your regular rate of pay will be just fine with me."

Callie tried very hard to do no more than just nod. She was still afraid that if he saw her sigh with relief, he might suppose that she needed him more than she actually did. He might change his mind and try to ask for more money after all.

Establishing a few inflexible rules should eliminate that idea.

"I don't allow any tobacco," she continued. "Smoking or chewing."

"No, ma'am."

"No playing cards or dice, or other sorts of gambling."

"Seeing as how there aren't any other farmhands right now, it's not going to be all that much fun betting against myself." With a wink, he added, "Anyway, I cheat."

Harden smiled, but Miss Jackson didn't return it. Oh, well, what had he expected?

He still had to wonder about what he was getting himself into. Wasn't there an easier way to accomplish what he had been sent to do? Maybe. But then what would be the cost in lives?

He had a great deal of respect and admiration for folks who quietly lived what they believed. But it was just his luck that his prospective new boss would turn out to be a grim-faced, penny-pinching, puritanical spinster.

It could have been worse, he reminded himself with a silent chuckle. He could have gotten here earlier and worked for crotchety old Aunt Samuela instead.

Well, he really ought to be more sympathetic, he decided. Looking as she did, Callie Jackson wouldn't seem to have too much else to keep her occupied besides church work.

"You'll take a bath weekly."

He shook off his speculations with that unexpected regulation. He realized he had to pay close attention to *everything* that went on here if he was going to succeed. But he never expected the rules to extend this far.

"Oh, at least!" he readily agreed. "I sincerely hope that anyone else you hire agrees to these minimum bathing requirements, too."

"I'll see that they do, Mr. Daniels."

Apparently she wasn't aware of the implications of what she had just said. He would have let it pass, but the thought of Miss Jackson insisting on his personal bathing habits brought some other intriguing possibilities to mind.

"Are you going to conduct an inspection to make sure I comply with that rule, ma'am?"

She sat there with her mouth hanging open for just a

moment. Her pale complexion was unusually flushed. Her green eyes probably couldn't get any larger.

Then she blinked, snapped her mouth shut, and glared at him with indignation.

"And . . . and we . . . I don't allow any . . . any . . . I . . . um . . ."

Callie heard her voice waver and could have kicked herself. She was stammering so badly it must appear as if they were holding an election for village idiot and she was the prime candidate.

"You can't just go running off to town any time you feel like . . ." Her throat almost closed up on her, she was so nervous speaking the words. "Any time you feel like running off to town. Do you understand, Mr. Daniels?"

"Oh, no, ma'am. I can't agree to that at all."

"What? No one ever told Aunt Samuela no, so . . . so don't go thinking just because she's gone that you can dictate the terms of your employment to me. You're . . . you're just a farmhand!"

"And you're just my boss. You're not the czarina of Russia reigning over some feudal estate, and I'm not one of your serfs, bound to the land."

"What are you talking about? What does that have to do with anything?"

"As long as I'm in your employ, I'll work for you just as hard as I possibly can."

"Of course. I . . . I won't accept anything less." She tried to sound as forceful as he, but she had the feeling she was failing miserably.

"But I'm still my own man, Miss Jackson," he continued.

"Well, of course you are."

Somehow she wouldn't expect anything less from him in that matter, as well. But she still had to maintain some semblance of control, just as Aunt Samuela had. She'd told him the same things she'd overheard her aunt tell each new farmhand. But since this man didn't fit the rules like the others, she had to make up new ones as she went along.

"But I still expect you to let me know where you're going, when you leave, and when you expect to return—"

"No, Miss Jackson," he stated firmly. "I come and go as I please."

"But—"

Harden shook his head. "No buts about it. I come and go as I please."

He leaned back in his chair and studied her. She was twisting the edges of her shawl again, just as she'd done when she was so nervous standing on the sidewalk outside, just as she'd mangled her handkerchief at the funeral. It was so pathetically easy to read her thoughts and emotions.

She'll give in soon, he figured. This woman was undoubtedly used to being told exactly what to do, and doing it. She was too fearful to act on her own, too timid to rebel, too weak not to relent. He wouldn't have any trouble eventually getting her to let him do exactly what he wanted, exactly what he had to.

Her bright green eyes clouded with unspoken doubts and fears as she seemed to be thinking about her alternatives. The way he saw it, she really didn't have any. He felt a twinge of remorse.

Ordinarily, when he had a job to do, it didn't seem to matter much if he hurt a few feelings or stepped on a few toes to get it done. It shouldn't matter now, either. After all, once his job was finished here, he'd never see her again. But for some reason, he hated like the dickens to get tough with this meek little spinster.

"Very well," she conceded with a sigh.

It seemed her shoulders slumped with defeat. Then he watched her lips suddenly tighten into a hard line and her brows draw into a deep frown.

"But . . . but this still doesn't mean you can leave the farm before your chores are done."

She tapped her finger firmly on the tabletop, accentuating her point. Maybe Aunt Samuela hadn't squashed all the life out of her after all. He almost expected Callie to start shaking a hickory stick at him like some stern old school-marm. He hoped he wouldn't laugh in her face.

"Of course not, ma'am."

"And you'll be ready to get back to work again bright and early every morning."

"Of course."

"And do a full day's work."

"I always have."

"Well, now that you're hired, Mr. Daniels," Callie said as she rose to her feet, "let's see that you continue to do so."

Mr. Daniels quickly stood.

She had already spent far more time in this place than she would ever care to—or than her aunt would ever have allowed.

"Fetch your things," she told him. "I'll expect you for dinner at six this evening. You'll start first thing tomorrow morning."

Without another word, Callie turned and walked away.

"Oh, my heavens!" she mumbled to herself. "I did it!"

She tried so hard to walk slowly when what she really wanted to do was break into a run and not stop until she was safely home. But she knew her shaking legs would never take her that far. She was lucky she made it out the door without keeling over.

Once outside, she headed down the sidewalk, tightly grasping the railing for support.

If any of the good ladies of the Society could see her now, leaving Hawkins Saloon, weak in the knees and mumbling to herself from nervous relief, they'd certainly mistakenly think she'd succumbed to the temptations of Demon Rum while she was in there.

But no one had seen her. She'd even managed to hire a farmhand.

"Now, I just hope I don't live to regret it."

Inside Hawkins Saloon, Harden picked up his cup. The coffee was cold and tasted more like turpentine now than it had when it was hot. But he drank a toast anyway to his unbelievable good luck. This couldn't have turned out any better if he'd driven the farmhands off at gunpoint himself.

He had his job as close to Fielding as he dared get right now, and the freedom to come and go as he pleased every evening. He'd finish what he started out to do much more easily and a lot faster than he'd ever expected.

He knew Callie would need to hire some additional men, and he hoped she eventually found them. But right now, he hoped not. He didn't mind working or even bunking in with strangers, if their feet didn't smell too bad and they didn't snore too loudly. But he didn't relish the idea of some nosy farmhand interfering with his real work.

On the other hand, if she didn't hire some more men now, what would Miss Jackson do for help when he finished his job and left?

He couldn't allow himself to think about that now. He still had too much else to do. That was her problem, anyway, not his.

He reached down and picked up his saddlebags, which he'd kept lying on the floor beside his chair, and slung them over his shoulder. He was ready to go.

Protecting her hand with a wadded-up dish towel, Callie lifted the lid off the pot and savored the aroma of the chicken soup.

Prudence meowed and rubbed against Callie's leg.

"You'll just have to wait," Callie told her as she replaced the lid.

She opened the oven and pulled out the pan of biscuits.

"They're just perfect," she said as she set them on top of the stove to keep them warm. "But everything'll be colder than the pump handle in winter if Mr. Daniels doesn't get here soon. I just hope it tastes as good as it smells. I've been cooking for Aunt Samuela ever since I was a little girl. I'm not a bad cook, I guess, unless that's what *really* drove the farmhands away."

Prudence sneezed.

"I do *not* care what Mr. Daniels thinks of my cooking," Callie protested. "He's just a hired hand."

If she didn't know better, Callie would suspect that Prudence laughed at her.

"Think what you like, you silly ball of fur. I just can't have the poor man thinking he's got to work with nothing better in his stomach than burnt stew and biscuits that are as hard and flat as little river stones."

Prudence flicked her tail with obvious disdain.

"I know, you never eat the biscuits anyway, and Mr. Daniels will eat what he's given. After all, Aunt Samuela always told the men to eat what they were given and like it. I see no reason to change."

But she wasn't Aunt Samuela, and Harden Daniels certainly wasn't Mack, Willy, Pete, or Josh.

"He told me he could read and cipher. But what does a drifter like him know about Russian serfs or czarinas?" she wondered aloud. "And where in the world is he, anyway? He was told to be here at six."

The mantel clock in the parlor chimed the quarter hour.

"Fifteen minutes late," she noted. "Aunt Samuela would've already served dinner, and if there was any left, he'd have to eat it cold."

Wiping her hands down the front of her apron, she strode through the large parlor and out onto the front porch.

The sky was an eerie half-light, shadowed by the clouds that had been threatening all day, but still hadn't given up a drop. When this storm broke, it was going to be a downpour.

"Where in the world is he?"

She looked down the road that stretched away toward Cottonwood. Not a stray dog, not a jackrabbit or a squirrel, not even a breeze disturbed the dust. Not even a bird flying overhead cast a shadow on the empty road.

"If he can't even be on time for a meal, how reliable can he be with anything else?" she demanded as she paced back and forth across the porch, twisting the ends of her apron.

"What if that cup of coffee was just a clever trick? What if he stayed in Hawkins Saloon and now he's dead drunk? What if he changed his mind, gathered up his things, and took to wandering again?"

He was her only hope to save her farm. Without him, what would she do? She didn't think she had the courage to go back to Hawkins Saloon looking for prospective hired hands a second time.

Away in the distance, she spotted someone approaching.

"It's about time!"

She crossed her arms over her chest and tapped her foot impatiently.

"I'll give him a piece of my mind to feast on for being late, and he can hope he'll have enough appetite left for my good dinner."

As she watched the approaching figure, she noted that not only was it too tall to be Mr. Daniels, but it also looked much too wide to be just him.

"Goodness gracious! For a solitary drifter, how much baggage does the man have?"

She frowned and squinted, trying to see better in the gathering dusk. The clouds on the horizon blocked the setting sun.

"He's just leading his horse," she noted with relief.

Suddenly she realized the baggage seemed to have legs and was walking with him.

"Oh, my goodness! What in the world is Mr. Daniels doing with two children?"

A little girl with blond hair walked along on his right. A smaller boy, with hair so light it appeared white, trudged along at his left. They both carried what they'd probably call baggage, but the bags looked like little more than a change of clothing tied up in a big handkerchief.

Callie stood on her porch, waiting for them and their explanations. She kept her arms crossed and her foot tapping.

Suddenly, the two children dropped their small bags and

headed toward her at a run. They slammed into her, throwing their little arms around her waist. Both of them squealed with delight.

"Mama!"

4

"*Mama?*" Callie shrieked with surprise.

Frugal and Refrain appeared from beneath the porch, barking like mad.

"What are you talking about?" Callie demanded, trying to step away from her small attackers. "Who are you? How in the world could you ever think I'm your mother?"

"You're not," the little girl told her.

"But you will be," the little boy said, grinning up at her with an unmistakable gleam of hope in his bright blue eyes.

If they squeezed her any more tightly, Callie was afraid she wouldn't be able to breathe.

"Well, I hate to disappoint you, but—"

"What's the matter, Miss Jackson?" Mr. Daniels asked with a laugh.

He dropped his saddlebags, as well as the children's two small bundles, at the bottom of the front porch steps. He looped the reins of his horse over the hitching rail by the gate.

"Don't you like children?"

"No! Yes." She was too busy trying to disentangle herself from the two children to pay much attention to what she was saying. "I mean, I don't know." She turned to the dogs. "Frugal, Refrain, now hush!"

Whimpering, they retreated back under the porch.

Suddenly, the little boy pulled back. A grimace of distaste squeezed his pudgy features.

"She don't *feel* like a mama," he protested.

The little girl drew back as well. "You're right."

"She don't feel like our mama at all." He shook his head.

"Do you remember her?" the little girl asked quietly, almost reverently.

"A little." He shrugged his small shoulders. "Enough to know this lady don't feel like her. She don't feel like nobody's mama."

"No, I guess she doesn't," the little girl admitted.

"That's because I'm not!" Callie protested.

Ignoring Callie's protests, the little boy asked his sister very quietly, "Bea? Now what'll we do?"

The children stood there, silently staring at each other in obvious puzzlement and disappointment.

"Well, I'm here for dinner, Miss Jackson, just like you said." He gave her a broad grin. "I'd be pleased if you'd show me where to stable my horse, and after dinner, I'd be pleased if you'd show me where I'll be bunking down so I can get some shut-eye so I'll be ready to work first thing in the morning, just like you said."

Things were not going at all as she had planned. *And whose fault was that?* she asked herself. She intended to let him know exactly what she thought of him.

"You're late for dinner, Mr. Daniels. I thought I'd made it pretty clear: Tardiness will not be tolerated."

Mr. Daniels just gave her that maddening grin of his and nodded toward the little girl and boy.

"It couldn't be helped. I couldn't fit us all on the horse, and children tend not to travel as quickly as adults. I think it has something to do with short legs," he added with a confidential wink.

"My legs are *not* short!" the little boy insisted. "They fit me."

Mr. Daniels did have a point, Callie had to silently admit. Well, that might excuse their lateness, but it still didn't explain their presence.

"Lying will not be tolerated, either, Mr. Daniels. I don't think you were quite honest with me."

"Lying?" His dark eyebrows rose with surprise. "Well, we talked about being sober, prompt, and chaste, but you never told me you expected your farmhands to be *honest*, Miss Jackson. That's not fair, you know. You can't go changing the rules *after* you've hired me."

"What? Oh!"

Then Callie noted his white teeth shining through his broad grin. She felt so stupid. How could she not have realized he was joking? The man was a fool, full of inappropriate jokes. Of course, Aunt Samuela had always told her, all jokes were inappropriate.

But jokes or no jokes, there was another, more immediate problem.

"Mr. Daniels, you should have told me from the start that you had two children."

"I don't."

"Then what do you call them?" she demanded, pointing at the little boy and girl who stood wide-eyed, watching Mr. Daniels and her.

"Children," he replied with a grin, "but they're not mine."

"Then what are you doing with them?"

"I met them wandering around in town, asking after a Miss Jackson. I told them I was heading in this direction, too, so we decided to travel together."

Callie looked from Mr. Daniels to the children and back.

"I could expect a man like you to be drifting through town alone, but what are two small children doing out here on their own? Why isn't someone watching out for them?"

"Why don't you ask *them?*" Mr. Daniels suggested.

She had watched how mothers in town dealt with their children, but they held them and hugged them. Callie didn't think that was such a good idea right now with these two. They might decide to grab her again, permanently declare her Mama, and never let her go. Then how would she breathe?

She tried to remember how her aunt had treated her when she was a child. She hadn't turned out so bad. That must be the proper way to do it.

She frowned at the two children.

"Stand up straight and don't fidget. Now, answer me, and don't mumble. Who are you?" she demanded. "Where did you come from? Why have you come to my farm?"

"I'm Beatrice Mobley." The little girl didn't seem to mind Callie's stern expression at all. In fact, she was smiling brightly up at her. "Most people call me Bea. I'm ten years old. This is my brother Walter."

"Most people call me Walter."

"He's only four."

"I'll be five soon!" he protested.

Ignoring him, Beatrice continued, "You must be Miss Jackson."

"Yes," Callie replied cautiously.

"Miss Sam . . . Samu—"

"Samuela?" Callie offered.

"Miss Samuela Jackson," Beatrice finished, nodding vigorously.

"I'm Callie Jackson, her niece."

"No, ma'am. We need to see the other one," Beatrice insisted.

"That's not possible. You see, my aunt passed away a few days ago."

"Oh, dear." Beatrice frowned with worry.

"Oh, our mama died once, too," Walter offered. "Our dad, too."

"I'm sorry," Callie replied. "But, you see, my aunt never

said anything to me about the two of you. That's why I don't understand why you're here, or why you need to see her."

"He sent us here to live with her."

"He?" Callie glared at Mr. Daniels. "Did you send these children—"

"I told you, no," he insisted.

"No, no, no," Walter broke in. "Not *him*. The *man!*"

"What man?" Callie demanded.

"The man at the orphanage."

Beatrice reached into the pocket of her tattered coat and pulled out a carefully folded piece of paper. She glanced at it, then at Callie, then back to the paper several times. She was frowning, as if she really couldn't believe what was written there.

"Which orphanage is that?"

"The one in New York."

"That narrows it down nicely, don't you think?" Mr. Daniels remarked.

"Oh, hush." Turning back to the children, she asked, "You're from New York?"

Beatrice nodded.

What in the world were two little orphans all the way from New York doing on her doorstep? That paper the little girl carried might contain some information that would clear up all the confusion.

"Can you show me your paper, please?" Callie asked, holding out her hand.

The girl shook her head and clutched the paper desperately to her chest. "Nope. Without it, we don't know where to go."

"But you're already here. You don't have to worry about where to go anymore." Callie waited for reason to sink in. "Now, may I *please* see your paper?" she repeated, extending her hand a bit farther.

But Beatrice still held back.

"Don't worry. Tearing it up isn't suddenly going to rid me

of you, so I won't do that. I just need to read it. It might help me understand what's going on around here."

"Go on. Give it to her," Walter said in what he probably thought was a whisper, but which Callie could hear very well. "Her name's Miss Jackson, too. That's close enough."

"Hush up, Walter," Beatrice told him through gritted teeth. "No, it's not."

"Go on. Don't worry," Mr. Daniels repeated Walter's advice. "If she starts to rip it up, I'll stop her."

"*You'll* stop me?" Callie repeated.

"If I have to," Mr. Daniels replied with a conspiratorial wink at the children.

What would he do? Once again, the thought of Mr. Daniels grabbing her up in his arms and subduing her sprang into her mind. She tried to keep her hand from shaking as she held it out to Beatrice for the cherished paper.

The little girl slowly handed Callie her precious paper.

"This is none of your concern, Mr. Daniels," Callie told him as she unfolded it.

"But, well, gee, when you assumed these children were mine, you sort of made it my concern, too."

Callie pressed her lips together and studied the paper more carefully than the little bit of writing on it warranted.

She read her aunt's name and the name of Cottonwood, Kansas. Obviously this was all someone had given these children to direct them on their way.

The name of Mr. Horatio Van Bokelyn meant nothing to her. At first the Brooklyn Orphanage meant nothing to her, either. Then she recalled a conversation she had overheard what seemed a long time ago.

It had been when Will first arrived at the farm, and Aunt Samuela was laying down the rules to him. He'd come from New York. Both his parents were dead, and he had no other relatives who were willing to raise him. He'd stolen an apple and instead of sending him to jail, some kind-hearted judge had sent him out West with a few other orphans where they could work on farms and mend their evil ways.

Apparently, Aunt Samuela had looked on orphans as a way to obtain cheap labor, but she hadn't sent for any in a while.

Was that how Beatrice and Walter had come to be sent here? Just what she needed: a farmhand she knew absolutely nothing about and two miniature felons!

"What did you steal?" Callie asked.

"Nothing!" Beatrice cried in protest.

"Her orange last Christmas!" Walter tearfully confessed.

"That was *you?*" Beatrice demanded angrily, giving him a punch on the arm.

"Stop!" Walter yelled, punching her back.

"Yep, you sure do have a way with children," Mr. Daniels said, stepping in and separating the two.

"Oh, hush! All of you!" Callie insisted.

But he was right. It seemed as if everything she said upset these two. She tried not to frown at the children anymore.

"Now, let's try to discuss this calmly. I'm sorry, but there's obviously been some kind of mistake."

"It's no mistake. Miss Jackson—Miss Samuela Jackson— sent for us," Beatrice explained quite simply.

"No, no. My aunt would have sent for workers—"

"No!" Beatrice stamped her foot emphatically. "The man said she wanted *us*—my brother *and* me. Both of us. Together."

Aunt Samuela had made it very clear to Callie on many occasions that she was only doing her bounden Christian duty in caring for her orphaned niece. Affection never entered into it.

"My aunt would've sent for someone old enough and big enough to work on the farm. There's no way on earth she would have any use for one—let alone two—small children," Callie insisted.

How could Aunt Samuela have wanted these two when she'd made it pretty clear she hadn't even wanted her own niece?

Beatrice's bright blue eyes glistened with tears, but she

lifted her chin proudly and declared, "She *sent* for us. She *wanted* us!"

"Yeah!" Walter chimed in. His lower lip was already quivering uncontrollably. It wouldn't take much to set him off.

"She wanted us," Beatrice continued, her voice cracking with emotion. "Even . . . even if you don't. Even if you don't believe anybody would want . . . us."

Beatrice sniffed. Apparently this was all Walter needed. He started to howl and sob.

"You do have a way with children, Miss Jackson," Mr. Daniels remarked.

"No, no. That's not what I mean. Really, really. I'm sorry!"

Callie tried frantically to hush the crying children, but nothing seemed to work. Even Frugal and Refrain emerged from under the porch again to add their howls to those of the children.

"Hush, Frugal! Get down, Refrain!" she shouted.

At least the dogs obeyed, but the children just kept yowling.

In desperation, she turned to Mr. Daniels.

"All right, you think you're so smart where children are concerned. Now what do I do?"

"How should I know? They're not my children."

"Well, they're not mine, either. I don't know what to do with them."

Mr. Daniels just grinned and shrugged.

Curse him! He seemed to be enjoying her predicament.

The children's weeping pierced her eardrums like little arrows. Her nerves were getting thread thin. She felt her own eyes filling with tears of frustration. She pressed her lips together and blinked hard. She *wouldn't* let Mr. Daniels see how this was affecting her.

"Chin up, little man," Mr. Daniels said. "You can be a brave fellow."

He scooped the howling Walter up in one arm. The little

boy laid his head on the man's shoulder, but still didn't stop crying.

Callie wondered how Mr. Daniels could stand that caterwauling so close to his ear.

Mr. Daniels held out his hand to Beatrice, who took it without an argument. Without an invitation, without even asking Callie's permission, he led them into the house.

Callie bent down and lifted Mr. Daniels's saddlebags. They were surprisingly heavy, but not so much as to be unmanageable. She retrieved the children's meager baggage, too. Apparently, none of them had much to call their own.

If Aunt Samuela were still alive, how in the world could Callie explain to her three complete strangers making free with her house, and herself acting as some sort of footman or bellhop to them?

She trudged into the house behind them. She needn't wonder when she'd lost control of this situation. She knew that, from the very start, she had never been in control.

Mr. Daniels deposited the weeping children on the sofa in the parlor.

"Oh, nice kitty," Walter said. His howls subsided to mere sniffles.

"Her name is Prudence."

Walter wrinkled his nose and sniffed. "What a name!"

"My aunt liked to give the animals instructive, edifying names," Callie explained. "Prudence means careful thought before action. So every time I call the cat, I'm reminded to think before I act."

"I'm sure you use that a lot," Mr. Daniels commented.

"Prudence, Prudence," Walter called, reaching out for her. With a swish of her tail, Prudence deftly avoided him.

"Your dog's name is Frugal," Beatrice said.

Callie nodded. "My aunt was very . . . careful with her money."

"Your other dog's name is Refrain," Mr. Daniels commented. "Did that mean your aunt liked music?"

"No, actually his name is Refrain from Evil."

"I should have expected as much," he said with a chuckle. Then he turned back to the children.

"You know, Walter, Beatrice, yesterday I had the most interesting meal here. Apple cobbler and huckleberry pie."

"Just pie?"

"Do you need anything else?"

"Nope."

"But we had something else to eat, too. We had roast gopher with pickled birds' feet in toadstool gravy, too. Yum!"

The children giggled.

"I want the kitty," Walter said, making another grab for Prudence.

"No, no. You can't eat the cat," Mr. Daniels teased. "I know there's got to be some cake or pie left."

Walter glanced about, as if already searching for goodies. Callie hoped that was what he was doing, and not that there might be a chance he actually *was* referring to a taste for the cat.

Mr. Daniels turned to Callie. "Isn't there?"

"I . . . I think so." She was so surprised by the abrupt change in the children that she found it hard to do a quick mental inventory of her cupboard.

As he leaned closer he whispered in her ear, "There'd better be, or you'll be in deep trouble with these two."

He didn't touch her, but she could feel his warm breath on her neck. He might as well have touched her, because she almost twitched with the little shiver that ran down her sides. She took one step to put some distance between them.

"Not as much trouble as you're in with me," she muttered, "for making promises that you don't know whether or not I can keep."

"Then I guess you'd better check, huh?"

She pressed her lips together. She didn't need this stranger telling her what to do.

She figured, even if she had lost control of everything

else, she could at least be in control of the meal she herself had made in her very own kitchen. She dumped the baggage in a corner of the parlor and went into the kitchen to dish out dinner. She didn't expect Mr. Daniels and the children to follow her.

"No, wait. The children and I . . . Aunt Samuela and I always ate in the dining room. The children and I will eat there." She tried to stand in the doorway, arms akimbo, as if barring him from entering. "Farmhands . . . farmhands are *not* allowed in the house."

"An old rule? Or are you making up new ones as you go along?" he asked with a grin.

He stood there, looking down on her until she felt as if he'd swoop her up and carry her out of his way.

"No, no," she finally managed to answer. "It's always been—"

"Aunt Samuela's rule, right?" he said as he and the children ranged around the table.

"Yes."

"Well, you're too late. I'm already here."

"The door works both ways."

"All right," he said, rising and heading for the door. "I'm sure you and the children will have a lovely meal together."

She *couldn't* keep him here. But she couldn't very well send these two small children out to the bunkhouse to eat. Walter didn't even look old enough to cut up his own meat. On the other hand, she wasn't all that happy with the thought of nightly meals alone with two small children, either.

"Wait!"

Mr. Daniels stopped. Even though he had his back to her, she knew with uncanny certainty that the darn man was grinning all over himself in triumph.

"I'll make an exception, but just for tonight," she warned. "Hereafter, you'll eat in the bunkhouse."

"Like everyone else?" he asked, looking around the table.

"Like everyone . . . oh, thunderation!"

She turned and quickly began to ladle soup into thick white bowls while Beatrice began passing around the biscuits.

"Now, just hush up and eat." She really didn't want to talk about it anymore.

Mr. Daniels turned to the children and said cheerily, "I personally can attest to the tastiness of the apple cobbler. However, I would warn you both to avoid any possum casserole."

"Ick!" Walter declared.

Beatrice giggled.

"Sorry to disappoint you, but Widow Marsden took that home with her," Callie told them. Nobody but a stranger would expect that parsimonious old miser to give anything away.

Mr. Daniels released a very audible sigh of relief, making the children laugh even more.

Then Walter released a big yawn.

"Oh, don't do that," Beatrice protested as she yawned, too.

"I wanna lay down and go sleep," Walter said. "I wanna sleep with the kitty."

His head was already lolling against the back of his chair. Any minute now Callie expected him to land face first in the chicken soup.

"We've been riding that train for four days," Beatrice explained. "It'd be nice to sleep lying down for a change."

"Well, now, I'm a stranger to these parts, myself. But I'd be willing to bet next week's wages that, in a house this size, there's bound to be a spare bed or two."

"There's . . . there's a big bed with a pillow for each of you right upstairs," Callie told them.

She didn't think it would be such a good idea to tell them right now that it had been Aunt Samuela's bedroom, and that, only a few days ago, she'd died in there.

"See, somebody wants you," Mr. Daniels assured the children.

"No, you don't," Beatrice said sullenly. "You just feel sorry for us now. You'll send us away first thing tomorrow morning."

Callie could hardly deny what the child said when it was probably true.

"Hush up, Bea," Walter mumbled sleepily through several sniffs. "They got cake."

"We don't just have cake," Callie said, trying to sound as inviting as Mr. Daniels had. Even if she was planning on sending them back, that didn't mean she had to be inhospitable this evening.

One thing she had to admit: Mr. Daniels might be able to irritate her, but he certainly seemed to know how to handle children.

"We've got apple cobbler and huckleberry pie, some lemon cake, and a little cinnamon peach cake."

"If you can stay awake long enough to eat it," Mr. Daniels said.

"Can I have cake for breakfast?" Walter murmured as his head flopped onto the table, barely missing his bowl of soup.

Mr. Daniels laid down his spoon. "Well, what do we do with these two now?"

Callie rose. "The bedroom's this way."

Mr. Daniels carried Walter out of the dining room, through the parlor, and up the stairs. Beatrice managed to stumble sleepily along behind them. Callie directed them to the hall on the right.

"There's nothing in here," Beatrice mumbled.

Callie had to agree with the child. Aunt Samuela hadn't believed in frivolous adornment for the body or the habitation.

"There's a bed," Callie told the little girl. "That's all you need right now."

Callie tucked the quilt around both children. They were asleep within seconds after their heads hit the pillows.

Callie thoughtfully studied the two exhausted children.

She'd needed men to help her work the farm, and here Providence had sent her two small children. They were even too young to get a decent day's work out of. Providence must either have a wicked sense of humor or be completely out of its mind. What was she going to do now?

"Come out of the room. Let's let them sleep," she whispered.

She couldn't bring herself to touch him, especially not in Aunt Samuela's very own bedroom. She motioned Mr. Daniels out the door.

She grimaced as she closed the door behind them. Apparently Mr. Daniels mistook her expression of concern for the children as distaste.

"Do you have something against children, Miss Jackson?" he asked.

"I . . . I don't know anything about children," she admitted. "Aunt Samuela and I certainly never had any around the house. Our neighbor to the west is a bachelor. The neighbors to the east have a son a little younger than me, so he doesn't count. Of course, if you knew him, you'd figure real quick he doesn't count for much, anyway."

Mr. Daniels grinned and scratched his head. "Well, ma'am, I haven't been in Cottonwood all that long, but every other place I've been, there were always lots of other people's children. Did you ever pay any attention to any of them?"

"I never had any reason to. Actually, I . . . I sort of try to ignore them whenever possible."

"Ignore them?" Mr. Daniels didn't bother to hide his disbelief very well. "How can you ignore children?"

"Believe me, it's not easy. Actually, there've even been a few occasions when I've gone out of my way to avoid some people's children," she continued to confess.

He chuckled. "Yeah, I can understand that."

"They sit behind me in church and pull the ribbons on my hat. Or they whine and complain during the hymns. Or they kick the back of the pew during the whole sermon."

"But Bea and Walter are pretty quiet now. What are you going to do about them?"

She was silent a moment while she thought. "Someone definitely made a big mistake."

"I'd say so."

"The only thing I can figure is, Aunt Samuela must have sent for an orphan again, expecting to get another adolescent boy to work on the farm. But this Mr. Van Bokelyn got mixed up and sent her these two instead."

"Well, I can see how that could happen. A ten-year-old and a four-year-old would equal up to fourteen. A body could get some decent work out of a fourteen-year-old boy."

Callie just stared flatly at him. "I don't think that's exactly how it works. But it makes just about as much sense as anything else that's happened today."

"That might explain how they got here," Mr. Daniels agreed. "But now that they're here, what are you going to do with them?"

"Leave them here, for now. But I'm in no position to keep them."

"Why not?"

She stared at him again. "You've seen I haven't the faintest idea how to deal with children. I'm not even sure I like being around them, and I don't think they like being around me. You heard them say they don't think I feel like a mother. How can you think I'd keep them where it's pretty obvious they wouldn't be happy?"

"So what will you do?"

"Tomorrow I'll start trying to find another place for them to live."

"Another orphanage?"

Callie could hear the censure in his voice. "Can you think of a better solution? I don't hear you volunteering to raise them."

"I think I'm in even less of a position to care for them—"

"That's all right. We don't even have an orphanage in Cottonwood. But don't worry," she added quickly. "I won't turn them out onto the street or anything. I'll try to find a place with people who know how to take care of small children."

Mr. Daniels laid his hand on her shoulder. "So you're not completely heartless."

She pulled away quickly. It was unnerving having this man touch her. His very breath had given her warm shivers when he'd whispered in her ear. His touch burned into her flesh, making her heart pound in her throat.

Her aunt had been right in keeping her sheltered from the men in town. The farther she stayed away from Mr. Daniels, the better. She picked up his saddlebags and tossed them at him.

"Come with me," she said, heading out the door. "I suppose you must be tired from traveling, too."

"And from not sleeping well last night," he reminded her.

"At least you didn't fall asleep in your chicken soup."

"I've had a lot of practice sleeping sitting upright," he told her.

Callie decided it wouldn't be a good idea to make any further comments about Mr. Daniels's sleeping habits.

"Come along. I'll show you where the bunkhouse is." She headed toward the door. "You can keep your horse in the barn."

"Thanks. I don't think I'll have much trouble finding an empty bunk," he told her, laughing, as he followed her toward the barn.

After he'd unsaddled and fed his horse and bedded him down for the night, he followed Miss Jackson to the bunkhouse.

A flash of lightning lit up the sky. A weak roll of thunder rumbled in the distance.

Harden felt large drops of rain dotting his denim shirt. He turned to Miss Jackson. Little droplets splattered her face. They both began to run toward the bunkhouse.

He pushed the door open, moved aside to let her enter first, then slammed the door shut behind him.

The bunkhouse was completely dark inside. Suddenly, a warm glow illuminated Miss Jackson's face. The golden flame of the lantern softened the angles of her features and lit up the raindrops on her skin like tiny stars. Running for the shelter of the bunkhouse had loosened the tight bun she kept her hair imprisoned in, and the dim light blurred the severity of the edges.

Harden felt the sides of his mouth twitch. *You know, in the dark,* he thought to himself, *Callie Jackson isn't half so ugly.*

Nope, he warned himself. *Don't get too involved in speculations.* Men who speculated unsuccessfully in gold just lost their shirts. Any unsuccessful speculations here, and he could risk losing his life.

Lightning flashed again, more brightly. This time, the thunder sounded much sooner. The storm was getting closer. He pulled his gaze away from her and looked around.

"So this is my new home."

Callie set the lantern on the table in the middle of the room. "Is it too fancy for you?"

"Probably," he replied. "But after a man's slept in mud up to his ankles, he's not too particular about whether the bunkhouse has a carpet on the floor or curtains in the windows."

He'd probably take the bunk farthest from the door, he decided. That way, he'd be able to get a good look at anyone who entered, and they'd have a distance to go to get to him. Just enough to buy him some time.

He tossed his saddlebags onto the bunk, claiming it for his own. The mattress wasn't so thick that his saddlebags sank into it, but at least it was thicker than a sheet of paper.

He started roaming around the room. The heels of his boots clunked on the bare wooden floor. The rain pattered against the sheets of tin on the roof.

The washbasin was clean. So was the floor. He paused to look at the sampler hanging on the wall between two of the bunks.

"Blessed is the man that hath not walked in the counsel of the ungodly, nor stood in the way of sinners, and hath not sat in the seat of the scornful," he read aloud.

He moved on to the next one.

"The wages of sin are death."

Thunder rumbled again. Was somebody trying to tell him something? He stroked his chin thoughtfully.

"Cheerful pieces of decoration," he remarked. "No doubt, the farmhands appreciated the constant reminders."

He moved along.

"In Adam's fall we sinned all," he read aloud again. "Worked by my hand this eighth day of June, 1849, Carolyn Jackson."

He turned to her.

"So your name's really Carolyn."

"Yes."

"How'd you get the nickname Callie?"

"I don't think that has anything to do with your being employed here, Mr. Daniels."

He coughed. "Maybe not."

After a brief pause, he continued, "1849, huh? You must've been all of—what—six? Seven years old?"

"I was five when I made that."

Harden nodded. "I guess Aunt Samuela kept you busy right from the start, huh?"

In reply, Callie pointed to the next sampler hanging on the wall.

"Idle hands do the Devil's work," he read, accompanied by another crash of thunder. "Yep, around here, I can believe it. I'm sure, as many times as you've told me you don't allow hard liquor on the farm, one of these samplers has to warn against the evils of drink."

Callie pointed to a sampler hanging on the opposite wall.

"Do you have any samplers warning against the evils of fornication?" he asked, chuckling.

Miss Jackson, unsmiling, just glared back at him. "I hope

you'll be comfortable here, Mr. Daniels. The cows get milked at five. Breakfast is served afterward."

"Yes, ma'am."

The rain sounded more like the rush of a swollen river. The lightning overhead flashed in such quick succession that it appeared to be an Independence Day celebration. The entire room vibrated to the seemingly perpetual roll of the thunder.

Callie sat bolt upright. The children burst through the door and pounced on her bed.

The flash of lightning and the loud clap of thunder overhead made them all jump. Walter squealed and threw his arms around Beatrice.

"The world's gonna 'splode!" he shouted.

"Don't be stupid, Walter," Beatrice scolded.

But Callie noted Beatrice was clinging to Walter just as tightly as he was clinging to her.

"Worlds don't explode."

"This house will," he maintained.

If Callie had run screaming into Aunt Samuela's bedroom when she was a child, she'd probably have spent a week eating off the mantel. But Callie had the feeling that was not the way Mr. Daniels would deal with this problem.

"We'll be fine," Callie tried to assure the children. "The house is sturdy. We're far enough away from the creek not to have to worry about flooding. The worst thing that can happen is the roof will leak."

Suddenly the sky lit up as if all the fireworks had gone off at once. The thunder changed from a rolling boom to a sharp, ear-splitting crack. But this time the intense darkness didn't return after the lightning flash was over. An eerie, yellow-red glow lit up the farmyard.

As the children huddled with each other, Callie sprang from her bed and dashed to the window.

"Oh, merciful heavens! The bunkhouse is on fire!"

5

"*MR. DANIELS IS* in the bunkhouse!" Beatrice cried.

Callie sat frozen, staring out the window at the mounting flames. Her throat was so tight with fright, she could barely whisper, "I know."

She didn't want to agree with the girl too readily and make the man's danger all too real. She didn't want to scare the children or feel any more afraid for him than she already did.

"You've got to save him!" Beatrice cried, tugging frantically at Callie's sleeve.

"You gotta!" Walter insisted, tugging frantically at the other.

"I know," Callie repeated.

She also knew she didn't have very much time.

"Stay here," she ordered the children as she sprang out of bed.

"But Mr. Daniels needs our help," Beatrice protested.

"Stay here!"

"But—"

She spun around and glared at them. "Or first thing tomorrow morning, you'll be heading back to that orphanage in New York!"

Mr. Daniels might have a pleasant way of calming the children, but if she really wanted them to obey, she didn't have time to cajole.

She didn't have time to bother with shoes and hose, either. But by the time she'd pulled a skirt on over her nightgown and sped out to the back porch, the rear roof of the bunkhouse was already completely engulfed in flames that were relentlessly making their way toward the front.

She stared up in awe. The top of the brick chimney was shattered, no doubt where the lightning had struck. The torrential rain wasn't doing a bit of good to extinguish the flames.

Mr. Daniels had claimed the bunk in the rear as his own. Was he lying dead on his bed—or dead on the floor? How would she find him? Was he even still inside?

Maybe he'd sneaked into town for a drink, she tried to reassure himself. Or gone outside for a smoke? Oh, yes, of course, she chided herself. Who wouldn't go out in the pouring rain?

Now she knew she was clutching at straws. But she could still hope the stubbornly independent man had already broken at least one of Aunt Samuela's rules.

Mr. Daniels was clever. But if he'd managed to get out, why hadn't she seen him standing around or even lying on the ground?

There was only one way to find him. She bolted off the porch, heading blindly through the rain.

The air cracked around her. Callie felt her arms and the hair on the top of her head prickle. She had to do something before the lightning struck again. But what? She could just picture herself at her own funeral, soaking wet and fried to a crisp.

Just as she slammed flat against the bunkhouse door, the

lightning broke harmlessly overhead. She was safe—for now.

The door was cool against her back. The fire hadn't reached the front of the building yet. Slowly, she opened the door.

A draft of hot air and smoke burst across her face, sucking the breath out of her. She fell to her knees. The air was cooler closer to the floor, and easier to breathe. She drew it in with deep, grateful gulps.

"Mr. Daniels!" she cried into the smoke-filled darkness. No answer.

"Mr. Daniels!" she repeated.

Still no answer. All she could hear was the roar of the flames as they consumed more and more of the bunkhouse.

"Mr. Daniels, I'm getting pretty sick of not getting any response from this bunkhouse. Now, answer me!"

Above the roar of the approaching flames, she heard a hoarse cough. She'd found him! But she couldn't be too relieved. He was still in the burning building. He was still very much in danger. She herself might die in the attempt, but she had to get him out of there. She had no choice.

Hitching up her skirt, she began to crawl across the floor. "Ouch!"

She bumped her head against the table leg. She shook her head to clear her vision. Then she realized the obscurity came, not from her dizziness, but from the increasing smoke. She crawled faster.

"Mr. Daniels! Where are you?" she shouted, trying to be heard over the incredible noise. "Call out, or at least keep coughing so I can find you. Ouch!"

She bumped her head against the front of a chair seat.

The farther she crawled into the bunkhouse, the denser the smoke grew. It was becoming increasingly difficult to breathe.

Suddenly, she tumbled over two long, lean legs and a set of narrow hips. Her skirts tangled between her legs and his. She landed flat on top of his body. Without her corset, she

could easily feel his firm muscles pressing against her
breasts and his chest rising and falling with each labored
breath he took.

"Mr. Daniels?" She peered down into his face.

"Who else were you expecting?" He tried to laugh, but it
degenerated into a fit of coughing.

"How can you joke at a time like this?" she demanded.
"We've got to get out of here—now!"

"Right." But instead of rising, he closed his eyes.

"Mr. Daniels, don't you dare die now!" She shook his
shoulder. "I can't carry you out and, in all good conscience,
I can't just leave your body here for cremation without some
kind of Christian service." She shook him again, harder.
"Mr. Daniels? Mr. Daniels? Harden!"

His eyes opened to mere slits. His nearness and the
approaching flames made her increasingly nervous.

She quickly drew back. "I thought you were dead."

"Just a little dazed." He opened his eyes a bit wider. Then,
as his vision cleared, he suddenly blinked in surprise. "What
in tarnation are you doing here? It's too dangerous. You
shouldn't have come—"

"We can argue about that later. Can you walk?"

"Not with you lying on top of me."

With a gasp, Callie almost sprang to her feet. But he
seized her hand and pulled her down.

"It's not such a good idea to stand up," he warned. "You
can't breathe up there."

"I know." But how could she breathe down on the floor,
with him touching her, holding her so close to his body?

She scrambled off to huddle beside him.

His voice seemed to be getting weaker, but his fingers
closed tightly around hers. She noted the calluses and the
strength of his grasp. She only hoped he still had enough
strength to get himself out of here quickly.

"Come with me. Can you crawl?"

"Yep, ever since I was real little." His weak laugh gave
way to more coughing.

"Stop joking! Stay low and follow me."

She could only believe it was her own desperation that gave her the courage to talk so sharply to him, even to seize his arm and pull him up to all fours beside her. But as soon as she turned around to look for the door, all her courage fled.

It was impossible to tell where she was. The smoke was too dense to see her way to the doorway or to any windows, or even to see the legs of the bunks. She had bumped into the table and a chair on her way in, so she knew she couldn't rely on their placement to guide her out of the building.

Everything was cloaked in smoke. Even the floor looked the same.

Almost the same.

Suddenly she had hope again.

"Come along!" She gave his arm an insistent tug.

"Where?"

"This way," she insisted, still tugging on his arm to urge him to follow.

"How do you know which way is out?"

"The floorboards." She pointed down. "They run cross-wise to the door. Even if you can't see it, you can feel it. Just keep moving across them."

"Are you sure?"

"It's my bunkhouse. Trust me," she told him, urging him forward. "Now, come on!"

She knew she had to stay close beside him if they were both going to get out alive. She was trying to crawl with one hand because she had the other wrapped firmly around his arm, guiding him out. She still needed to keep her shoulder pressed against his, just in case they lost each other in the smoke. She had never pressed her body against a man's this closely. His shoulders were broad, lean, muscular—and she knew she'd better concentrate on something else if they were going to get out of here in time.

They had only crawled a few feet when his elbows buckled beneath him. He reached up and held his head.

"I don't know if I can keep up," he said with a groan.

"I'll help you." She tugged at his arm, but he continued to sit, staring at the floor as if he was very dazed. She draped his arm over her shoulders, so that he was practically resting on her back.

"We'll never make it out."

"Yes, we will. I'm stronger than I look."

"No! Go on. Save yourself."

"Don't be a martyr." She dragged him along. "It doesn't suit you."

But even as she scolded him, she had the horrible feeling that maybe he was right. Maybe they were both going to die.

A blast of hot air coursing through the doorway hit her in the back of the head, fairly propelling her through the opening. A wave of fresh, cool air rushing in at the bottom filled her lungs.

At last! They were out of the building.

"We're not clear yet. The building's going to collapse."

She urged him farther out into the yard. The cool rain drenching her burning skin and smoldering clothing provided a welcome relief from the smothering heat of the bunkhouse.

"Come! This way!" she heard the children yelling. "Come!"

She wouldn't have believed it was possible for only two children to surround Mr. Daniels and her, but they seemed to be all over them.

"I thought I told you to stay inside," Callie scolded as they grabbed and tugged at her clothing.

"Can't, can't," Walter replied as he helped his sister pull them along.

"We had to rescue you," Beatrice explained.

"Gotta help," Walter maintained. "Without you, we got no place to live."

"You . . . you didn't really mean it when you said you'd send us back, did you?" Beatrice asked anxiously.

How could she send them back now when they were working so bravely in the pouring rain to help them?

"Not yet."

At last, Callie collapsed onto the back porch steps. She sat, her elbows resting on her knees, and her chin in her hands, watching the bunkhouse as the flames shot out the front door and engulfed the building.

Mr. Daniels had the unmitigated nerve to collapse beside her. Her nerves were already stretched taut as a bow. This man had the power to heighten her senses to the breaking point. Now that they were both safely out of the bunkhouse, she didn't need him coming any closer.

But he didn't lean against her for support. He didn't even close his eyes as he sat slumped back against the porch railing.

He was watching her very closely. There was a definite puzzlement showing in his eyes that she couldn't fathom. What was there to be puzzled about?

"Are you all right?" he asked.

"I'm fine. But your face is smudged," she told him, hoping to draw his attention away from her.

"So's yours."

She wasn't sure where, but she reached up to rub both cheeks, anyway.

"You missed," he said, indicating a vague area on her left cheek.

She rubbed her cheek a little harder.

"Nope. You still missed."

He reached out a single finger and slowly brushed it across her cheek. She might as well have still been in the bunkhouse. He might just as well have swept a burning brand across her cheek for all his touch seared through her skin and into her soul.

She drew back sharply. She hoped he wouldn't mistake the look she gave him to mean that she hated him and wanted him to leave. She just wanted him to understand that he shouldn't touch her like that. It could lead to far too many problems. She already had as many as she could handle.

"Your hair's a little singed, too," she told him to distract herself from these troublesome thoughts.

He reached up and gingerly touched the top of his head. "A piece of the roof fell and hit me when the lightning struck. I've got a bump back there the size of a goose egg."

"No wonder you passed out. We'll get you a bandage."

"Here, drink this." Beatrice pushed a glass of water into Callie's hands while Walter handed one to Mr. Daniels. "It'll make you feel better."

Callie's throat was dry, but when she took a sip, she found she was far too nervous to swallow.

"This is horrible."

Mr. Daniels took a sip, then studied the contents of the glass. "Oh, it doesn't taste too bad."

"No, no! I mean the fire, the bunkhouse."

Mr. Daniels reached out to pat her arm in consolation, but apparently changed his mind and drew back. Callie knew she should be grateful he'd understood her warning glance, but she was surprised to discover that some perverse part of her missed the feel of his hand against her skin. When would he touch her again?

"Don't worry," he told her. "At least the fire didn't spread to the barn or the chicken coop, or especially to the house. We can always build another bunkhouse."

"But your saddlebags were inside."

"That's nothing."

She stared at him in amazement.

Nonchalantly he brushed soot and ashes from his sleeves. He reached down to brush the dirt from his trousers, but everything was wet. He only ended up smearing the mess over more of his clothes.

"All your cheerful, uplifting samplers were in there, too."

"Don't be too disappointed. Aunt Samuela kept me very busy. There are plenty more in the house."

He grinned. "I should've figured. So we're both fine. You have your samplers, and I still have my horse."

"But your clothes, your shaving things, any money—"

Harden shrugged. "I can always get more next payday."

"How can you be so unconcerned over the loss of everything you own in the world?"

Harden shrugged again. He hadn't quite lost everything.

"Oh, I've been through worse."

He tried to keep his voice light. But he'd tried for almost a year now to bury those memories, and he still wasn't too successful with it. Better to think about a more positive side.

"I guess it's a good thing all the other farmhands left, after all. I doubt if we'd have been so lucky getting them all out."

"Yes, I suppose I should be grateful for blessings in disguise," Callie agreed. "No matter how small they are."

With a deafening roar and a fountain of sparks, the bunkhouse collapsed on itself. For a long time, Callie just stared at the blackening heap.

"Why did you do it?" he asked her.

"Do what?" She looked puzzled.

"You saved my life."

"No, no."

"Yes, you saved my life," he insisted.

"If that's what you'd like to think."

She shook her head firmly. Freed from the constraints of her severe bun, her auburn hair curled about her face and glistened with raindrops like lost particles of a shattered halo.

Harden longed to reach out again, to touch her glowing hair and wipe away another little smudge of soot she'd missed on her other cheek. If he did, she'd probably just cringe away from him again. She didn't seem to be the feisty kind of lady who'd slap his hand away. On the other hand, maybe her actions would surprise him as much as her sudden change of appearance did.

Nope, he decided, a person would have to work really

hard at dressing as badly as she did. The improvement in her appearance was strictly by accident.

"You know, some people hold with the belief that when you save a man's life, he's beholden to you for the rest of his life," he told her.

"That won't be necessary, Mr. Daniels. I'll be happy if you just stick around and help me work my farm."

"I've also heard that other people believe that when you save a man's life, you're responsible for him for the rest of your life."

"Well, I don't know about my lifetime, but, of course I'll see that you're paid and fed—while you're here."

What sort of tie had she created between herself and Mr. Daniels tonight? she wondered and worried. And for how much of her lifetime?

Harden watched her as she sat there. Her hair had come completely undone and flowed loosely over her shoulders. Her skirt was soaked, and there was a little rip in the side.

When she'd been lying on top of him, Harden had thought she felt too soft and pliant for everyday dress. As he studied her now, he knew the reason why. All that covered her soft, generous figure was her thin nightgown and her skirt.

The wetness of the fabric made it cling to her, accentuating the outline of her breasts and the darker rounds of her nipples, puckered and pressing against the thin, damp fabric. In spite of all he'd been through this evening, he found it difficult to take his eyes off the obvious physical attractions of the very plain woman who had saved his life. What a pity she hid such a beautiful body under such ugly clothes.

Suddenly, she crossed her arms tightly over her chest. When he managed to raise his eyes to her face, he saw her staring at him. But she wasn't angry, only . . . what was it? Hurt?

"Why did you do it, Miss Jackson? Why did you risk your life to save mine?"

"I . . . I had to. I mean, what else could I do?"

"You could've stayed outside where you were safe."

"No, I couldn't have."

"You should've left when I told you to."

"No. I didn't have a choice." She drew in a deep breath and tried to explain. "You know darn good and well you were too dazed to make it out of that building by yourself."

"Maybe."

"Very well, if your masculine pride prevents you from admitting you might have needed help with anything, especially from a woman—yes, you were perfectly capable of getting yourself out of that building. But, you see, I had to try to help you because you're completely invaluable to me."

He grinned and rubbed the back of his head. "You know, if I were a less scrupulous man, I might think this would be a good time to ask for a raise."

She only stared at him in great seriousness. "If you died, I wouldn't have anyone else to help me work my farm. I need you to work my farm, Mr. Daniels. If I lose my farm, I won't have anywhere to live."

So that was it. He was nothing more than a useful tool to her, he thought with chagrin. This cool lady had probably given about as much thought to saving him as she'd give to pulling a new shovel from a burning shed. And why not? That's all he was to a lot of people. That was all he'd ever been: a useful and highly effective tool.

"If I lose my farm, you'll have to go back to wandering around, telling everyone how desperate you are searching for another job."

She glanced over to Beatrice and Walter.

"The children wouldn't have anywhere to stay—not even until I could find them a new home. I can't leave little children to sleep in barns or along the side of the road."

"But did you ever stop to think about what would happen if *you* didn't get out?"

Very quietly, but without a bit of hesitation, she replied, "It really wouldn't matter."

From the way the sadness shadowed her eyes, Harden thought she looked as if she might release a deep sigh. But she pressed her lips together and continued.

"Some kind-hearted people in town would eventually take the children into their home. You'd move on, and eventually somebody would take pity on your pathetic desperation"—she gave a teasing little laugh—"and offer you another job. Someone would inherit the farm, or the ladies of the Society would sell it and donate the proceeds to a worthy charity, so at least somebody might benefit from my death."

She turned to him. The mist in her eyes came from more than just the rain or the disaster of losing the bunkhouse.

"Everyone else would get along just fine without me."

She rose quickly and headed across the porch. A hard shield rose to cover her loneliness and vulnerability. He understood exactly how she felt.

"Now, stop asking annoying questions," she scolded. "There's nothing we can do about the bunkhouse. I have to get the children—and myself—out of these wet clothes before we catch our deaths from pneumonia."

Callie ushered the children back into Aunt Samuela's bedroom and began fishing through their meager baggage for a change of clothing. She found another pair of trousers for Walter with large patches at the knees and a shirt with frayed sleeves that were much too short.

Beatrice grabbed her bundle and ducked behind the dressing screen. "I'm no baby. I can do this myself!"

"I ain't no baby, either," Walter fussed.

"I know, I know," Callie agreed as she struggled to pull his wet clothes off his squirming body. "But I think this is just something a mama does."

"You're not a mama. You said so."

"Beatrice is busy, and I don't think Mr. Daniels would do much better at being a mama. It looks as if I'm all you've got for now."

Walter twisted his lips as he thought. "Maybe you're right. But you're still not like *my* mama."

Callie finished buttoning his shirt. "No, I'm not," she had to agree. "Nobody else will be, Walter. But someday, somebody could come real close. My mama died when I was born, but her sister—my aunt Samuela—raised me. So, see?"

While Aunt Samuela had never exactly been a doting mother, Callie supposed she'd come as close as she was capable. She wondered how very different her real mother might have been.

"I wanna sleep with the kitty," Walter said.

"I can't find her. I think she's hiding from you."

"Why?"

"Oh, Walter, I can't imagine why anyone would try to hide from you!" Callie hoped the storm had passed completely over so that she didn't risk getting struck by lightning for that horrendous lie.

"What about me, Miss Jackson?" Mr. Daniels asked from the doorway.

She knew the aggravating man couldn't resist following her, posing more questions to which it was becoming increasingly difficult to find the answers.

"I'm sorry, Mr. Daniels. We only have one cat, and if she sees fit to hide, well, there's not very much I can do about it."

"That's not what I mean, Miss Jackson. I'm not too partial to catching pneumonia myself."

"It pretty much stands to reason, Mr. Daniels. If I don't want to see you dead, of course I wouldn't want you to be sick, either. I wouldn't get much work out of you either way."

"But, well . . . I need your help."

"Your hair's not on fire, and I don't see any blood running down your face. I'll get you a bandage as soon as I've dressed the children."

"But I need help getting dressed, too."

She wanted to give him a scornful glance, but she knew that running her gaze over his lean body would only stir up once again those feelings that Aunt Samuela had never warned her about. Right now, she had a few more pressing problems to resolve.

"I think the children need my help a little more than a grown man, who ought to be able to undress himself."

"I've been doing that since I was very young, too, and I'm pretty good at it."

For just a moment, Callie feared Mr. Daniels would volunteer to give her a demonstration of his skills.

"But you're forgetting something," he continued, grinning at her like the cat who'd swallowed the canary.

"What's that?"

"All my clothes were in my saddlebags. I don't have a dry stitch to put on."

It was bad enough she could still remember how firm and warm he felt beneath her. She didn't want to think about Mr. Daniels without any clothes on at all.

She held up Walter's bundle. "I don't think there's anything in here that would fit you."

"You're absolutely right. But I don't think it's a good idea for me to be running around here in Nature's own."

Callie felt her cheeks flush hot with the very thought of Mr. Daniels and anything to do with Nature.

"I . . . I'm sorry," she stammered as she devoted a great deal of attention to tucking the blanket around Walter. She turned down the wick of the lamp. "There's nothing I can do for you."

"I seem to recall you once told me the same thing about finding a job on your farm. And, lo and behold, here I am, working for you after all. So, I never give up hope, Miss Jackson." He chuckled again. "I never give up."

"Well, you just keep hoping some dry clothes will show up, Mr. Daniels," she told him as she motioned him out the door.

Somehow it seemed impossible to touch him in Aunt

Samuela's very own bedroom. She led him into the kitchen, where she fished a few rolls of bandages out of the cupboard.

Mr. Daniels sat on one of the kitchen chairs. Somehow it seemed easier to approach him now that they were out of Aunt Samuela's bedroom.

But it was still difficult to stand close to him, with his blue eyes level with her breasts, gazing up at her. She stood behind him. She could get a better look at his injury that way, she reasoned. It was also a lot easier to breathe without Mr. Daniels's face shoved right into her bosom.

His broad shoulders spread out in front of her. His hair was dark and, in spite of the singed edges, curled softly over the back of his head and around his ears.

What sorts of things went on inside Mr. Daniels's head? Callie wondered. *The same things that went on in any other man's head, probably.* She could tell that from the way she'd seen him looking at her in her damp nightgown. *Just like any other man,* she thought with a sigh. She'd been hoping that someday, somewhere, somehow, she'd at least meet *one* who was different from the rest.

"There's good news. You don't have any bald spots."

Mr. Daniels chuckled. "My uncle George would've liked to have had somebody be able to say that to him."

Callie laughed. She reached out and tentatively touched his head with a single fingertip.

"There's more good news. That bump doesn't look as bad as you think. It's really only about the size of a pigeon's egg."

Mr. Daniels released a sigh of relief.

"I'll still give you a bandage if it'll make you feel better." She began wrapping a single strip around his perfectly healthy head.

"Thanks, but I don't think you have enough bandages to substitute for a set of dry clothes."

The man was persistent, if nothing else.

"I told you before, Mr. Daniels, only my aunt and I lived

here. If I'd had an uncle who'd recently passed away, I might still have some of his clothes that you could use. But as it is, I don't think you'd look too good in one of my aunt's old dresses."

Mr. Daniels's chuckles turned into coughing again. She knew she had to help him. She knew if she didn't find some way of drying him off, she'd be back to working the farm by herself, with only Bob in Pieces to help whenever he could, at least until the bank repossessed her property.

"I suppose I could find you a place to change and a place to sleep for the night," she offered.

"I can sleep in the barn," he insisted. "I just need some dry clothes."

"Well, I don't have any," she replied sharply. She was getting awfully sick and tired of hearing this same old complaint. "Even if I did, they wouldn't do you a darn bit of good if the very first thing you did in them was run out to the barn in the rain."

Callie nodded toward the window. The pane was streaming with rivulets of rain highlighted against the storm-swept night sky beyond. With each lightning flash, the rivulets turned to streams of stars.

"I don't want you to get the wrong impression if I invite you to stay in the house. But, after all that's happened to you, I'd feel very remiss in my humanity if I let you sleep in the barn tonight."

He eyed her cautiously. "I'd really rather go to the barn."

"I'd really rather have you go to the barn, too, Mr. Daniels. But if we look at this logically, as much as I dislike breaking yet another of Aunt Samuela's rules, you're just going to have to stay in the house tonight."

"I don't mind the barn. Really."

"I'm sorry if you think we can't offer you the same caliber of companionship, sparkling wit, and scintillating conversation as the hogs and mules—"

"It's not that. I just don't want to be any trouble."

"You've already been that. And I've got a bad feeling

you're not through yet. But there's no fire to warm you in the barn, no bunk to sleep on, not even a folding cot, and no blankets to wrap up in."

"I've been—"

She held up her hand. "I know. You told me. You've been through worse. Well, if you're that particular about your accommodations, we'll set you up in the barn tomorrow morning. For now, you can follow me."

"Is there another bedroom in this house?"

Very quietly, she answered, "No. No . . . we never needed more."

"Well, Walter and Beatrice have pretty much taken over the one bed. I don't suppose you're going to be willing to share."

"Don't even consider it."

She spun around on her heel and headed out of the kitchen. She didn't even turn back to see if he was following her.

But he was following her, all right. She expected as much, especially if he thought she was heading toward a bedroom. The man was incorrigible, even in jest. Thank goodness there was a lock on her own bedroom door, just in case.

At the end of the hall, she pushed open a narrow door and entered.

"I think you'll be comfortable in here for tonight," she told him as she lit the lamp.

Harden poked his head inside the room. A small sofa, probably only big enough to sit two, was shoved into one corner. Under the window sat a small table with a lamp on it. A sewing machine with a battered trunk beside it sat in the opposite corner. The plain, whitewashed wall was adorned with more of the stern samplers. It was amazing how many things they had managed to stuff into such a small space.

"Gee, I don't know." He chuckled. "I've never slept in a closet before."

"It wasn't exactly meant to be a cozy bedroom. We made

all our clothes, so Aunt Samuela decided that a sewing machine was one of the few newfangled inventions that might be worthwhile. But she said it would be sinful pride to display it in the parlor, so she put it in this little room."

He strode into the room and sprawled across the sofa.

"No lice. No chinches. No bedbugs," he observed as he bounced. "No foul smells. The cushions are thicker than a letter from home."

"It's got to be better than the barn."

"I guess it'll do—for now."

He bounced back up again and began unbuttoning his soaked shirt.

"Mr. Daniels!" Callie cried, taking several quick steps backward. "Stop!"

6

"CALM DOWN. I wouldn't take my clothes off while you're still here." He grinned mischievously. "At least not all of them."

"You're incorrigible," she accused again.

Mr. Daniels's fingers ceased unfastening the buttons, but his hands still stayed poised at his chest. Between his rough knuckles she could see the dark hairs curling across his bronzed chest and down toward his belt buckle. Obviously, Mr. Daniels was not a man who enjoyed working with his shirt on.

"Aunt Samuela had a rule—"

"*Another* one? About keeping one's clothes on?"

"Aunt Samuela required the farmhands to keep their vests on and their shirts buttoned."

He grinned at her and tugged at the two halves of the front of his shirt. "It'd be a bit hard to take off a shirt with the neck still buttoned, wouldn't you say?"

Callie didn't want to think at all about Mr. Daniels taking off his shirt—or anything else.

"I think I've broken enough rules for one day. I'm going to get you a sheet to wrap around you."

"When you say that, do you mean to wrap around me, or that you'll personally wrap it around me?"

"I should've wrapped that bandage around your mouth," she told him. "Honest to goodness!" she muttered as she headed for the door. "If I'd known you were going to be this much trouble, I'd have hired Zack Keegan or Eugene Redmond instead."

"Who?"

"I'd have gotten some work out of them—at least until payday."

"What?"

"Never mind." She closed the door with a loud slam behind her.

Harden stripped off his sodden vest and damp shirt. He folded them into a neat bundle and placed them on the floor.

He pulled off his wet boots. He was silently grateful he'd been so exhausted earlier that he'd just collapsed onto his bunk without removing them.

It was just a darn shame he hadn't been able to salvage his saddlebags. There was so much that he needed badly that he just couldn't replace. Not easily. Not in this small town. Not without attracting unwanted attention.

"Mr. Daniels?" Callie called, rapping sharply on the door. "Mr. Daniels, are you decent?"

"No, but I'm dressed," he replied with a laugh. "Well, sort of."

"Cover yourself," she warned. "I'm opening the door and tossing in a sheet and a pillow."

"Did it come from your bed?" He laughed again.

"No," she answered quickly and very, very firmly.

The door squeaked. A feather pillow bounced off his head and landed on the floor. Then a cool, fresh sheet slapped him in the face. Before he could disentangle himself, the door slammed shut again.

Through the wood he could hear her giving instructions. "Please leave your wet clothes in the hall outside the door—the *closed* door," she amended.

Harden tugged at the damp denim until he'd managed to remove his trousers. He wrapped the sheet around him, then opened the door.

The hallway was empty. How could Miss Jackson at one time be so brave and save his life, and yet at another time be such a timid soul that she couldn't even stay around long enough to risk seeing him in nothing but a sheet? He didn't look that bad.

He laid the clothing on the floor outside the door, then went back inside to settle down to sleep.

The sofa wasn't half as uncomfortable as he'd feared it would be. It had to be more comfortable than dodging cow pies or road apples in a pile of hay in a stall. But if he wanted to get his job done, he'd have to move into the barn.

How could he come and go to do what he had to do if he was living under the same roof and the watchful green eyes of Callie Jackson?

She was always trying so hard to live up to her aunt's steely example, when the woman was made of anything but steel. But it would be just his rotten luck to have her stumble onto something secret, or interfere with his carefully laid plans, and ruin everything—not to mention putting his life and hers in danger.

As he dozed off, recollections of her soft breasts pressing against his chest through the thin fabric of her nightgown flitted through his mind. How could he sleep here, knowing that she was only a doorway away down the hall?

What did it matter? She continued to be as cold as ice, as rigid as an iron pike. Thoughts of her made him feel rigid, too, but he felt anything but cold as ice. He might as well sleep—or at least try to.

*   *   *

The fresh-washed sunshine of dawn flooded the room. Harden blinked and threw his arm over his eyes. Yesterday had been trying. Last night hadn't been so great, either. He'd spent it flipping from one side to the other on the narrow sofa. But he never expected his head to be pounding this badly.

Then he realized the pounding wasn't coming from inside his head. Someone was knocking on the front door.

Well, it wasn't his house, he thought as he tried to turn over and shield his face from the sunlight pouring in the window. Next time he stayed in a strange house, he'd make sure to pull the curtains before he went to bed.

Miss Jackson was undoubtedly up already. She'd answer the door.

But the pounding continued.

Harden groaned and stretched. He certainly wasn't dressed for receiving company. He wasn't sure where Miss Jackson had hung his clothes, or even if they were dry yet. Well, he reasoned, somebody had to answer the door.

The bandage had worked itself off during the night—and no wonder, with all that tossing and turning. It was a wonder he hadn't flipped right off the sofa onto the floor. But he figured covering his head was the least of his problems.

He wrapped the sheet tightly around himself, flipping one end over his bare shoulder.

"Harden, my lad, you look like a Roman senator or a Greek philosopher," he joked aloud as he opened the door and stepped into the hall. "I'm coming. I'm coming," he muttered as he headed down the stairs.

He glanced left and right, hoping to encounter Miss Jackson coming to answer her own door, but she was still nowhere in sight. He hoped she was getting dressed quickly.

"I hope it's not the minister," he continued to mutter. "Or little Miss Jemima Finchcroft, poor dear. She'd probably faint dead away if she could see me this way. Either that or she'd grab hold of me and ravage me on the spot."

Harden was still chuckling to himself at such an idea when he pulled open the door.

"My goodness!" Mildred Preston cried, clutching her hand to her breast.

Olive Luckhardt took one look at him and screamed.

The tall, thin young man standing behind her just stared. His Adam's apple bobbed up and down as quickly as the needle of that sewing machine upstairs probably did.

"You're that drifter!" Mildred exclaimed, obviously quickly recovered.

"You're Mildred!" Harden countered.

Callie stood at the top of the stairs. She watched Mildred shoulder her way past Mr. Daniels into the house. Olive Luckhardt and Herbert Tucker followed her like some rear-guard action.

She could pretty much figure why Mildred and Olive were here. She had a horrible premonition of why they'd brought along Herbert Tucker, too.

"What have you done to Miss Jackson, you worthless scoundrel?" Mildred demanded as she continued to press onward, driving Mr. Daniels back from the door. "I thought we'd sent you away. But here we find you've used your clever wiles to insinuate yourself into her good graces, preying on the poor child's grief at the loss of her only aunt to worm your way into her home. Did you ravage her, you savage, unprincipled cad? Did you murder her in her bed as she lay sleeping, you perverted evil-doer?"

"No, ma'am. Really," Mr. Daniels declared. "She's alive. She's breathing. She's moving. She's fine."

He grasped his sheet tightly around him. Callie almost laughed aloud. As if that flimsy piece of material could protect him—or anyone—from the righteous indignation of the formidable president of the Cottonwood Methodist Ladies' Evangelical, Temperance, and Missionary Soul-Saving Spiritual Aid and Comfort Bible Society and her loyal minions!

Callie was afraid Mildred would intimidate him so badly

that he'd throw up his hands in surrender and lose his sheet. Why, she shuddered to think what would happen then! Yet, the more the thought ran through her head, the more she found herself pondering its eventual occurrence.

It was difficult enough to keep her mind on the problem at hand without constantly noticing Mr. Daniels's broad, tanned shoulders, partially concealed and then revealed by the flapping sheet. He'd looked so thin in his worn, baggy clothing. But now she could see he was all muscle and sinew, not beefy flesh.

She also knew that if he turned around, the sheet wouldn't hide his chest as much as his shirt had. It certainly did nothing to hide the way his back narrowed to two small dimples just above the edge of the sheet. If it came down that far in the back, how much did the front reveal?

She drew in a deep breath. She'd changed her mind from her earlier speculations. Right now, she so hoped the sheet was fastened tight enough to stay where it was.

"Then where is Callie?" Mildred demanded.

Mr. Daniels was looking around frantically.

Mildred gestured at his own covering. "And what are you doing dressed—or rather undressed—like that?" she demanded. "What have you two been doing?"

"Mildred! It's all right," Callie interrupted, figuring it was about time she stopped admiring and started defending herself and Mr. Daniels. She came down the stairs as quickly as she could. "Really it is!"

"It certainly doesn't *look* all right," Mildred maintained.

"Innocent people have no reason to take their clothes off!" Olive declared.

"Don't innocent people bathe?" Callie asked as she interposed herself between Mr. Daniels and his accusers.

Olive and Mildred just stared at her with skeptical frowns.

"What are you doing here so early in the morning, anyway?" Callie asked to distract them.

"Everyone in town could see the glow from some sort of fire here last night," Mildred said.

"Lightning struck the bunkhouse," Callie explained. "But thank heaven that's all the damage that was done."

Mildred glanced about. "So I see. But, naturally, we all feared the worst."

"Naturally."

"We came here, out of Christian love and charity, to make sure you were all right, and what do we find?" Olive demanded. "Some half-naked man answering your door!"

"No, no," Callie protested. "It's not what you think."

"Callie Jackson, I might not have a college education—as a matter of fact, I only went for three years to that little red one-room schoolhouse back in Lexington, Kentucky. But I sure know a naked man when I see one!"

"There's a perfectly logical—and *very* innocent—reason for all this," Callie said.

"For your sake, I certainly hope so," Mildred said.

She stomped toward the sofa in the parlor and planted herself firmly on one side. Following in Mildred's wake, Olive took her station at the other end of the sofa.

"I, for one, would love to hear it."

For her sake, Callie thought, she certainly hoped, once they heard it, they would believe her.

"But you must admit," Olive insisted, "it looks *mighty* suspicious."

Only to someone who's looking for the worst, Callie thought, but she clenched her jaw to keep from telling Olive so.

Tight-lipped and stern-eyed, Mildred and Olive sat there, glaring at Mr. Daniels. Herbert Tucker, obviously overwhelmed by the rather loud display of overt hostility and incensed sensibilities, took a seat to the side and watched everything with wide, curious eyes.

His wide-eyed stare and pumping Adam's apple only contributed to the way the shock of blond hair rising from the top of his head made him look like an ostrich.

"By the way, Miss Jackson," Mr. Daniels asked with a broad grin, "where did you put my clothes?"

Right now, if I had them I'd like to shove your socks in your big mouth and wrap your shirt sleeves tighter and tighter around your throat until I strangled you, Callie thought. Instead, she smiled sweetly and replied, "Drying by the stove in the kitchen."

"Then I guess I'd better dress and get to my chores," he said.

"I guess you'd better," she dismissed him.

Go ahead, you coward, she silently shot after him. *Leaving me alone to explain my way out of this.*

On the other hand, she was so very glad to see him heading for the kitchen. Without having to look at him in that ridiculous and unbelievably provocative outfit, she would be able to think properly.

"Now, if *that* doesn't look suspicious, I don't know what does," Olive said, eyeing him skeptically as he made his way through the doorway. "Having a farmhand—that your late, lamented aunt would *never* have allowed in the house in the first place—getting dressed in the kitchen."

"He can hardly get dressed on the front porch," Callie replied, giving her chin a defensive lift. "I . . . I don't think it's at all suspicious, and it's certainly not my fault that lightning struck my bunkhouse last night, and Mr. Daniels and I both got drenched in the downpour when I helped him escape from the burning building, leaving him nowhere else to sleep, so he had to stay in the house instead of crossing the yard again to get to the cold, damp barn, getting even wetter, and possibly catching his death of pneumonia, and then his death would be on my conscience, so I had to hang the only clothes he had left—because the rest all burned in the fire—in the kitchen where they could dry by the stove because it certainly wouldn't have made any sense to hang them outside in the rain, and then he only had a sheet to wrap up in."

She drew in a deep breath.

Mildred and Olive just stared at her in amazement. She couldn't blame them. She herself couldn't remember ever having said so much at one time, except maybe that time she'd had to recite Samuel Taylor Coleridge's "Rime of the Ancient Mariner" at the Independence Day celebration the year she was ten, except she hadn't talked so quickly then. But now she felt as if, somehow, she'd tapped into a wealth of speed and eloquence. If she could just manage to convince Mildred and Olive . . .

"My, my. All that excitement in one day," Olive remarked.

Callie couldn't miss the woman's skepticism.

"My dear, you could've at least wrapped him in something that was a little more difficult to see through!" Mildred suggested.

"Only one day, and you're already doing things that, in the eyes of the ladies of the Society, could result in the loss of your farm." Olive shook her head.

"Only *some* of them," Callie interjected hopefully. She raised a prayer of thanksgiving that Widow Marsden hadn't come with them this time.

"Or, at the very least, that could result in making it extremely difficult to find you a suitable husband," Mildred amended sadly.

Callie shot Herbert a furtive glance. She didn't want to be rude and ignore him completely. On the other hand, she didn't want to appear as if she might actually be assessing his worth as a prospective spouse.

"But I've already told you. I don't want a husband," Callie insisted.

She watched Mildred and Olive shoot Herbert Tucker apologetic glances. She could tell Herbert swallowed hard because she saw his prominent Adam's apple bobbing up and down again.

"Begging your pardon, Miss Jackson," Herbert said. "But even if you're not in need of a husband, it appears to me you could at least use a good carpenter right now."

"I'll keep that in mind, Mr. Tucker," Callie replied. "The chimney was badly damaged. I could really use a good bricklayer now, too."

Callie had to grin as she watched Mildred squirm in frustration. She knew perfectly well that the only bricklayer in town was already very happily married, with his third child due any day now.

"You'd do well to keep Mr. Tucker in mind," Olive told her. "He's a fine craftsman, doing quite well for himself in his business. He's only twenty-five, been a widower for two years, is a regular churchgoer, has a house in town, no children, and all his own teeth."

"How nice," Callie answered with a forced smile. She could hardly be unkind to the man when he was merely an innocent fellow victim of yet another of Mildred's match-making schemes.

Herbert gave her a wide grin, as if trying to corroborate Olive's testimony. "I . . . I'd even be willing to overlook certain . . . indiscretions," he offered.

The smile quickly dropped from Callie's face. The man was hardly a victim. He was a predator, too.

"How generous of you."

She glared at him. How *dare* he be so willing to believe the worst about her on so little evidence! That certainly eliminated him completely from any possibility of being a prospective mate—as if he ever was one.

Then she shifted her glare to Mildred and Olive.

"But there's absolutely *nothing* to overlook."

"My dear," Olive said, leaning forward to pat Callie's hand. "Even if *we*—why, even if every single member of the Cottonwood Methodist Ladies' Evangelical, Temperance, and Missionary Soul-Saving Spiritual Aid and Comfort Bible Society—believed every word you said—"

"That would be quite an accomplishment!" Callie interjected.

"Callie! You simply can't have strange men parading

through your house, answering the door with no clothes on!" Mildred exclaimed.

"Mr. Daniels got no clothes to wear," Walter declared from the top of the stairs. "He got them all wet playing in the rain."

"We all got wet," Beatrice explained, "but we were the only ones with more clothes to put on."

Mildred and Olive's head spun around so quickly, Callie thought they looked like her weather vane in a bad storm.

"He didn't want to put on Aunt Samuela's dress," Walter added.

"Course not. He'd look silly in it."

The children skipped across the room to stand in front of the sofa.

"Callie? What is this?" Mildred demanded.

"They're children."

"I know that! What are they doing here? What are you doing with children?"

"I'm Beatrice Mobley," she introduced herself with a deep, very proper, and rather graceful curtsey. "How'd'y'do, ma'am? Pleas't'meetchoo."

"Well, aren't you just the sweetest little angel!" Mildred declared. She turned to Olive, as if daring her to contradict her.

Then Beatrice jumped up, perched herself on the arm of the sofa beside Mildred, and sat there grinning at her.

"Most people call me Bea. I'm ten years old. This is my brother Walter. He's only four—but he'll be five soon!" Beatrice added quickly, before he could repeat his earlier protest.

Walter executed a deep, equally proper, if terribly awkward, bow.

"What a fine young man you are," Mildred said.

"Most people call me Walter. She's already told you how old I am."

He clambered over the furniture to squeeze himself between Mildred and Olive.

At least it was a lot easier to explain the presence of these two than to explain Mr. Daniels, Callie thought with relief.

"What . . . how did you come to be here?" Mildred asked.

"We took the train from New York."

"No, no, I mean—" Then Mildred stopped, apparently realizing the silliness and futility of trying to correct them. "All the way from New York? But why?"

"Miss Jackson—"

The women's eyes turned to Callie.

"No, not her," Beatrice said. "The dead one . . ."

"Samuela?" Mildred asked.

Beatrice and Walter nodded vigorously in unison.

"She sent for us from an orphanage in New York. We came here to find a home."

If Callie had thought Mildred's eyes couldn't grow any more round with surprise or disbelief, she was definitely wrong. If Olive's mouth hung open any wider, Callie was afraid a flock of martins would fly by and nest in it.

Walter leaned closer to Olive. "Mmm. You smell like breakfast."

"Breakfast?" Olive repeated. She frowned at Callie. "What's that supposed to mean?"

"How should I know? They just arrived last night. I've never had breakfast with them."

"Breakfast smells like coffee and apple pie," Beatrice explained.

"Well, I did have coffee and a few apple turnovers— mind you, just a few—before I came here," Olive admitted.

"That's what we always had for breakfast before . . ." Beatrice leaned closer to Mildred and whispered, as if trying to keep Walter from hearing, "Before our mother died."

"Oh, you poor, motherless little lambs!" Mildred exclaimed. "What happened to your father?"

"He died, too, when Walter was just a baby."

Walter leaned closer to Mildred. "You smell like my mama's closet."

"What's *that* supposed to mean?" Mildred demanded, obviously rather insulted at being compared with something a lot less favorable than Olive's deliciously fragrant image.

"I have absolutely no idea," Callie said.

Walter sat there and sniffed in the atmosphere around Mildred.

Beatrice just shrugged. "Stop that, Walter! You look like some kind of idiot dog trying to hunt."

Walter sat much more quietly, but still turned his head and drew in a sneaky little breath from time to time.

"Well, if you'll all excuse me," Callie said, rising to her feet. "I have to start my day working this farm, and part of that job is getting breakfast for these children."

"You haven't given these children breakfast yet?" Mildred demanded, her disbelief very evident.

"As I recall, there was a bit of excitement around here earlier this morning that prevented me from preparing the usual breakfast."

"Apple pie?" Walter asked, quickly scooting off the sofa and heading for the kitchen. "You promised me apple pie last night."

"Hush up, Walter," Beatrice scolded. "You said before, this one's not like Mama. We don't know what we're liable to get."

"Indeed you don't," Mildred said. "Callie Jackson, I have absolutely no idea why your aunt sent for these poor, dear children, or what you could possibly do for them now. You don't know a thing about children."

"No, I don't. But I do know about fixing breakfast. If you'll all excuse me," Callie said. "I think you can see that I'm far too busy running my farm, taking care of these unfortunate orphans, and saving the life of my farmhand to be doing anything that could ever possibly be mistaken by the ladies of the Society for inappropriate behavior."

"I . . . I suppose so," Mildred replied as she quickly rose. She prodded Olive's arm. "Don't you agree?"

"I suppose so. For now."

"Yes, indeed. For now. But, mind you, Callie," Mildred warned her, "we'll be keeping an eye on you."

Callie had never doubted that for a minute.

"Well, we certainly have many, many other—more important—things to attend to, don't we, Olive?" Mildred said as she sailed toward the front door with Olive and Herbert trailing in her wake.

"Oh, yes, indeed. Always."

Callie closed the door behind them and leaned against it. They'd missed finding her dead so they could sell her farm and be charitable at her expense. They'd missed finding her in a compromising position with the farmhand so they could sell her farm and be righteously indignant, as well as benevolent, at her expense.

Callie almost had to chuckle as she realized the thing that had probably aggravated Mildred and Olive the most was Callie's rejection of their proposed suitor.

Aha! The first attempt of the Cottonwood Methodist Ladies' Evangelical, Temperance, and Missionary Soul-Saving Spiritual Aid and Comfort Bible Society to marry her off had been foiled. She chuckled with triumph.

Then she realized that in no time at all they'd be back with another one. Their supply seemed inexhaustible.

"Are they gone?" Mr. Daniels asked, grinning at her from the doorway to the kitchen.

"Yes. Where have you been?"

"Getting dressed. I could hardly do that in the parlor in front of the ladies, could I?"

Callie just shook her head in exasperation. The infuriating man had an answer for everything.

"Did it take you that long to get dressed?" she asked.

"I was doing my chores. What did you expect?"

"You couldn't stay and solemnly swear to your—and *my*—innocence?"

"It would've looked a lot more suspicious if I sprang to your aid like some knight in shining armor with a personal stake in the outcome than if I just minded my own business, kept my mouth shut, and went off and did my job like an ordinary farmhand."

"I didn't want you to be a fully armored knight on a white charger. I just wanted a small protestation of complete innocence. I don't need any dragons slain around here."

"Maybe you're right," he agreed with a playful gleam in his eyes. "It would be pretty hard to explain to the ladies of the Society why Mildred was lying dead on your parlor floor with a lance in her side."

"You're incorrigible!" Callie declared, giggling. "So now you've had your first real encounter with Meddling Mildred."

"Is that what you call her?"

"Not to her face."

"I didn't think so."

"I didn't start it, either. I understand that's been her sister's nickname for her since they were children."

"So it's a talent she was born with."

"Apparently. Other people in Cottonwood recognized it, and the nickname stuck."

"So, now that I've survived an attack by Meddling Mildred, do I get my breakfast?"

"I guess so."

"Yeah! You told me you had pie," Walter reminded her.

"I've got another good point," Harden said.

"What's that?"

"This little incident should have proved to you the wisdom of my staying in the barn in the first place."

Callie threw a log into the firebox of the stove. She moved the coffeepot forward over the increasing heat.

"Is that your way of saying 'I told you so'?" she finally asked. She waited, hands on hips.

He chuckled. "I guess it is. I appreciate you letting me spend the night in that nice, warm, dry spare room of yours, ma'am. But as soon as I'm done milking the cows and slopping the hogs, I'll be moving into an empty stall."

"Very well, if you're so insistent. But I need to ask you:

Are you coughing anymore? Do you have a fever?" she demanded.

"No."

"Then I hope you'll be very comfortable in the barn tonight."

"I suppose that's your way of saying 'I told you so.' "

She just grinned at him.

"Mr. Preston, you will never guess what has happened!" Mildred announced as she slammed her hat onto the small round table in the center of the vestibule.

The Reverend Mr. Abner Preston, comfortably settled in the big chair in the parlor, didn't lift his head from the book he was reading.

"Yes, dear."

"I never would've believed it myself if I hadn't seen it."

The Reverend Preston turned the page.

"Yes, dear."

"Olive Luckhardt was there, and Herbert Tucker, too. You can ask them if you don't believe me."

The Reverend Preston silently turned another page.

"A volcano suddenly erupted right in the middle of Forest Hamilton's cornfield," Mildred announced. "It's already demolished his house and is heading for Gibson's gristmill."

"Yes, dear."

"Emory Johnson sprouted a huge turnip out of the top of his head and plans to take it to the county fair in September if he can just figure out how to keep it in the root cellar and still do his chores."

"Yes, dear."

"Mr. Preston, are you listening to me?"

"Yes, dear."

"Oh, Abner, *listen* to me!" Mildred cried, slamming her hands on the tabletop.

Why should it be that every lady of the Society hung on to her every word like gospel, but her very own husband of

twelve years ignored her completely? It was just one more
splinter in the cross she had to bear.

"I'm listening, dear," he replied, still not lifting his head.

Mildred had to swallow several times before she could
compose herself enough to say what she had to say.

"Callie . . . Callie Jackson has two children."

The Reverend Preston looked up. At last she'd managed
to say something that could get her husband's attention—
and it had nothing to do with her.

He stuck his thumb into the book and closed the pages.
He removed his glasses and stared at Mildred. "But Callie's
not married."

"Neither was Charlotte Douglas, and she had three of
them. That doesn't seem to make any difference to *some* of
these people!"

"But we just saw Callie at the funeral two days ago, and
she didn't look—well, you know—in *that* condition. Doc
Hanford hasn't said anything. And she hasn't said a word
to me about having them baptized!" His eyes widened
with horror. "You don't suppose she's gone over to those
Lutherans, do you?"

"No, no, not two children of her own," Mildred corrected.
"Samuela sent for two orphans from New York. Now
Callie's saddled with the additional burden of raising them
and still trying to run her farm with only that one rather
suspicious-looking farmhand. But that's a whole other story.
I swear, the girl hasn't the faintest notion of how to raise
children."

"I don't think too many people do," he replied. "I think
the Lord just provides that sort of information as one needs
it."

"It's just not fair!" Mildred protested.

The Reverend Preston opened his book again.

"Year after year, I watch you join in holy matrimony
dozens of young people, and a year or so later—and
sometimes quicker than that—they're coming back to you

for a baptism and, in a little while, they're back again, and again, and again."

She sniffed and started crumbling the brim of her hat.

"While year after year, I wait and wait and wait for the blessing of being able to stand before that baptismal font with our own baby. And it . . . just . . . never happens."

"I've prayed about it, dear," he said without looking up from his book. "We'll just have to take it on faith that we're two of those unfortunate people to whom the Lord has decided to give other blessings instead of children."

Mildred pressed her lips together and gave her hat one more twist.

"Well, I don't think much of His decisions," she stated.

Snatching up her hat, she ran up the stairs, into her bedroom, and slammed the door behind her.

She wouldn't cry—not this time. She'd already shed enough tears, said enough prayers, been to enough doctors, listened to enough old wives' tales, even actually tried some of the silly things they recommended. She sat on the edge of her bed very still and very quiet so she wouldn't break down and scream.

If the Lord had decided to give her blessings other than children, she'd sure like to know what they were.

Maybe the Lord would've seen fit to bless her with children if He hadn't already given her the dubious blessing of a husband who completely ignored her.

Harden sat on a bale of hay in the barn, twisting the metal ring on the harness back into place with a pair of pliers. Motes of dust sifted down from the hayloft overhead, softening the outline of Callie's figure highlighted in the slanting rays of afternoon light.

It still didn't soften the severe bun into which she continued to pull her hair. It didn't make her plain black clothing any more stylish. But Harden figured a person would have to start somewhere with helping Callie. A little bit of softness just might be it.

"First thing tomorrow, I'm hiring another farmhand," she muttered as she stuck her pitchfork into the dank straw.

"You'll have to warn him he'll be sleeping in the barn."

"His sole purpose for being here will be to clean out the barn."

Harden chuckled. "Then I think he'd probably like to sleep somewhere besides where he works."

"No, no, I mean it," she insisted. "That's it. That's all he'll have to do, but—my goodness—then I'll never have to do this again."

"You don't have to do this now, either, you know," he told her.

"Yes, I do," she insisted.

Callie in her plain black dress with her hair pulled back might be able to do this sort of work. The Callie he'd seen last night, loose and glistening with raindrops, the Callie he saw right now, softened in the morning light, should be sitting among sun-drenched wildflowers and grass sparkling with dew, with butterflies fluttering around. Maybe with a cheery little bluebird perched on her shoulder just to complete the idyllic picture.

"If I don't do it, who will?" Callie asked.

"Isn't that what you hired me for?"

"Partly. But there's only one of you and chores enough for four men. Beatrice is already clearing away the breakfast dishes, bless her heart. Unfortunately, Walter's too little to be much good for anything right now."

"You'd better not let him hear you say that."

She lifted the pitchfork and tossed its load at the wheelbarrow. The pile of manure landed on the other side.

"You missed," Walter called out with a giggle.

Callie looked around for where his voice had come from.

"Am I going mad that I hear voices?" she asked Harden. "Or is that child actually some sort of changeling pixie who can appear and disappear at will, sending his voice wherever he wants, to confound mere foolish mortals like me? I really wouldn't put anything past those two."

Harden chuckled and pointed up. Walter was sitting in the hayloft, dangling his feet over the side through the hole in the ceiling.

"Thank you for pointing that out, Walter," Callie told him.

Harden heard Walter giggling. He was finding it hard not to laugh himself.

"How'd you get up there?"

"I climbed."

"Don't fall and kill yourself."

"Course not!"

"Does this mean you're starting to feel some sort of affection for the children, Miss Jackson?" Harden asked.

She just glared at him. "I didn't send for them. I don't think it would be fair for me to be stuck with the cost of his funeral."

She moved around to the other side of the wheelbarrow and forked up the stray bundle. Then she moved along, cleaning up straw as she went.

Even picking up manure, she moved with a delicate grace that made even her worn cotton dress flow like black satin. What would she look like in satin, Harden wondered, skimming across a candlelit ballroom floor?

"Hey, what's this for?" Walter called.

"What's what?" Harden replied, still wrestling with the contrary harness ring.

"This rope."

"Which rope?" Harden had already been up to the loft. There were a lot of different ropes up there.

"This big one here, hooked to this big nail in this big board."

"Don't touch it!" Harden shouted, dropping the pliers and harness.

"Touch what?"

"Touch the rope."

"Okay."

"No!"

Before Harden could reach the ladder to stop Walter, the ceiling opened and the pile of stored hay came tumbling down on top of Callie.

7

CALLIE COULD HEAR muffled sounds. She opened her eyes. The light was dim and strangely yellow, but at least she could still see.

What had hit her? One minute she was having such a jolly time cleaning out the barn. The next thing she knew, she was waking up under a pile of hay. The only thing she could remember was Mr. Daniels saying something to Walter about not touching the rope.

The rope that held the hayloft door closed! That was the only thing she could figure. Callie tried to release a sigh of frustration. If she ever got out of here, she'd wring Walter's overly curious, ornery little neck.

If she got out alive.

She tried to move her arms and legs. The straw prickled her skin. At least she could wiggle her fingers and toes, but not enough to work her way out from under the mound of hay by herself. She knew how much hay was in the loft, and now it was all on top of her. Pitchfork by pitchfork, she knew hay wasn't that difficult to move, but an entire load was unbelievably heavy. She was afraid she'd never move again.

She'd scream. Then Mr. Daniels would know she was still alive and try to dig her out of here faster, before she suffocated to death. If only she could draw in a breath!

Each time she opened her mouth, little pieces of straw slipped in. She tried to spit them out. With every breath she took, the dust rose up and choked her. If she wasn't dead now, she soon would be.

Would Mr. Daniels need help getting her out? Would he even have the time to get help before she died? Beatrice and Walter were too little to be much help. Where in the world was Bob in Pieces when she needed him? Where in the world were Mildred, Olive, Widow Marsden, or any of the other fine busybodies of the Society? Even Miss Jemima, with her little clawlike hands, could scrape off a bit of hay and save her. Why couldn't they come nosing around here when she really needed them?

Somehow, Mr. Daniels alone would have to dig her out. Somehow. She'd just have to pray. She closed her eyes. That was the proper thing to do when one was praying. She wouldn't want to find herself at the Pearly Gates, facing St. Peter, only to learn she was denied entrance just because she hadn't closed her eyes while praying.

Worse yet, she remembered when she was just a little girl, going with Aunt Samuela when old Mr. Sturgis had died and nobody had found him for a week. She'd seen him lying there dead in his bed before anybody had come to clean him up. His mouth was hanging open, and his sunken eyes were staring heavenward, even though anybody in town could have plainly told you that the old curmudgeon had undoubtedly ended up going in the other direction.

Callie knew she'd never been a truly pretty woman, but at least if she managed to keep her eyes closed, she thought she'd leave a better-looking corpse.

She closed her eyes and waited for Mr. Daniels or the angel of death, whoever reached her first.

"I'm sorry."

Oh, dear! Saint Peter was telling her she'd missed her chance at Heaven by one unclosed eyelid.

Why did Saint Peter sound like Walter? Oh, no! Maybe she ended up like Mr. Sturgis after all—headed in the wrong direction!

"I'm sorry! I only wanted to see what the rope was for," she heard Walter cry.

Someone was pulling on her arm. She opened her eyes. Walter knelt at her side, brushing hay away with one hand and tugging at her arm with the other.

Tears were streaming from the little boy's eyes.

"I'm really, really sorry."

Callie drew in a deep breath of clean air. One just wasn't enough. She was so glad to be able to keep breathing.

She turned to Walter. "It's all right. I know it was an accident. The next time, please ask first."

Walter smiled, sniffed, and rubbed his dripping nose on the back of his hand. "I did. *He* told me to pull the rope." He turned accusingly to Mr. Daniels.

"Oh, Miss Jackson, you don't think—"

She turned her head. Mr. Daniels was still standing over her, removing huge scoops of hay in his powerful arms.

"Of course not."

With each scoop, she found she had increasing mobility in her arms and legs. She started to push herself up onto her elbows.

"Are you all right?" Mr. Daniels asked. "No cuts? No bruises? No bumps?"

"I . . . I don't think so," she replied, looking around her. She felt the top of her head. "Not even the size of a robin's egg."

He shoved aside the last pile of hay. He gave a start and stared at the ground beside her. "Well, you're a dang sight luckier than you'd ever imagine, that's all I can say."

"What?"

Mr. Daniels stooped down and picked up what was left of the pitchfork. The weight of the falling hay had snapped the wooden handle in half, leaving the sharp prongs of the head sticking upright in the straw, about half an inch away from Callie's side.

Even without the hay, it was almost impossible to breathe.

"Oh, merciful heavens!" Callie gasped. She swallowed hard as a shiver of horror coursed through her. She felt sure she was going to vomit.

"I think I'd better get you back to the house. Can you walk?"

She nodded weakly. "Since I was very small." But suddenly her arms and legs felt weak and completely useless. Her knees buckled under her as she tried to rise.

He chuckled.

"Then it's time you took a break," he told her. "After all my efforts, I wouldn't want you to faint and fall and hurt yourself anyway."

"*I* don't faint," she declared defiantly.

Before she could say anything else, Mr. Daniels bent down and scooped her up into his arms.

"Oh, no! Don't! Stop! Put me down immediately!"

One strong arm caught her around her ribs, crushing her to his chest. His other arm pressed firmly against the backs of her knees as he lifted her from the barn floor. She'd never felt so completely helpless and yet so completely safe in her entire life.

"Really. Put me down. I can walk!"

The more she protested, the more tightly he held her as he carried her across the yard toward the house. She had to do something to prove she wasn't completely in his power.

She'd show him she wasn't relying completely on his strength alone. She could provide some support for herself. She reached her arms up to encircle his neck. In order to do that without discomfort, however, she realized she also needed to tuck her head against his chest.

Accident or not, she shouldn't be doing this. She shouldn't be allowing Mr. Daniels to be doing this. A man and a woman in each other's arms! What would Aunt Samuela say?

But it felt so wonderful. She never imagined a man as lean and wiry as Mr. Daniels could be so strong. She had never imagined how good it would be to feel his muscles moving across her back and side, or under her legs as he supported her in his arms.

Suddenly, Callie began retracting all her earlier wishes for assistance. If Bob showed up, after a few expressions of concern for what might have transpired, he'd probably just laugh her predicament away. But now was definitely *not* the time for Mildred, Olive, or any of the other ladies of the Society to pay a visit!

"Beatrice! You missed it! It was really 'citing!" Walter cried as he burst into the house ahead of them. "I saw it all, and you didn't."

He went running madly through the house, searching for his sister, to taunt her more.

"I knew from the first time I laid eyes on them, these children were going to be a lot more trouble than they were worth," Callie muttered. "The sooner I find someone else who can take them in, the better."

"It really wasn't his fault, you know."

"I know," she answered very softly.

But how could she explain to Mr. Daniels that complaining about Walter and Beatrice kept her mind off what she really wanted to think about? How could she tell him how very warm and comforting it felt to be in his arms after such a horrible experience? How could she explain to him when she didn't even understand herself how she could feel comforted and at the same time newly and vividly alive in his arms? How could she let him know that she enjoyed the heat of his body, the strength of his muscles, the very masculine scent of him?

"Oh, Miss Jackson!" Beatrice cried as Mr. Daniels carried Callie into the parlor. "You're filthy!"

"Thank you for drawing that to my attention."

"You can't put her on the good sofa," Beatrice told him.

"She's getting awful heavy. I'm going to have to put her down somewhere soon."

"But you'll ruin the upholstery."

"My, my, aren't you the good little housekeeper?" Mr. Daniels teased.

"She's got horse manure on her. Do you want to put her in *your* bed?"

Mr. Daniels coughed. "Gosh, Beatrice. I don't think that's the question you ought to be asking me."

"Here! Here!" Walter exclaimed, offering Beatrice the sheet Mr. Daniels had used to wrap up in earlier.

She spread it out to protect the upholstery. Then Mr. Daniels lowered Callie to the sofa.

"Are you feeling all right?" he repeated.

"Of course I am," Callie insisted. She pushed herself up into a sitting position. "I was only a little stunned. I'm not some sort of invalid who has to lie around all day after almost being smothered to death."

She held out her arms, brushing off bits of straw.

"Look, barely a scratch. So, thank you all for taking care of me. I think I ought to get up and get back to work now. It's probably time to begin supper."

"I can do that," Beatrice declared proudly.

"You can?"

She nodded emphatically. "My mama could cook. She was a good cook. She taught me."

"Ordinarily, I do the cooking."

"Yeah?" Beatrice, hands on hips, confronted her. "Ordinarily, you probably aren't out in the barn, scooping up straw and horse manure, either."

"Ordinarily, you don't have piles of hay dropped on you,

either," Mr. Daniels said. "Maybe you ought to let Beatrice take care of things just this once."

"But—"

"If she burns the potatoes, we'll just eat beans," he continued. "Remember, I've been through worse."

"You keep telling me." Callie leaned against the back of the sofa. It did feel mighty good to rest her weary bones. "Maybe you're right."

"Good. You stay here. I've got a few things to clear away in the barn," Mr. Daniels told her. "Walter will keep you company."

The little boy started to settle in beside her on the sofa. Then he sniffed. "You smell like the barn. You need a bath."

"Whose fault is that?" Callie demanded.

Walter grimaced. "You were working in there, anyway."

"Walter, why don't you go help Beatrice in the kitchen?" Callie suggested.

"Oh, please!" Beatrice protested. "Why don't you go help Mr. Daniels?"

"Gee! Don't nobody want my help?" Walter stamped his foot.

"Come along, Walter," Mr. Daniels said, holding out his arm to usher the little boy from the house.

"Aw, you're only saying that 'cause you ain't got nobody else to pass me off on."

"No, sir. We menfolk have to stick together. I don't think it's safe for us fellows to be inside the house when the womenfolk are cooking or bathing."

Walter bolted out the door ahead of him.

Beatrice knocked, then poked her head inside Callie's bedroom. "Supper's ready."

"Oh, thank you for taking care of all this, Beatrice. My goodness, that does smell good," Callie said.

She didn't want to sound too surprised and hurt the eager little girl's feelings, but she was pleased and surprised to find such a wonderful aroma arising from the kitchen.

Beatrice responded to the compliment with a self-satisfied smile. "Thanks. You smell good, too."

"Thank you." Callie figured her tuberose toilet water was just a little different odor than the cabbage she smelled.

"Did that bath make you feel better?"

"Yes, indeed."

"Or do you still want me to bring you up a tray?"

"No, no. I'm tougher than I look. It's going to take more than a pile of hay to keep me from coming down for supper."

"Are . . . are you coming down like that?" Beatrice asked tentatively.

"Like what?"

"Like *that.*"

Beatrice's upper lip curled as she gestured up and down. Callie took that as an indication that her entire appearance had been weighed in the balance and found wanting. But it was a dress she'd worn dozens of times before, and no one had complained. What could be wrong with it now?

Callie glanced down at her dress. All the buttons were fastened, and all of them matched up to their appropriate buttonholes. She looked at herself in the mirror. She'd washed all the dirt off her face. She'd brushed all the bits of straw out of her hair and smoothed it back into her usual bun.

"What's wrong with how I look?"

"Nothing. It's just . . . well, it's just . . . you don't seem to be doing anything to help yourself."

Callie stared at her, puzzled. "What should I be doing to 'help myself,' as you put it?"

"Well . . ."

Beatrice heaved a deep, thoughtful sigh. Then she began circling Callie, studying every aspect of her appearance. Callie was starting to feel like a horse or cow at auction time. She also had the feeling she was going for a very low bid.

"You got a nice figure, ma'am. But, well, that dress don't do a darn thing to show it off."

Aunt Samuela would be horrified at the thought of showing off anything—much less her body!

"Clothing's meant to hide the sinful, naked body, not show it off," Callie repeated automatically.

Beatrice grimaced horribly. "What muttonhead told you that hogwash?"

"Aunt Samuela."

"Oh." At first, Beatrice looked as if she wanted to hide under a rock to save herself further embarrassment. Then she glared at Callie. "The old maid?" she said accusingly, without any further hint of apology or remorse.

"Well, yes. I guess so. Only it might be more polite to refer to her as a maiden lady."

Beatrice crossed her arms over her chest and eyed Callie knowingly. "Whatever. But it just goes to show about how much *she* knew about dressing up, doesn't it?"

"It's not just Aunt Samuela's idea," Callie asserted. "Even in the Bible it says Adam and Eve covered their nakedness."

"Yeah, with *leaves!*"

Beatrice started holding her hands over various places on her torso, as if setting leaves in place.

"Do you know how big a leaf is? Do you have any idea how much a leaf actually covers? Do you know of any really, really *big* leaves?"

"But—"

"Come to think of it, when Mama used to take me and Walter to church, I seem to recall, in all those paintings and even the stained-glass windows, Adam just had on that one little teeny tiny leaf." She held up her thumb and forefinger with a very tiny space between them. "And Eve always had bare bosoms."

"I will *not* do that!"

"Either that or they were standing behind bushes. I don't think you want to spend your life standing behind bushes— although in that dress, I think maybe you ought to."

"I think, in our modern world, we've progressed a bit beyond wearing leaves," Callie told her.

"Yeah, we sure have!" Beatrice's eyes lit up with a light that Callie found slightly alarming. "There's cotton, linen, and wool. Satin, velvet, and brocade. And lots of beautiful colors besides green. There's stripes and dots and flowers and plaids."

"How do you know about all this—cooking, dresses, trays for sick people in their bedrooms?"

"I told you, my mama worked in a big, fancy house in New York, on a street with a number. I think it was something like Five or Fifth. I think she was like a maid or something to this really rich old lady. She cooked for her, and helped her dress, and ordered the other servants around, and made sure all the parties had lots of music and really weird food that grown-ups like to eat. Do you believe, one time Mama told me the old lady actually served *fish eggs!* And her guests ate them!"

Beatrice pantomimed a quite awful retching gag.

"Walter and I could live there, but we had to stay in the kitchen in the basement during the day, which wasn't too bad because there was a little window way up high, and you could see the people's feet through it. And we stayed in the servants' bedrooms on the top floor at night, which was really beautiful because we could see all the stars up above, and down below we could see all the candles in the rich people's houses and all the gaslights along the streets. We had to be very, very quiet all the time and not touch anything. But sometimes, when the rich old lady was napping, and Mama was working someplace she wouldn't see us, we'd sneak out and see such *wonderful* things. Oh, Miss Jackson, you have no idea!" she finished with a reverent sigh.

"That's all well and good for rich old ladies from someplace fancy like New York. But I'm not rich or old." She gestured down at her dress. "And this is all I've got."

"Well, you're sure not doing much with it."

The child certainly was relentless and remorseless in her criticism.

Callie studied herself with new eyes in the small mirror that hung over her dressing table. Her dress certainly didn't look like the dresses of the other ladies in town—not like Mildred's or Olive's or even Miss Jemima's, she realized. The shoulders were too broad and high. The waist wasn't where it ought to be. The skirt wasn't full enough.

No doubt about it. The dress was very old. The fabric had already been turned once, and the ribbons and buttons had been replaced several times. Even if she wasn't one to follow every frivolous whim of fashion, at least she oughtn't to wear clothes that were rusty and threadbare, at least not to dinner.

It had never bothered her before, but suddenly she found herself questioning the wisdom of Aunt Samuela's fashion sense—on the advice of a ten-year-old girl, of all people!

"We've got that good sewing machine," Callie offered tentatively. "It's a shame to let it go to waste."

"Oh, definitely," Beatrice agreed enthusiastically.

"Maybe I ought to go into town and get some more material soon," she suggested.

"Some new patterns, too."

"Maybe I ought to make myself a new dress."

"Oh, at least one."

"But there's nothing I can do about it now."

"No, you're right about that." Beatrice couldn't hide her disappointment about the dress. Then her little face brightened again. "But, well, I'm not done yet."

Callie viewed with dread what she truly believed sounded like a threat.

Beatrice flung open both doors of the wardrobe and stood there, staring.

"Well, you don't have much, and what you do have . . . Ick! Everything's dark."

"Not everything," Callie defended. "There are a few white—"

"You've just *got* to have a better-looking dress." She

started pushing dresses out of the way, rejecting everything she touched. "Aha!"

She pulled out a deep green calico dress.

"But that's my Sunday dress."

Beatrice eyed it with extreme distaste. "Sunday, huh? How in thunderation do you expect them to let you into heaven in something this unfashionable when all the other angels'll be wearing dazzling white robes and sparkling wings?" she demanded.

"I . . . I always thought they supplied the uniform."

Beatrice gave a deep sigh. "Oh, well. It'll just have to do. You put that on when I leave," she ordered.

At first, Callie thought Beatrice might be satisfied, and they could go eat supper. But the little girl just stood there, fists on hips, glaring at her.

"What's wrong?"

"Miss Jackson, you just *got* to do something about that *hair!*"

Callie's hands immediately flew to her head. "What's wrong with my hair?"

The little girl guided her toward the chair at the dressing table and urged her to sit down.

"Nothing. You really got beautiful hair," she hastened to assure her. "That's why . . . well, that's why it's such a darn shame to do such a horrible thing to it."

"Horrible thing?"

"Just pulling it back so tight, tying it in that awful knot. Why, that's about as bad as putting a butterfly in prison!"

"What?"

No one had ever talked to her like this before about things she'd never really given much thought. And yet, deep inside, now that the subject had been brought out into the open, Callie had to grudgingly admit that she saw the rightness of the little girl's reasoning. That darn tight knot always had given her a headache, anyway.

"What do you suggest we do instead?"

Beatrice's hands started flying around, reaching for brushes and pins on Callie's dressing table.

"Oh, just let me show you!"

Callie could hardly ask the child for credentials, but she had to learn a little more about her background before she let her go experimenting with her hair.

"Did you used to do this with your mother?"

"Oh, no. This is sort of like something you'd do for a big sister or a real good friend. Nope. This isn't mama stuff."

"It smells great in here!" Harden exclaimed as he and Walter entered the house.

"Oh, boy!" Walter immediately headed toward the kitchen. "We're having cold cannons!"

"Cold cannons?"

"I found some potatoes and a cabbage in the springhouse," Beatrice explained. "When we had that, Mama always made something she called colcannon."

"Colcannon," Harden repeated in recognition.

"Haven't you ever eaten it before?" Walter demanded.

"Oh, yeah, lots of times," Harden told him. "I just heard it called something else."

Walter planted himself firmly in his seat at the table, grabbed his fork, and started drumming his feet impatiently against the legs of the chair.

"I'm sure if it tastes half as good as it smells, there won't be any left," Harden commented.

Should he sit at the table, too? Harden wondered. There were four places set, but Beatrice had taken care of that. He wasn't sure what Callie would have to say about continuing with these arrangements. He'd been so stubborn about sleeping in the barn. Would she use that as an excuse to send him out to eat there, too? He'd just have to wait to find out.

Where was she, anyway? he wondered.

Beatrice was busy setting out a big bowl of colcannon and dishes of pickled beets and corn relish, and a basket of hot bread, and cold butter. As a matter of fact, she seemed a little too intent on her job. Something was definitely going on that was sure to surprise him. He didn't have to be some kind of medium to know that when Callie showed up, everything would be made crystal clear to him.

"Miss Jackson!" Harden exclaimed, springing to his feet.

She stood in the doorway, hanging back as if afraid to enter. He'd never expected the revelation to be *that* clear!

Her dress wasn't black. Where had she gotten a green dress? It was almost as old as her black one, but it sure looked a heck of a lot better on her. It made her green eyes glow like emerald fire and her auburn hair burn like copper flame.

It wasn't just the dress. Part of her hair hung long and free down her back, and it curled up slightly at the ends. The rest had been gathered up at the back in a mass of curls and ribbons. Someone—and he had a fairly good suspicion who—had carefully coaxed out a few delicate curls to wrap gently around her face.

"Do you like it?" she asked slowly, her voice echoing uncertainly.

"Like it? Why, Miss Jackson, you . . . you should let a pile of hay fall on you every day!"

Oh, my goodness! What a stumble-tongued, mouse-brained clod he was to say such a thing!

"I mean . . . I mean, you look so different. So much better."

Oh, for heaven's sake! He did it again!

Maybe he ought to just shut up, take his food outside to eat like the pig he was, and leave the compliments to the poets.

"I'm so glad you like it, Mr. Daniels," Callie replied. Apparently he hadn't insulted her enough to drive her away. She took her seat at the head of the table.

Her shy little smile and the faint blush to her cheeks told him she was very pleased with his lame compliments. Maybe she wasn't much of a literary critic. But she certainly was beautiful.

"I . . . I had a little help," she admitted.

"Looks like you had a *lot* of help," Walter said

Harden and Callie both looked toward Beatrice, who was sitting there, grinning broadly with pride.

"Well, miss, I'd say you've acquitted yourself quite nicely this evening," Harden told her.

"She didn't quit. She finished it," Walter protested.

"She did it very well, too," Harden managed to say without laughing at Walter.

"We're going shopping," Beatrice announced.

"We are?" Callie asked.

She knew she'd been unconscious for a while, but that had been out in the barn. She couldn't remember making any definite plans.

"We need new material for new dresses."

"Can I go?" Walter asked.

"You don't like to look at material for dresses," Beatrice told him.

Walter grimaced. "Ick! Course not!" Then his eyes brightened. "But they got candy at the store, too."

Aunt Samuela had never been much of a one for indulging in sweets. Callie tried to remember the last time she'd had candy. Probably the Christmas party two years ago at Mr. and Mrs. Hooper's house. While Aunt Samuela was visiting, Callie had found a small dish and eaten a piece or two. She couldn't remember any time before that. All she knew was that chocolate tasted wonderful! Maybe if they went into town, she could buy just a little bit more.

"I guess we might be able to go into town sometime soon," she agreed.

The children cheered.

"You come, too!" Walter insisted, grabbing hold of Mr. Daniels's arm.

"Oh, I don't know," Harden said. "I have an awful lot of work to do around here."

"No, no," Walter protested. "What kind of work you got?"

"Well, for instance, I've got a whole pile of hay to move back up into the loft."

Walter twisted his lips around, then ducked his head to stare intently at his colcannon and shovel a goodly portion into his mouth.

"I don't have any money until payday, either," Harden said.

"I . . . I think we might be able to arrange an advance on your pay," Callie told him.

"I'd be much obliged, ma'am," Harden replied.

Aunt Samuela would turn in her grave if she could hear her now! The farmhands *never* got paid until after the work was done.

But this was her farm now, and her work, Callie decided, quite boldly for her, actually. She could pay whoever did the work whenever she felt like it.

"Oh, you don't need any money to go shopping," Beatrice told him. "We used to do it all the time in New York. It doesn't cost any money to shop. It only costs money when you actually go to *buy* something."

Harden laughed. "On the other hand," he said, "I really could use some new clothes, too. I'm getting a little tired of washing out the same shirt every night, hoping it'll be dry by the morning."

"I seem to recall more clothing was your primary goal last night," Callie said.

"I guess I'll have to decide."

Callie wasn't sure what she hoped he would choose. If Mr. Daniels stayed at the farm, she'd be faced with the prospect of a trip into town alone with the children. Who knew what kind of mischief the children would get into? Walter might decide to drop an ax on her foot or an anvil on her head or rob the bank.

On the other hand, if Mr. Daniels did decide to accompany her, what would the stern ladies of the Society think if they saw her socializing with a mere farmhand? According to Aunt Samuela, there were only two sorts of people—the merchants in town and the landowners out of town—with whom one did associate, and the people who worked for them, with whom one did *not* associate.

Two of the ladies of the Society had already caught her in a very compromising situation with Mr. Daniels and decided to ignore—or at least forgive—the indiscretion.

It probably wouldn't be a very good idea to be seen with him again so soon. In the warped minds of some of the ladies of the Society, even the most innocent of pastimes could be turned into an orgy of lewdness and debauchery. Callie marveled at the unbelievable imagination a feat like that required.

"You gotta come with us, Mr. Daniels," Walter insisted.

"No, no, thanks. It's not much fun trying to shop without any money."

"Sure it is," Beatrice declared. "We used to do it all the time."

"I'll take your word for it."

Harden grinned and tried to look as if he were concentrating on eating his dinner.

Should he go into town to buy new clothing? He certainly needed some.

On the other hand, if Callie and the children were away from the farm for a few hours, it would give him the perfect opportunity to stroll on over to Otis Fielding's farm. It would be so much easier to get the layout of the place in broad daylight. Then it would be easer for him to do what he had to do by night.

He'd sleep on it. He had a little time yet before he had to decide.

Callie had managed to convince Beatrice that, since she'd made dinner, it was only fair that Callie take her turn at cleaning it up. Of course, the really difficult part had been in convincing the children that it was time for bed.

Callie dried the last dish and replaced it in the cupboard. She hung the damp dish towel on the little rack.

She looked out the kitchen window. It was good to see stars again after the torrential rains of the night before. After that horrible accident in the barn, it was good to see anything.

She wandered out onto the back porch. She was surprised to find Harden already out there, gazing up into the sky.

"Oh, I'm sorry to disturb you," she said. "I thought you'd gone to move a cot into the barn."

"I'll do it later." He stepped back and leaned against the porch railing. "It's just too pretty an evening to waste stars like these."

"You're very strange, Mr. Daniels," Callie commented.

"I'm supposed to be. I'm a stranger."

"No, no." She allowed herself to laugh. "I mean, I've never heard any other farmhands talking about serfs and czarinas and wasting stars."

He shrugged. "I'm not surprised. I understand your aunt kept you pretty sheltered from the farmhands. You wouldn't have known if they spoke Greek or sculpted marble or played the bagpipes."

She laughed a little harder. "You're absolutely right. Do you speak Greek, Mr. Daniels?"

"Thunderation, no! I picked up a little Spanish once— just enough to keep me from getting killed."

"How . . . astonishing! How did you ever get into such a dangerous situation?"

Harden pushed himself off from the porch railing and started to pace back and forth. "It wasn't dangerous. I didn't get killed."

"But—"

"I don't mean to be rude, ma'am, but it's a darn shame to discuss danger on such a beautiful night with such a beautiful lady present."

She smiled at him, but the look in her eyes let him know in a way no words could, exactly how full of hogwash she thought he was.

"I'm not beautiful."

"I wish you wouldn't say that."

"Why not? It's true."

"Truth, like beauty, is often in the eyes of the beholder."

She gazed into his eyes. From the way he was looking at her, Callie knew where he believed beauty dwelt.

Miserably self-conscious, she reached up and began pulling at her mass of hair. The curls and ribbons began to tumble loosely over her shoulders. Instead of making her appear less finely dressed, she feared it made her look more like a woman of complete abandon. She began to regret what she'd done, but there was no sense in trying to undo it. The best she could manage would be to pull it back in a bun again. She just didn't seem to have Beatrice's knack, and she wasn't about to wake the child up.

"You don't talk like a farmhand, Mr. Daniels."

"You don't look like an old maid, Miss Jackson."

"It was Beatrice. She went to such a lot of trouble to . . . fix my hair and my dress. She's such a helpful little girl. I'm sorry I can't keep them here, but they truly do need a family—a mother *and* a father—who could provide for them."

"Someone who could keep Walter in check. That kid's a son of a gun," Harden added with a chuckle.

"Yes, and as with any gun, a body could get killed with him around!" She laughed. Then, much more seriously, she said, "This time, I'm thanking you for saving my life."

Harden reached out and placed his hand on her arm. "I was glad I could be there. Poor little Walter was so worried for you and so sorry for what he'd done."

"I feel sorry for Beatrice and Walter."

"Me, too."

"And, in a way, I envy them."

"Envy them?"

"They remember their mother. Even Walter, as young as he is, has some recollection of her. I don't have anything. Not a ring or a lock of her hair. Nothing. And at least they know who their father was."

Harden was silent, waiting to hear what more she had to

say. He knew she had a lot more to say—probably things that no one had ever bothered to listen to before.

"I've never known any other home than the one Aunt Samuela made for me."

"It's . . . it's a nice home," he said, glancing about. Even though he wouldn't be able to see anything in the dark, at least he could indicate the extent of the well-run little farm.

"I never knew my real mother. I understand her name was Paulina."

"Samuela, Paulina?"

"Apparently my grandfather had had his heart set on sons, and he had been devastatingly disappointed."

"I see." Harden waited.

"My family all came from Ohio," she continued at last. "When my grandparents and Aunt Samuela moved out to Kansas, my mother and father stayed in Cleveland. Aunt Samuela went back to help my mother when she had me. But my mother died when I was born. My father . . ."

She stopped again. Harden waited.

"My father blamed me for her death. He told Aunt Samuela to take me away. That . . . that he never wanted to . . . lay eyes on me again."

Harden expected to hear her sob. He never expected her to rest her head on his shoulder.

8

HARDEN HAD ALREADY warned her he wasn't averse to taking advantage of a situation. Even if he wasn't thinking about doing anything that would compromise Callie, he sure as heck wasn't about to push her away.

"My grandparents were so incensed that they had my name changed back to Jackson."

"I can't hardly say as I blame them."

"Neither can I."

"What was your father's name?"

"Aunt Samuela never told me."

"How about any doctor's record of your birth?"

"She told me she was so upset that when she left Ohio, she left without anything. She didn't dare send for it afterward. Not knowing the name of the doctor who delivered me, I don't think it's likely I'd be able to find it now."

"Baptism records?" he suggested.

"Not from Cleveland. Aunt Samuela had me baptized here."

"Did you check the church records?"

"They only go back to 1862. Part of the church was burned in a raid on the town, and the records were destroyed."

"Is there anyone you could contact in Cleveland who might know your father?"

Callie shrugged. "I have no idea. I never bothered to find out, and, after the way my father acted, I don't really know why I should."

Her soft lips were set in a hard, determined line.

Harden nodded. "I can't say as I blame you. But maybe, after all this time, he's changed his mind. Have you ever thought of trying to get in touch with him?"

"Yes, I have. But when I brought it up to Aunt Samuela a few years ago, she almost had a conniption fit. After she calmed down, and after I thought about it for a while, I realized that he'd had a lot more opportunities over the years to try to find me than I had to find him."

"So you gave up?"

"I released him," she corrected. "I wish him well, wherever and whoever he may be."

Her laugh was feeble and, no matter how much she declared she'd put her callous father out of her mind, was tinged with bitterness.

"Looking back, I see now that I really didn't need him. I had a complete family without him."

Harden refrained from remarking that he didn't see all that many of them hanging around. "What happened to them all?"

"Aunt Samuela told me my grandmother died while she was back in Cleveland. I vaguely remember my grandfather. He really didn't pay much attention to me. You know, I can't ever remember him hugging me. I don't believe he ever actually called me by my name. Come to think of it, he never really spoke to me. He'd always tell Aunt Samuela what he wanted me to do, and she'd tell me."

"What happened to him?"

"He died when I was about eight. The tombstone in the cemetery says he wasn't quite fifty. He was bald and always smelled like camphor. I know he wore other things, but I mainly remember him in a red flannel shirt and a black vest. He looked so strange at the funeral, laid out in that white shirt and fancy black suit. Aunt Samuela had a hard time convincing me it was really him."

"So, you were a stubborn child." Seeing what a timid little thing she'd turned out to be, Harden couldn't help but be surprised. He wondered what had happened to her to break her spirit, or was she just hiding it very well.

"Not really."

As she shrugged, she cuddled closer into the crook of his arm. Harden resisted the almost overwhelming urge to run his hand up and down her arm, enjoying the feel of her soft, warm flesh.

"I've never told anyone about this. Why am I suddenly telling you?"

"I'm a very good listener."

"I . . . I *trust* you, Harden."

"Why haven't you ever told anyone else?"

"In the first place, who would I tell? Who would listen? They would just say they were the complaints of a spoiled little girl."

"No, they're not," he told her softly. "It's the story of a little girl who was hurt by being so neglected. Didn't anyone ever hug you?"

"No."

"Not even Aunt Samuela?"

Callie was so quiet for a moment that Harden was afraid she'd never speak to him again. Then she said, "After my grandfather died, the only real change I noticed was that Aunt Samuela moved into the big bedroom. I stayed in the little room she and I used to share. I've been alone ever since."

"That's why there are only two bedrooms in this house."

She nodded. "And why we never needed any more. We knew we would *never* be needing any more."

"Will you be moving into her big bedroom now? I mean, once the children have gone to another home?"

She shrugged. "I doubt it. Even if I changed the beds and mattresses and moved the furniture around, I couldn't sleep in there comfortably. That'll always be Aunt Samuela's room to me."

"I don't think her restless shade will rise from the grave and command you to vacate the premises immediately."

"If I thought she'd really do that, that would be where I'd entertain all the fellows Mildred brings over."

She laughed and leaned just a bit closer to him.

This time he felt bolder. He moved his arm to cradle her to his side.

"How do you know you don't want to get married, Callie?"

"My father abandoned me. My grandfather ignored me. I don't think I have a great deal of good luck with the men in my life."

"But a husband—"

"You saw the fellow Mildred brought over. Would you really expect me to marry him?"

"What about a man who was a bit more . . . handsome?"

She gave him a scathing glance. "In the first place, you haven't spent much time in Cottonwood. There aren't any better-looking single men. In the second place, do you really think that mere physical appearance would influence my decision?"

Harden reached up and stroked his chin thoughtfully. "All things considered, no, not you."

"And in the third place, would a man who was truly handsome ever want to marry a woman as plain as I?"

"He'd have to be insane or a complete moron not to see

how very beautiful you truly are. You deserve better than to be married to a man who only sets store by mere physical appearance."

He had to be bold to take her in his arms. He'd have to be patient and move very slowly so as not to scare the timid, sensitive woman away.

Slowly, he moved his hand up her arm, then gently turned her to face him. She didn't resist until at last they were face-to-face. Then she made a tiny move as if to pull away, but stopped. She stood there, silent, and watched him.

"Did Aunt Samuela tell you such horrible things about men that you'd pull away from me when I haven't done a thing?"

"She told me men could do horrible things."

"Do you believe I will?"

"I don't know. I don't really know you well enough."

"So you're taking Aunt Samuela's word for it. You know, she never met me, so how would she know?"

"Aunt Samuela was an old maid. She didn't know anything about men."

"Do you?"

"I . . . Of course not!" Her answer was half laugh, half protest.

"Then how do you know you don't want to . . . get married someday?"

"Aunt Samuela warned me about . . . about the things men did, the things they thought about when they were with a woman."

"Such as?"

"Such as . . ." Callie couldn't answer him.

It was difficult enough when she was by herself to consider some of the things Aunt Samuela had told her. It was even more difficult to think about them when she was in Harden's arms.

"Such as having a man put his arms around you?" Harden asked.

"That . . . that was one of them."

Harden wrapped his arms gently about her shoulders. "There. Is that so horrible?"

"No, but—"

"And if I held you a little tighter, do you think that would hurt anything?"

Very slowly she replied, "No. As long as you don't squeeze too hard and crush my ribs."

She smiled at him. She probably expected him to laugh at her little joke, but he couldn't. There was something very serious that he needed to tell her.

"I'd never want to hurt you, Callie."

He reached up to cradle her small chin in the palm of his hand, until he was looking directly into her face. Slowly he lowered his lips to hers.

She held her breath. He shouldn't do this, but the brazen man seemed to have absolutely no self-control. *She* shouldn't be doing this. But she lacked as much resolve as he.

It felt so good just to be near him! No one had ever held her—certainly not like this! She'd missed so much, growing up with such cold, unfeeling people. Even Aunt Samuela's warnings against feelings had turned out to be so wrong.

Harden was warm and strong. She felt secure in his arms, yet at the same time she felt more incredibly alive than she'd ever felt in her whole safe, dull, uneventful life.

Slowly his lips met hers. Warm and soft, yet insistent, taking possession not only of her body, but her heart.

He moved away just slightly, just enough for her to take a ragged breath. He was breathing rather deeply himself, she noticed. Could she actually have that sort of effect on a man? Could any man have this effect on her? She was afraid to think it might be so. Then what would she do? For now, that didn't seem to matter much.

She reached up, entwining her arms about his neck. He pulled her closer to him. She could feel his muscles against her breasts, and the concave of his stomach, and the bulge beneath pressing into her flesh through the soft, green cloth.

Instead of pulling away as she knew she should, Callie found her own feminine flesh responding to his with a tingling rising through her stomach up to her heart. She pressed her own body closer to his.

Her heart was pounding too loudly in her tightening throat to make it easy to swallow. She could only gasp for a breath as his lips met hers again. They were still as soft, and perhaps even a good bit warmer, than the first time. But the force of his feelings as he kissed her made her body tingle with excitement and anticipation.

Aunt Samuela wasn't just an old maid, she was a *crazy* old maid who had absolutely *never* had any idea what she was talking about!

Harden began to move away. Callie wished he could stay and hold her forever. She wished that together they could explore these new feelings and each other, could pursue them, maybe perfect them—or at least get darn good at it.

Suddenly, completely unbidden, Mildred's warning echoed in her ear. He was just a drifter, and she knew it. He had no morals, no scruples, just as Mildred had warned her. He was probably only intending to stay until he made enough money to get him to the next town, just as Olive had warned her.

He had no money now, and she wasn't about to let him use her as he might use one of the ladies at Hawkins Saloon if he'd had the money to pay them. That wasn't part of the terms of his employment here.

She knew precisely where activities of this sort would lead, and she'd been blissfully traipsing down that primrose path right beside him. Oh, without a doubt, she was headed for perdition. Aunt Samuela would have told her so in no uncertain terms.

She was going to lose her farm if she kept up this sort of activity.

She took another step backward. She felt a little pang of disappointment and utter loneliness as he let her go.

Well, she figured, that's the way things were. She'd just have to get used to being alone again.

She pulled back just a little more.

"Maybe . . . maybe I'll . . . move the sewing machine into Aunt Samuela's old room." She tried to speak normally, but it was mighty hard to do when she could barely breathe, and she wanted to break down crying with the intensity of the conflicting emotions she was feeling.

He let her move away, but only a step or two. He didn't try to kiss her again, but he still held her gently about the waist.

"That's an awful lot of room to sew for just one person." He looked down at her.

"Maybe I'll make a dress for Beatrice and a shirt for Walter while they're still here."

He should be angry, she thought, *about not getting what he was aiming for. He should be disappointed.* But his expression was a different sort of disappointment.

He didn't look like a man who had been denied something that he figured was his just due. He didn't look like a man who had been tracking a creature that had ultimately eluded him.

He looked more like a little boy who had been promised something wonderful, then been told he couldn't have it, after all. There was more hurt than anything in his eyes.

She had no idea what that meant. All she knew was that she couldn't let her involvement with Mr. Daniels go any further. She backed up enough so that he had to release her.

"Good night, Mr. Daniels." She tried to sound gentle, but not as if she might change her mind. "We've had an awful . . . busy day. We've got a busy day ahead of us tomorrow, too."

He stood there watching her for a few moments. His pale blue eyes held an unbelievable longing in them. She could almost feel the pain as they moved away from each other. She wondered if he could feel hers.

"Good night, Miss Jackson," he said as he stepped off the

porch. "If you need me, I'll be trying desperately to sleep in the barn."

Frugal and Refrain barked a joyful greeting.

Callie flung open the kitchen door. Bob never had been one to stand on ceremony. He always maintained he was "back-door" company.

"Bob! It's good to see you again."

"How y'doin', Miss Callie?"

"I'm fine, just fine. Come in." She stepped back to allow him room to enter. "I've been putting up blackberries the children picked this morning."

"Smells good."

"Put some on a slice of bread and tell me how you think the jelly turned out."

"Thanks. Don't mind if I do," Bob said, reaching for the loaf of bread and helping himself.

"How have you been, Bob?"

"Real curious," he answered as he smeared jelly on the bread.

"Curious?"

"About how that new farmhand was workin' out for you." He took a big bite of bread and jelly.

Callie swallowed hard and hoped that, being as she was standing in the shadow of the porch, Bob couldn't notice the hot flush she could feel rising up her cheeks.

"Mr. Daniels?" she asked, trying to keep her voice from cracking with nervousness.

"Say, this is real good. Yeah, that's the feller. Unless you've hired a couple more since I was here last."

"No. It's just Mr. Daniels and I."

"I found where she was hiding! I get to hold her first!"

Callie heard Walter shouting as his footsteps stomped down the stairs.

Prudence came shooting through the kitchen and out the door. Walter was hot on her trail.

"No, me. She likes me better!" Beatrice protested as she came thundering after him.

Both children shot out the door in pursuit of the cat. The dogs, barking loudly, took off in pursuit, too.

"Oh, poor Prudence," Callie wailed.

"Just you and Mr. Daniels, huh?" Bob asked. "It sure looks like you two been busy—and awful fast, too."

"Oh, Bob!" Callie felt her cheeks growing hotter and hotter.

"Just kiddin'. Didn't mean to embarrass you, Miss Callie. I found out about the children the day they arrived. They was just hangin' around the train station askin' for Miss Jackson. I'd have brung them out to you, myself, but Mr. Daniels said he was goin' that way, anyway. I guess he felt as sorry for 'em as I did. They looked so lost and forlorn."

"They *are* lost and forlorn."

Bob watched the children climbing the big cottonwood tree in pursuit of Prudence while the dogs barked and shimmied around the base of the tree.

"They look pretty much at home to me."

"Oh, no. They can't be," Callie protested. "I can't keep them here."

"Why not?"

"I don't know anything about children! They need a mother and a father to raise them properly. And there are plenty of people in town who ought to be willing to take them. Don't you think?"

Bob scratched his head. "Maybe."

Why did he have to say that? Callie silently lamented. *Why did he have to say it that way?* It was almost as if Bob could read her thoughts.

"I don't know why you're so worried, anyway."

"You'd be worried if you had two strange young children show up on your doorstep, too."

"Yeah, especially since I ain't got one."

"Oh, Bob. Help me again, please."

"With children?" He laughed, but Callie noticed he was

starting to look a little worried too. "I've done most types of work, but I told you before, I ain't a nanny. I couldn't change a baby with a magic wand."

"They're not babies, and they don't need changing. Just looking after."

"Honest to goodness, Miss Callie," Bob protested, deep pleading in his voice. "I've never had none o' my own. I don't know nothin' 'bout raisin' kids."

Then he started to look brighter.

"I don't know what you're frettin' so about, anyway. All you got to do is turn this problem over to the ladies o' the Society."

Callie stood there for a moment, contemplating what Bob had just suggested. Then she smiled.

"You're absolutely right! Interfering in other people's business and ordering around other people's lives is what they do best. Why, it's just their cup of tea!"

"Speakin' o' the ladies and tea, I almost plum forgot why I came all this way. Mrs. Preston asked me to come out here and invite you to her house for dinner tomorrow night."

"Oh, dear, just what I need," Callie said with a deep sigh.

"Don't you want dinner?"

"Yes, but I know if I go there, I'm going to be getting a whole lot more."

"More?"

"Oh, come on, Bob. You know very well this is another thinly disguised attempt at matchmaking on Mildred's part."

She didn't want to spend the time now trying to explain to Bob that she would also have to suffer the well-intentioned attentions of Beatrice, who was just going to love dressing her up again.

"Come now, Bob. Forewarned is forearmed."

"Yeah, but who needs four arms?" He laughed.

Callie didn't. "No, no. Tell me who he is, so I can at least be prepared. Who else did she send you to invite?"

Bob grinned and grimaced.

"Oh, please, tell me. We both know good and well; it's not as if it's a surprise, anymore."

Bob grimaced again. At last he said, "Andrew Nesbitt."

"Oh, no! I swear, I've got a good mind to poison Mildred's tea."

"Oh, don't go on so, Miss Callie. Andy Nesbitt's not too bad if you don't sit downwind from him."

"But I'll be sitting across the table from him!" she wailed. "I don't know how long I can try to eat and still hold my breath at the same time."

Harden could smell the molasses in the baked beans drifting out across the farmyard. Would Callie have put little chunks of bacon in, too, like his ma used to do? It was hoping too much to think that she might have a plate of some slices of big, juicy tomatoes on the side, or a plate of beaten biscuits, or a big bowl of fried okra. His mouth was watering already.

Frugal and Refrain were barking madly. They were usually good watchdogs who didn't bark at every passing carriage or rider, but only at those things that really bothered them. Something had to be wrong. But it didn't look as if there was any trouble going on at the house.

Harden shrugged. It was probably just the children, chasing poor Prudence again. If the darn cat were truly living up to her name, she'd exercise a little more caution about staying away from those children.

On the other hand, he didn't see Beatrice or Walter anywhere around. Were those two little rascals already inside, gobbling up all the beans?

He'd dreaded this job from the first moment he'd been assigned to it. Outsmarting Otis Fielding wasn't going to be easy. The thought of coming to this little backwater town, to this farm run by two persnickety old maids, hadn't thrilled him.

But from the moment he'd entered the house and laid eyes on Callie Jackson, he'd had a different feeling. He'd finally gotten settled in—in the barn, if not the bunkhouse.

The food was good. He was free to come and go as he pleased. He felt pretty good here. If such a thing were possible for a man like him, he could even say he felt at home.

He couldn't wait to see what Beatrice had done to Callie this time. There had always been a gem under that deliberately plain coating of dross of hers. He'd seen it from the first day he'd met her. It was just amazing how the little girl had managed to bring out all Callie's natural beauty and made her realize she could do these things for herself. And maybe—just maybe—she was doing these things for him, too.

He felt so good he whistled as he sauntered across the yard.

Suddenly, he frowned. There were three strange horses—a black and two bays—hitched to the rail in front of Callie's house. Mildred and her cohorts would walk or use a buggy, wouldn't they? It certainly would be the ladylike thing to do. They were men's saddles. The one on the black horse was a lot fancier than the others.

Had Mildred been too busy to bring the men herself and just sent the prospective suitors over on their own? Maybe. But why in the world would she send three at a time? Poor Callie, beleaguered by not one but three undesirables!

Did Mildred think she'd just throw them all in together and let the lone survivor have Callie? That idea was even less appealing to Harden.

He stopped in his tracks. What did it matter to him? Callie had made it pretty clear she didn't want to get married to anyone. Heck, she was such a moral, upright lady, she didn't even want to fiddle around a bit. Even if she did, it could mean the loss of her farm. He couldn't do that to her.

No, no, no! None of this mattered. He'd gotten far too involved with people he should just be using to do his job, and then move on and forget about.

His years of training and experience took over. Much more cautiously, he approached the house.

There were other ways of entering a house besides the door. There were other rooms to enter besides the traditional kitchen or vestibule or basement. There were other ways of crossing a room besides just marching straight across it, although Aunt Samuela's penchant for sparse furnishings made his feat awful difficult. But Harden knew them all.

He slipped through the back door without having the screen door make a single squeak. He knew exactly where to step to keep the floorboards from creaking. He could pinpoint the exact position in the house of the voices he heard.

He knew Callie's voice, but he couldn't identify the other voices. One man was doing most of the talking.

The big man in the black suit standing in the middle of the room seemed to be in charge. The other two men just wore denim trousers and plain shirts. They weren't smoking big, expensive cigars, either. That was sort of a dead giveaway that he was the boss and they were just the workers. The man with the money was the man in charge, Harden noted. That always seemed to be true.

The two other men hung back a bit, watching Callie and the big man talking, as if they really didn't understand what was going on and were just waiting for something to happen that they *could* take part in.

"You do understand, I'm offering you far more than the farm is worth," the fat man said.

"Thank you for your more than generous offer," Callie said.

She was standing, too, obviously doing the best that poor timid soul could do to hold her ground against the man. But she was standing behind a chair as if she were hiding, and her white knuckles clenching the high back gave away her fear and nervousness. Her dress wasn't severe black anymore, just a blue calico, and it made her look so much more delicate, more vulnerable to these harsh men. Her hair curled around her cheeks, making her look softer, more easily hurt.

Harden wanted to spring to her aid, but he'd left his white charger in the barn, and he'd forgotten his lance. So he stood, watching, gathering information, and waiting for the right time to step in if he had to.

"But I just inherited the farm. I really don't have any intention of selling it, Mr. Fielding."

Fielding! This overfed, overdressed, overrated dandy was Otis Fielding?

Harden made a mental note. When he returned to Washington, he'd be sure to replace his current sources with more accurate and reliable ones.

How could this man be the mastermind behind the Army payroll robbery, the cold-blooded murder of a train conductor, a Pinkerton man, and several federal marshals? He didn't look as if he could take his mind off his next meal long enough to devise a clever plan to rob the payroll train. Thunderation, he didn't look as though he could bend over to tie his own shoes!

On the other hand, he did look as if he could afford to pay somebody to tie his shoes for him. Come to think of it, he could probably find somebody he could pay to do almost anything.

Fielding took a long, leisurely drag on his cigar. It wasn't one of the little cheroots that a man might roll for himself while sitting under the stars around a campfire with his friends in the evening, discussing which was the best cattle trail to Santa Fe. It was a big, long, black, Cuban cigar, the kind the butler lit for a gentleman who sat, after a sumptuous steak and oyster dinner, drinking brandy, while conferring with his business associates around a long, mahogany table laid with white linen, sterling silver, and Limoges dishes, deciding where to build the next factory and how little to pay their workers.

The rolls under Fielding's chin undulated as he shook his head. "I just do not know how a pretty little lady like you will ever be able to run a farm this size all by herself."

"As difficult as this may be for you to believe, Mr.

Fielding," Callie told him, "that's really none of your concern."

"But you're my neighbor. We sort of look out for each other around here. Don't we, boys?"

"Oh, yes, sir, Mr. Fielding," both of the other men enthusiastically agreed.

"I must say, since your aunt passed away, you certainly have changed, little lady. Why, you were just a drab little girl, and now you've blossomed into quite a lovely young woman."

Callie stared at him.

"Aren't you going to say thank you?"

"Why should I thank you? You didn't do anything to make me beautiful."

"Hmm." Fielding only puffed on his cigar, obviously unhappy with Callie's response. Actually, Harden thought it was pretty good. But if he laughed, he'd give his position away.

He also figured Fielding wasn't a man to be outdone.

"A pretty little thing like you needs a man to watch out for her. It's painfully obvious to me from that blackened heap in the farmyard that you need looking after."

"Why? Could a man have stood out in the rain and ordered the lightning not to strike my bunkhouse?"

Fielding was silent for a moment. "But if it had happened to a man—who'd know what to do in the event of a fire—well then, it wouldn't have been such a problem. But it's obvious you don't have a single, solitary notion in that pretty little head of yours about what to do in a situation like that, and you shouldn't. You should have a man to take care of you."

"I think I handled it fairly well myself, Mr. Fielding," Callie said. "I even managed to save the life of my farmhand."

Fielding gave a loud harrumph, then took another long draw on his cigar. He puffed the smoke out into the air with a grin of satisfaction.

"Farmhand. Yes, indeed. I heard all about your hiring a new farmhand. But what in the world could have happened to all your other farmhands?"

He paused for a long, long time, obviously waiting for her to answer.

"They left."

"Did they, huh?"

"Yes."

"Aren't you afraid your new hand will leave, too?"

"No."

Harden felt a strange warmth in his chest. She'd answered so quickly, so emphatically. She must truly have faith in him. When his work was done, and he had to leave, how could he convince her that her faith hadn't been misplaced?

"Where could those farmhands have gone, huh?"

"Out West, to make their fortunes."

"Is that what they told you, huh?"

"Yes."

Harden could hear the mounting tension in her voice.

"So, you actually think they went that far, huh?"

"I . . . I have no idea. It's not as if we've continued a lively correspondence."

"They can't write, anyway. But they're darn good farmhands."

"How would you . . . ?" Callie just drew in a deep breath of resignation in the very ugly face of the obvious. "That's impossible! Bob in Pieces saw them get on the westbound train."

Fielding chuckled. "But Bob didn't see them get off the train at the next town and ride back to my place."

"Worthless scum!" Callie muttered.

"Come now, little lady. They didn't lie to you—not exactly. My farm *is* to the west of yours."

Callie said nothing. Harden was having a hard time keeping himself from just stepping out and shooting the bastard—if he only had his gun!

Fielding started strolling around the parlor as if he

already owned the place. He was raising a cloud of smoke that was hovering just below the ceiling. Harden didn't care how expensive the cigar was, it was going to make the place stink for weeks.

"Now, I've offered you a fair price. Why don't you just admit that I'm a bit too clever for a pretty little lady like you and sell me this place?"

"I don't care what you say or do, Mr. Fielding. I'm *not* going to sell my farm."

"What a pity. But you will."

"Not yet."

"Someday."

"Don't hold your breath."

"I'm a patient man. I've got time."

"So do I."

"But I've got something you don't."

"Yes, I know. My worthless farmhands," Callie replied sarcastically.

"Oh, more than that, little lady." He grinned at her and paused again, as if trying to add more emphasis to his disclosure. "I've got *my* farmhands."

Callie pressed her lips together and viewed the men with narrowed eyes. "They don't look like much to me."

"Oh, they don't have to be pretty to get the job done. So I hope you'll remember my offer and let me know as soon as you can when we can go into town to transfer the money and sign over the deed."

"Never."

"I know I said I had all the time in the world, but there is a limit to my patience, little lady. Each time I have to make another trip here costs me more and more money. So, each time you force me to make another trip, the amount of my offer goes down."

"Then save us both the trouble, and don't come here again, Mr. Fielding," Callie told him. "I'm *not* selling my farm."

Harden stood on the other side of the door, marveling at

Callie's stern boldness in the face of a pompous autocrat like Fielding.

Suddenly, someone grabbed Harden by the scruff of the neck. His shirt tightened around his throat until he almost couldn't breathe. Before he could turn around to punch whoever it was, Harden heard the metallic click of a hammer being cocked. He felt the hard barrel jabbing into his side, right below his ribs.

9

"*EASY, EASY, FRIEND,*" Harden said, keeping his voice low and steady. Very slowly, he raised his hands above his shoulders.

Make no loud noises, no sudden moves, he warned himself. Not around this character. He might think he was a bodyguard to a rich and powerful man, but he was nothing more than a glorified hired gun.

Men like this were easier to set off than a string of Chinese firecrackers, and were just about as loud, and as potentially dangerous if a body got too close to them.

He didn't relish the thought of having his innards ventilated—not to mention the mess he'd make on Callie's wallpaper.

"What're you doing sneaking around here?" the man demanded, giving him a shake by the scruff of his neck.

With the cold, hard barrel of the gun pressing into his side, Harden decided it would probably be a good idea not to resist as the man hauled him into the parlor. As the man propelled him along, Harden tripped across the rug, heading straight for Fielding.

He couldn't fall! He wouldn't! That would be the worst possible impression to make, landing kneeling at the feet of the man he might eventually have to kill. He managed to pull himself up just in time, and stood face-to-face with Otis Fielding.

"Harden!" Callie cried.

"Harden, huh? Is that who you are?" Fielding demanded. He raised his head and, through half-closed, purple eyelids, examined Harden as if he were something he'd found on the bottom of his boot.

"Harden Daniels. He's my farmhand," Callie explained.

"So that's you, huh?" Fielding took a long puff of his cigar, then blew the smoke into Harden's face.

Harden held his breath to keep from coughing. He'd *never* show any weakness to Fielding!

"Answer me!"

To punctuate his boss's demand, the henchman pushed the barrel of the gun more forcefully into Harden's ribs.

Harden wanted to kick himself. He deserved to be dead. How could he have been so stupid! He'd been concentrating so completely on what Callie was saying and on what that obnoxious Fielding was saying to her—and on what effect it all could have on his job—that he'd broken his first and most important rule of surveillance. He'd neglected to keep an eye on *everyone* in the room, no matter how harmless, ugly, or dim-witted they might at first appear.

That was it! That might be his way out of this predicament for now. If only Callie would understand what he was trying to do and back up his alibi. He'd just have to depend on a woman who had made it pretty clear she wasn't sure if she could depend on him.

He stooped his shoulders down just a bit and started shaking his head slowly. He wished he had a pinch of chewing tobacco to make him drool, just to complete the picture.

"That's me, sir. Harden. Harden Daniels," he answered, with a big, proud, pie-faced grin on his face.

"What are you doing sneaking around here?" the sidekick demanded, jabbing the gun harder into his ribs.

"Ouch! Don't do that, friend. That don't feel so good."

"Then answer Mr. Fielding."

"What was the question?"

The henchman had to think just a bit before replying, "What are you doing sneaking around here?"

"Sneakin'? Aw, I don't do no sneakin', friend," he said. "I just work here."

"A likely story." The henchman shoved Harden again.

"Stop it!"

Callie was trying to sound commanding. If only she could know how miserably she was failing, Harden thought with increasing dismay.

"He belongs here," Callie explained.

"I belong here," Harden repeated, nodding.

"He's my hired hand. You have no right to do this to my farmhand, on my property."

"He's eavesdropping on *my* conversation. That makes it *my* business," Fielding insisted. "I want to know why he's listening."

"Yeah! Answer Mr. Fielding. What're you doing here?" the henchman demanded, giving Harden another push.

It took every bit of self-control Harden could muster not to turn around and flatten the dolt. Instead, Harden cringed, and pleaded, "Don't hurt me, friend. I ain't done nothin'."

"I ain't your friend," the man said, giving Harden another push. "Eavesdroppin' ain't 'nothin''."

"I wasn't droppin' nothin' from the eaves," Harden protested. "I wasn't nowhere near the eaves. I was just comin' in for supper and couldn't find my way to the kitchen. I'm . . . I'm new 'round here, y'know, friend, and I guess I just ain't got my bearin's yet."

"He can't find his way around the place yet?" Fielding

started to laugh. Then he grew very serious again and glared at Harden. "That's a little hard to believe."

"I was just followin' my nose to supper, sir. Don't know how I ended up in the fancy sittin' room 'stead o' the eatin' room. Guess that there smoke from that big fancy see-gar o' your'n done fouled up the works." He tapped his nose.

Fielding took a big puff, sending smoke billowing up to the ceiling. "He's a mite skinny for a farmhand, don't you think?"

"He gets his work done," Callie offered.

He turned to Harden. "You do, huh?"

"Yes, sir. I sure do." Harden started vigorously bobbing his head.

"A might dim, too, wouldn't you say?"

"He gets his work done," Callie repeated. "Slowly, but he gets it all done eventually."

"Where are you from?" Fielding demanded.

"Virginny, sir."

"Hmm. Southern boy, huh?"

"Yes, sir. That's me."

"Did a lot of fighting for your country, then, huh?"

Harden's head started swinging back and forth again. "No, sir. They wouldn't let me have no gun."

Fielding laughed more heartily. "Afraid you'd shoot your own foot off, huh?"

Harden shrugged. "Guess so, sir."

"I can't say as I blame them."

"They wouldn't even let me carry a flag or a drum," Harden complained petulantly.

Fielding chuckled again. "Afraid you'd go marching off in the wrong direction and get your whole battalion killed."

"Don't know, sir. All I knowed is, when I went to sign up to do some fightin', they just sent me on back home. They didn't tell me nothin', sir."

"I guess it wouldn't be much use trying to tell you anything anyway, would it?"

"Oh, yes, sir. You can tell me anything you want. I listen

real good," Harden proclaimed vigorously. Then he tapped his temple and grinned apologetically. "I just don't hang on to it for too long."

Fielding blew another puff of smoke in his face. This time Harden coughed loudly and clumsily waved the smoke away.

Then Fielding turned to Callie. He was laughing. His belly moved up and down in disgusting, undulating motions. Harden tried to stop the murderous urge he had to wrestle the gun away from Fielding's henchman and see how that fat blob undulated with several bullet holes going through it.

But he couldn't risk a stray bullet striking Callie. He just stood there and exercised the most self-control any human probably ever had.

"Please, just let him go," Callie pleaded. "He can't do you any harm. You can see the poor fellow's not right in the head."

"I should've figured a little lady like you wouldn't have the faintest notion of how to hire good farmhands," Fielding told Callie with a loud laugh. "You've even hired yourself a half-wit!"

"You can see he's too stupid to do you any harm. He probably doesn't even remember now why he came into the house in the first place," Callie said. "Please, let the poor fellow go."

The murderous expression wasn't quite so strong anymore in the dandified weasel's beady little eyes. Harden was relieved to see that, where argument had failed, Callie's pleading might be having some affect on Fielding.

"He might not be too bright. I think somebody said the doctor dropped him on his head when he was born. Either that, or he was struck by lightning. But he's a good worker," Callie defended him. "I mean, I have to tell him everything, and keep after him constantly, or the first thing you know, I find him out napping in the barn—provided he can remember where the barn is."

Fielding laughed. After one more cloudy puff of the cigar, he headed for the door.

"Come along, boys," he said to his hired guns. "I think I'm wasting my time coming here offering to buy this place. I don't even have to worry about chasing off or buying off your farmhands anymore. This one's liable to be heading for the outhouse one night, not remember where it is, and end up just wandering off across the prairie until he hits San Francisco."

Fielding laughed loudly at his own joke. The henchmen, too, obviously thought it was hilarious.

"Hell, little lady, you even had the plum lousy rotten luck to have your own bunkhouse catch on fire. My boys and I don't have to do a thing to help you out of here."

He laughed again.

Callie didn't see anything funny about it.

"If you're real lucky, that idiot farmhand of yours won't kill all your cattle and poison the well."

"He's doing just fine," Callie stated very seriously.

"Yes, indeed, little lady. You're doing a pretty good job of destroying your farm all by yourself. All I've got to do is bide my time, wait until the bank forecloses on the mortgage, and buy this whole place at auction for a song! And not even a very long song. It's hard to get a good price on a farm where half the buildings are burned to the ground. Good luck, little lady. You're going to need it!"

Harden stood there, uncomfortably hunched over, as he watched the men leave. Callie never moved from behind the chair.

He waited until they'd slammed the front door shut. Straightening his shoulders, he hurried to the window to watch them as they made their way down the front walk and mounted their horses. Just as he figured, Fielding rode the black horse. He watched which way they went until they were out of sight.

"Oh, my gracious!" Callie exclaimed as she collapsed into the chair. "I hate that man!"

"I can understand why," Harden replied as he came to kneel beside her.

He placed his hand on her arm. He wanted to wrap her up in his arms and never let her go. He wanted to run his hands over her soft, sweet body until he knew those crude men hadn't harmed her.

"Did they hurt you? Are you all right?"

"No, I'm not all right. I *hate* that man!" She fairly drummed her feet on the floor and her fists on the arms of the chair in frustration. "I wish I knew some way to get rid of him! I wish I could stand him long enough to invite him here for dinner and poison him! I wish I had the nerve to shoot him! If I could stand seeing him naked, I'd drown him in his own bathtub!"

"Why, Miss Jackson! I shudder to think what Mildred and the ladies of the Society would say about your lack of Christian charity for your neighbor," he said with a chuckle.

"Mildred doesn't like him, either." Her anger spent for the time being, she leaned her head wearily against the back of the chair.

"I can see why," he said much more seriously.

Harden had figured out pretty quickly that, no matter what other names he could think to call them, the other two men were basically Fielding's hired guns. What was Fielding so involved in that he needed several hired guns? Were they here to coerce other people into doing Fielding's bidding, or were they here to protect Fielding?

Apparently, Fielding had grown a lot more powerful in this town since the last report from Harden's sources had given him to understand. This wasn't going to be as easy a job as he'd first supposed.

Did he dare risk going into town and wiring for reinforcements? Who would notice? A simple telegram to "Mother" asking how "Aunt Grace" was would take care of that.

On the other hand, in a town this small, who *wouldn't* notice? What would a penniless drifter be doing sending telegrams to a family back East?

"Aunt Samuela never liked him, either," Callie told him.

"I don't think much of him, myself. I'm glad you saved my neck once again."

"I must admit I was worried at first. Mr. Fielding's so-called farmhands frighten me. But I couldn't let anything happen to my best farmhand."

"Thanks. Especially since I'm your *only* farmhand."

Callie knew it was a bold move on her part. She shouldn't do it. Aunt Samuela and the ladies of the Society would be scandalized. But she'd already held him in her arms and kissed him. She didn't think this extra little display of gratitude and affection would make that much difference.

She lifted her hand to stroke his cheek. His face was stubbled with his unshaved beard, but the skin beneath was warm and smooth. Yet the muscles and bones of his cheeks and jawline were stern and rugged. The man was such a mixture of contradictions. She could spend a lifetime studying his changes, or just be happy to spend whatever time he chose to stay around.

"It wouldn't matter how many farmhands I had. I still wouldn't want to lose you," she said very softly. "I couldn't bear to see that horrible man dragging you into the room. I was so frightened when I saw that gun jammed into your side."

"I wasn't too happy about it, myself," he admitted with a chuckle.

"Don't joke about that." She held her hand to his cheek and gazed into his eyes. "I worried so."

"Don't worry about me. I can take care of myself." He leaned closer to her and said more softly, "I can watch out for you, too, Callie. You don't have to worry about that scoundrel hurting you."

"I'm very glad to know that."

Harden leaned closer and placed a kiss on her lips. She raised her arm to pull him closer.

Suddenly, he pressed closer to her, wrapping her completely in his warm embrace. She entwined her arms about his shoulders, drawing his face to rest against her breasts. He cradled his cheek into the soft cleavage.

She smelled like flowers and the blackberries she'd been making jelly from all day. She smelled like the sunshine and rain that made the berries blossom and grow. He moved his arm up and across her back and down her arms, to feel the softness of her flesh and the smoothness of her skin.

He lifted his face to hers.

He needn't pull her down to him. She was already gazing steadily into his eyes. He felt a fire like the sun glowing in his loins as he watched a glimmer like starlight in her eyes, telling him she was feeling the same desire he did.

He kissed her. Rising on one knee, he kissed her again, pulling her closer to him.

He passed her hand over his shoulders, and down his chest. Her hand came to rest on his side, just below his ribs. The harsh memory of the feel of the gun disappeared quickly under her gentle touch.

"I couldn't bear to think of you being shot."

"Not there."

"Not anywhere."

Her hand continued to move slowly up his ribs, across his stomach, and up his chest, drawing agonizingly blissful chills of excitement to the surface, until he thought he'd explode from the sheer pleasure of her gentle touch. And she hadn't even touched anything really important yet! Oh, now he knew he was going to go insane with wanting her!

"Harden," she whispered in his ear.

"Callie, I want you." He tried to sound calm and in control, when all the while he knew his voice was hoarse with desire for her. "I need you."

"I . . . I want you, too, Harden. But—"

"We'll go slowly," he promised. "I've already told you, I'll never deliberately do anything to hurt you, Callie."

"I'm not sure."

"If you have any doubts—"

"I want you, Harden. Since the first time I saw you in that

sheet, I knew I wanted to see you in . . . something connected with sheets only . . . only slightly different. Is that horribly sinful?"

Harden chuckled. "It sounds pretty natural to me. Do you think I should move back in from the barn?"

"You can't. We can't." Clouds of worry began to fill her eyes, blotting out the starlight. "What will the ladies of the Society say when they find out?"

"Don't you mean *if?*"

She placed a single finger across his lips. "I mean *when.* Oh, yes, they *will* find out. Make no mistake about it. The ladies of the Society were the ones who figured out Benny Robinson was the one who painted Charlie Wilson's sheep blue last Halloween."

Harden chuckled. "Oh, well. Then we'll have to be very, very . . . prudent."

Callie laughed, too. Then, suddenly, her face grew wide-eyed again, and she was definitely on edge, listening.

"Someone laughed, and it wasn't the cat."

More laughter and little giggles emanated from the hallway.

"The children!" Harden sprang to his feet as Callie rose from her chair.

"The little eavesdroppers!" She was a bit faster. She bumped into him.

"The rascals!" He reached out to steady her, then drew his hands back quickly.

"Oh, my goodness!" Callie exclaimed. "How long have you two been watching?"

"Blue sheep?" Walter said, giggling madly.

"That's all right," Beatrice said, dragging a giggling Walter into the room behind her. "I saw Mama and Papa doing that once."

"You look funny," Walter managed to gasp out between giggles.

"And then, a little while later, she started getting fat, and then Walter was born."

"Are you gonna have a baby now, too?" Walter asked, still chuckling behind his hand.

"No!" Callie and Harden declared in unison.

"Sneaking around is despicable behavior!" Callie scolded. "Didn't your mother teach you not to do that?"

"No, we used to do it a lot at the rich old lady's house," Beatrice said. "We had to. That was the only way we got to see all the wonderful, expensive things she had there. We had to be very quiet all the time and not get caught."

"Well, you did get caught here, so it doesn't work, does it?" Callie demanded. "If you want to stay here, that sort of behavior stops now! There will be no snooping around here!"

"I know." Beatrice grimaced with disappointment. "There's nothing wonderful or expensive to see in this house."

Harden crossed his arms over his chest and fixed them with a stern glare. "How long have you two been spying on us, anyway?" he demanded.

"Long enough to know how silly you two look rubbing your faces all over each other," Walter answered, still giggling. He puckered his lips and made smacking sounds.

"Just from the part where you were glad she saved your life," Beatrice answered a little more sensibly. "You know, just from right before all the good stuff started."

Harden turned away, shaking his head. "You were right," he muttered to Callie. "They're not children."

"They're changelings," Callie joined in.

"We're hungry," Beatrice and Walter merrily chimed in together.

"Go wash up," Callie told them. "I'll have dinner on the table in two minutes."

The children, still laughing, bolted from the room.

"They're really midgets in disguise," Callie told him.

"They're imps from Hell," Harden corrected with a chuckle.

Callie shook her head. "I've just *got* to find them a new home."

"Have you tried the circus?" he suggested with a laugh.

"I swear, the next snake oil salesman who comes through town . . ."

"It's a darn shame there aren't any caravans of gypsies traveling around to steal them."

"Do you think I could sell them to the Indians?"

"I think the Indians are going to be having enough trouble of their own."

Harden looked around, then moved to stand closer beside her.

"I think we might be safe—for just a few moments." He reached out his arms to her. He wouldn't grab her up, no matter how intense the temptation was to hold her fiercely in his arms and make love to her. "Now, where were we?"

Callie turned around. She watched him with worry in her eyes.

"Oh, really, do you think we ought to . . . with the children in the house . . . and watching?"

"Yes."

With a soft, willing grace, she glided into his embrace.

"They're both washing. I think we're safe for a minute or two."

He placed both hands around her waist. He leaned forward and placed a gentle kiss on her cheek. She reached up and wrapped her arms around his neck. He kissed her again.

"Yes, I believe this is exactly where we were."

His lips glided over her cheek and down her throat.

"You were telling me how very grateful to me you were for convincing Mr. Fielding you were a half-wit," she told him.

"That's not what I mean."

"But you did it so well." She gave a little laugh.

"Thank you."

"You know, you were really good at acting—especially the role of the half-wit. Have you ever thought of a career on the stage?"

"Not exactly."

"Why, with that kind of skill, you could rival Edwin Booth."

Harden grimaced. "I don't know about that. I don't think his brother's done much to advance his career right now, anyway."

"No, you'll be better than him," she insisted. "If I didn't know you better, I'd have really been convinced you weren't quite right in the head. I'd have been willing to bet money you couldn't even tie your own shoes."

"Thank you, I think." He sounded much less enthusiastic this time. "On the other hand, you didn't have to be quite so . . . so vigorous in telling him all about my lack of good sense. Struck by lightning! Really!"

"Well, it did happen—sort of," she asserted. "I mean, the lightning struck the building you were in, and a piece of the building fell on your head. There's a connection there," she insisted.

"Tenuous at best."

"It seemed to work."

"Yes, but you must admit you did lay it on a bit thick." He gave her a mischievous grin.

She raised one eyebrow and eyed him, affronted. "I beg your pardon. I do my best for you, and this is the gratitude I get?"

"Did you have to tell him I was quite so stupid? Not being able to find the barn! Honestly! The next thing I expected was you to tell him I spilled food on myself when I ate."

"I'm sorry. I guess it was just too easy."

Harden laughed. "I was just hoping that, if they thought I wasn't too smart, they might think I was harmless and let me go."

She shook her head. "Every Saturday night, Sheriff Thompson has to throw several of Mr. Fielding's farmhands out of Hawkins Saloon for fighting. He doesn't dare throw them in jail for fear of what Mr. Fielding will do. Those men don't take pity on anyone."

"I realize that now."

"I had a feeling what your plan was, but I must admit I was afraid it wasn't going to work."

"Thanks."

"On the other hand, I certainly wasn't going to deliberately say or do anything that would make you look like a liar and get you into trouble."

"I appreciate that."

"I'm not sure why, but I figured if you wanted to pretend you were a half-wit, there had to be some good reason for it."

He gave her a little squeeze but made no response to her comment.

"Harden, did you have a good reason for it?" she pursued.

"I thought so at the time."

"And now?"

"It's probably still a good reason."

He nodded his head, but it was pretty obvious to Callie he wasn't about to tell her what that reason was. But she *had* to ask. She had to *know*.

"Were you actually eavesdropping on that conversation? Why would you care anything about Mr. Fielding? Why would you want to bother with a man you don't even know?"

"I wasn't eavesdropping. Not exactly. I was just curious. I don't care anything about this Mr. Fielding. But I . . . I care about you, and I was afraid three strange men alone in the house with you might be here to hurt you. I couldn't let that happen, but I'm not so brave—or so stupid—that I'd go running in to save you without a gun."

"Do you have a gun?"

"Of course not," he replied with a little laugh. "That's why I was being very, very cautious about seeing what they were up to."

She just watched him, waiting for further explanation.

"After all, I could hardly protect you if I was dead. Could I?"

"I . . . I guess not."

"I do want to protect you, Callie."

"Do you really think I'm in danger?" Her eyes grew wide with fear and worry. "I mean, his farmhands are a pretty rough lot, but they follow his every instruction. They don't act on their own. Mr. Fielding's sneaky and underhanded. I think he'd try to cheat me out of my farm, but . . . why are you so convinced he'd actually harm me?"

Harden shrugged and backed away. "I don't know. Maybe I just don't like the smell of his cigar."

Callie had just placed the bowl of steaming baked beans on the table and was preparing to sit down when she heard a knock on the kitchen door.

"Miss Callie?" Bob called.

"Bob!" She sprang to her feet. "I thought you'd gone back to town."

"Well, I almost did."

She opened the door. Bob limped in.

"But when I left here, I got to thinkin'. While I was around this end o' town, I might as well kill two birds with one stone. I stopped off at the Wilsons' place for a visit."

"How was your visit?"

Bob chuckled. "About the same. Moan, groan, and grumble, whine and complain."

"About the same, then?"

Bob gave a sharp little laugh. "Mr. Wilson's pretty handy at gettin' supper on the table for himself and his family, but he ain't too sociable about sharin'. Course, while ordinarily it would look like he'd just be fixin' a meal for three, at that house it turns into feedin' the Grand Army o' the Republic!"

Callie laughed. "Then I suppose you haven't eaten."

"No, I haven't, Miss Callie." He reached for a chair and dragged it toward the table. "It's mighty neighborly of you to invite me, too."

Callie just grinned and went to the cupboard to pull out another plate.

"Just pull up a chair and make yourself at home."

Bob had already settled in beside Walter.

"Who are *you?*" Walter asked.

"Bob in Pieces."

"Is that your *real* name?" the little boy demanded.

"Might as well be."

Callie had always been under the strong impression that it was Bob, in a waggish moment, who had given himself that name.

"I'm really Walter. That's my sister, Bea, but her real name is Beatrice."

"Pleased to make your acquaintance," Bob commented, helping himself to the beans and bread as they were passed around.

As Walter squirmed around in his chair, trying to pass the various dishes, he managed to knock against Bob's leg. Apparently, when Bob didn't cry out in pain, he kicked him again, just to see what was going on. The wooden sound brought a look of shocked surprise to his face.

"Is that your real leg?" he demanded.

"No, I work in a furniture factory and I'm tryin' to steal a table piece by piece."

"What?"

"Sure, it's my own leg. I paid for it with my own money, so I guess it's mine, if that's what you mean."

"No, I mean . . . I mean . . ."

Apparently, Walter couldn't decide what he did mean.

"But it's not a real leg—unless bein' a real artificial leg counts."

Walter looked thoughtful. "I don't think it does."

Bob shrugged. "Oh, well. It still works for me."

Walter leaned over and peered closely into Bob's face. "Are they your real teeth?"

"Sure are!" Bob shot Walter his familiar, toothy grin just to prove it. "I had my own hair once, too, but I lost it."

"Did you lose them all at once, or did they fall out one at a time? Did your mama punish you for losing it? Ours used to punish us for losing good, important things."

"I never had anythin' important, 'cept maybe my own two eyes and arms, and I'm sure thankful I still got 'em, even if I only got a couple o' fingers left on the ends of 'em."

"How'd you lose your fingers?"

"Well, I used to be a dentist until—"

"Ick!" Beatrice squealed.

"No, no. Sawmill accident when I was a lumberjack up in Minnesota."

"How'd you lose your leg?" Walter asked.

"Had an altercation with a cannonball in Mexico. Let that be a lesson to you, boy." He shook a warning finger under Walter's nose. *"Never* altercate with a cannonball."

"How come you still got your own teeth?"

"I made it a rule never to ask too many questions, son."

"Oh."

"By the way, this is my own nose, too." He reached out and lightly tweaked Walter's. "Is that *your* real nose?"

Walter let out a shriek, then burst out laughing.

Hoping to distract the comical Bob and give the children a chance to calm down and eat their dinner before it got cold, Callie said, "Bob, this is Harden Daniels, my new hired hand."

"Pleased to meet you, sir," Bob said through a mouthful of beans. "Say there, you look awful familiar to me."

10

CALLIE'S EARS PERKED up. She almost laid down her fork and stopped chewing so she could devote all her attention to Harden's answers to the questions Bob was asking. Good old Bob, with his friendly, easygoing manners, could get away with asking questions that she would never dare to pose.

"I've never been to Cottonwood before," Harden said. "I don't see how we could've met."

"Oh, I've been other places, and I'm sure you have, too. Where're your people from?"

"Virginia."

Bob shook his head. "Nope, never been there. Lived anywhere else?"

"Not to speak of."

"Never was a lumberjack up in Minnesota, was you?"

"No."

"Never been to Mexico?"

Harden gave a short laugh. "I never had an altercation with a cannonball, either."

Bob turned to Walter, pointing toward Harden. "See there, boy. That's a smart man."

"I never asked too many questions, either," Harden added with a chuckle.

Bob scratched his head. "I could've sworn—"

"Maybe I just resemble somebody you know," Harden suggested.

Bob pressed his lips together, as if that could help him remember. "Do you know who your pa was? No offense intended."

Harden nodded. "None taken. I sure do. My ma's first husband. Phineas Daniels."

"Daniels. Daniels. Nope. How about your ma's folks?"

"The Hardens. They named me after her family."

"Nope, nope." Bob shook his head, as if that might rearrange a few things inside and bring back the memories. "I might've lost a couple o' body parts, but I know I haven't lost my mind—at least not yet. Dang! If I could just remember."

"Maybe there's nothing to remember."

Bob shrugged. "Maybe."

Callie wished she could think of something that would prompt Bob's failing memory. He was usually so sharp. She figured Bob had been around for a long time and had been a lot of different places. In which one of those places had he encountered Harden? And what had Harden been doing there?

She realized she knew very little about the man she cared for so very much.

The men were silent. Bob was probably trying to figure out where he'd seen Harden before. Was Harden silent because he was trying to think up excuses why Bob *hadn't* seen him before? Even the children were quiet for a change.

She was starting to feel a definite tension.

"Beatrice, Walter, I'll bet you didn't know my aunt

Samuela was the founder of the Cottonwood Methodist
Ladies' Evangelical, Temperance, and Missionary Soul-
Saving Aid and Comfort Bible Society," Callie proudly told
them.

"Was she ever a lumberjack?" Walter asked.

"Same thing," Bob muttered through his beans.

"Why they got so many names?" Walter demanded,
squashing his beans with the tines of his fork. Then he
picked the fork up and licked the juicy amber mush off the
bottom.

Callie supposed his method beat scooping them up and
balancing them on the knife blade, or tossing them into the
air one by one and trying to catch them in his mouth.

"They couldn't decide on just one name," Callie told
them.

"So they just decided to use them all?" Beatrice asked.

"No. That was the whole point of the argument."

"Lasted for months, as I recall," Bob interjected. "Still
ain't over with yet, either."

"Of course, they all agreed the name should include
Cottonwood," Callie said.

"That's easy, 'cause that's the name of the town,"
Beatrice said with a broad smile, obviously proud of her
powers of deductive reasoning.

"They'd be stupid to call it New York," Walter agreed. He
stuck his tongue out at his sister.

"They all knew the name had to include Methodist."

"Yeah, that's easy, too," Walter agreed.

"And it had to be for ladies only," Beatrice interjected.
She stuck her tongue out at Walter. "No *men!* Right?"

"Aunt Samuela figured the men pretty much had the
whole rest of the church—and pretty much everything
else—all to themselves. She wanted something for just the
women."

"Good for her," Beatrice declared.

"When some of the men raised a fuss, some of the more

timid ladies balked at the idea, while others stood their ground."

"Like Harmonia Pringle," Bob added, "who threw her husband Zephaniah out o' the house until he agreed to vote in favor o' the ladies. As I recall, he spent three months sleepin' in the back room o' Frank Lang's barbershop. That was 'cause none o' the married men was allowed to keep him, and Frank's a bachelor. Otherwise, Zephaniah'd have been campin' out in his own backyard."

Callie continued, "Then all the men finally figured out, while they were having meetings deciding on all the big, important things, like how much to pay the minister, and if the new iron hitching posts out in front of the church should be painted black or white, they could call on the Society to supply the food for their meetings."

"Pretty sneaky," Beatrice observed with narrowed eyes.

Callie laughed. "They didn't figure on the ladies becoming so involved with the business of the Society that they wouldn't have the time to cook."

Beatrice gave an emphatic nod. "Serves them right!"

"Then the real problems started. Now that they had the Cottonwood Methodist Ladies, what were they supposed to do?"

Callie looked around. Beatrice was watching her with interest. Walter was more interested in his beans and applesauce.

"Evangelical," Beatrice supplied helpfully. She held up one hand, ticking off the terms of the Society on her fingers.

"That meant they wanted to follow the teachings of the Gospel."

"I can think of worse things to do," Harden interjected.

"Temperance." Beatrice ticked down another finger.

"The ladies of the Society voted not to approve of strong drink," Callie explained.

"Not even for medicinal purposes!" Bob lamented.

"I'll bet your aunt was a big supporter of that part of the name," Harden said with a laugh.

"They've been tryin' for years to close down Hawkins Saloon, not to mention the Red-Eye, the Rusty Nail, and the Stars and Garters. I'd say, seein' as how they been so unsuccessful, it was a sign from God to leave them valuable public institutions alone."

"Missionary," Beatrice continued.

"No, no. Wait a minute there," Bob protested. "Miss Callie, you can't forget abolitionist."

"That's right," Callie said.

"You mean their name used to be even longer?" Walter demanded incredulously, fairly spitting the beans out of his mouth and across the table.

Beatrice was busy doing a recount on her fingers.

"Yes, it was. It would have been even longer if they'd been able to figure out a single word that meant being against using tobacco. But they had a big fight about including abolition."

"Worse than Harmonia and Zephaniah," Bob agreed.

"The whole argument lasted more than a week. At one point, half the membership of the Society up and walked out."

"The Miller sisters still aren't talking to each other over that one," Bob added.

"It's pretty ironic that they ended up having to take that out of the name anyway in 1863," Callie explained.

"But Ruth and Alice still aren't speakin'," Bob said. "They just kinda nod, then look away real quick if they happen to pass in church or at the store."

"Soul-saving?" Beatrice continued.

Before Callie could reply, Bob jumped in. "Well, it ain't much fun goin' to church if you can't drag somebody else along with you to save his soul." He lowered his voice to a clearly audible, conspiratorial tone. "That's actually so you can have somebody's shoulder to lean on while you're sleepin' through the sermon."

Walter and Beatrice laughed.

"Oh, Bob!" Callie scolded. "What a horrible thing to tell these children."

"No, no," he insisted. "See, you got to have somebody next to you that you know real well—or who at least don't mind much. Last Sunday I dozed off on Flora Bancroft. Why, the howl she set up, you'd have thought I'd dipped my hand in the collection plate or down the front o' her dress instead o' just leanin' my head on her shoulder."

"Spiritual aid?" Beatrice ticked off one more item.

"Well, the spiritual aid and comfort kind of belong together," Callie told her.

Before Callie could continue her explanation, Bob laughed.

"The ladies put that in for the sole purpose o' givin' 'em an official-soundin' excuse to go pokin' their noses into everybody else's business."

His voice rose several octaves, and he fluttered his hands around as frantically as Miss Jemima. "Oh, my dear, you're in dire need o' spiritual aid and comfort. Do tell me *all* about your problems!"

"Bible?" Beatrice asked.

"That's sort of self-explanatory, too, don't you think?" Callie asked.

"Oh, wait! We forgot Missionary," Beatrice reminded them.

Once again, Bob jumped in. "That's just their excuse to go pokin' their noses into things that ain't none o' their business, even in foreign countries."

"Well, I suppose that explains it all, then," Beatrice said, lowering her hands to the table.

Callie hoped her beans weren't too cold by now.

"Well, not quite all," she said. "They even fought over the *Society* part."

"What's to argue about that?" Harden asked.

"Do you think they need a *reason* to argue over anything?" Callie countered.

"Good point," Harden replied.

"Some of them thought it should be *association,* but others thought that was too businesslike," Callie said. "Some thought it should be *club,* but some said that wasn't serious enough. Some wanted *organization,* but others said that sounded too scientific."

"How'd they finally settle on *society?*" Harden asked.

"That was Widow Marsden's suggestion."

"I haven't met her yet."

"You're just as well off. When Widow Marsden brought it up, she just pointed out to them that they would all be ladies of society. Widow Marsden's been trying for years to do something that would actually make her superior to somebody."

"Anybody!" Bob interjected.

"The word *society* certainly appealed to everyone's sense of superiority and won them all over."

Harden laughed. "I couldn't think of a better reason, myself."

"Of course, it's not over with yet. Now, some of the younger ladies want to add *suffrage* to the name," Callie said.

"Which words would they fit it in between?" Beatrice asked, tangling her fingers. Apparently, she was trying to keep her words and fingers all in the proper order.

"I'll bet they'll be fighting over that for a long time," Harden replied.

"The men have joined in again, too. They'll be fighting for a long, long time."

"Has Harmonia thrown Zephaniah out of the house yet?" he asked with a laugh.

"Not yet, but Aunt Samuela would have approved."

"Do you approve?" Harden asked her.

"I don't see why not. Aunt Samuela ran her farm by herself. She certainly should have been able to vote on laws that affected it."

"And you?"

"Since I suppose I'll be running my farm by myself, I

ought to be able to vote, too." She lifted her chin. "Come to think of it, you don't own a farm, and you can still vote. If any man can vote, why shouldn't any woman?"

Harden shrugged.

"What do you think, Mr. Daniels?"

She grinned defiantly at him from the length of the table.

Oh, my goodness! Where was this streak of stubborn independence coming from? she wondered. Would she be able to maintain it? Even after Harden was gone?

"I wouldn't hardly contradict my boss, now, would I?" he replied with a mischievous twinkle in his eye.

"You're slipping, Daniels," Harden muttered to himself as he lay in bed that night, staring up at the ceiling of the barn, mulling over the day's events. "Used to be, you never let anything interfere with getting a job done. Manassas, Chancellorsville, Chattanooga, even Andersonville. Nobody got in your way. You did your job. You collected your pay. You put a little aside for a rainy day, like your ma always taught you, and you squandered the rest on riotous living. Not a bad life for a bachelor."

He flipped over to his side.

"You've been alone a little too long," he scolded himself. "Maybe you should've availed yourself of the company of some of those ladies at Hawkins Saloon while you were there. But, no. When you had the chance, you were still trying to play the spy. You were too intent on being a hero again."

He flipped to his other side.

"You could always go back there," he reminded himself. "After the fuss you raised with Callie about being able to come and go as you pleased, it would sort of be expected of you."

He rose and made his way to the barn door. He opened the top half of the small door in the side. Leaning both arms on the ledge, he looked out across the moonlit farmyard toward the house. He figured that window on the right ought to be Callie's room.

She'd be up there, sleeping in one of those soft, white nightgowns of hers. Nothing he could actually see through, mind you. But he kind of liked it better that way. She was sweet and modest, and he had a good imagination.

"Yeah, you could go into town to Hawkins Saloon if you really wanted to," he told himself.

The trouble was, he really didn't want to anymore.

"If I was going anywhere, it'd be right across the farmyard and straight upstairs to Callie."

He grimaced and kicked in frustration at the bottom of the door.

"Ouch! You big dummy! Serves you right for walking around without shoes."

He grimaced again and limped back to his cot.

"That's your trouble, Daniels. You got so wrapped up in a pretty face, sweet smells, and a soft, feminine body that you neglected your duty. You came here to get back that payroll shipment from Otis Fielding. But he's intent on taking Callie's farm. You shouldn't be worrying about her. Just do your job."

He sat on the edge of the cot, nursing his sore toe. Then he stooped over and picked petulantly at bits of straw on the barn floor.

He couldn't stand the thought of that oily varmint hurting her or letting those weasels he called farmhands hurt her.

Harden clenched his fists. He could feel his jaw tightening, and his blood pounding angrily at his temples.

He had to make sure Callie didn't begin to suspect the real reason why he was here. The less she knew, the better. He couldn't let her get hurt because of his job.

He fell back onto his cot and stared at the ceiling in frustration.

He also couldn't allow watching out for her to interfere with the job he had to do. It was time to get back to work.

*   *   *

Callie awoke before dawn. The owls and crickets had quieted down, and the meadowlarks hadn't started singing yet. The world was so silent, she could almost believe it had stopped spinning.

Maybe that was a good thing, she tentatively decided. If the earth had stopped spinning, time would stop. Everything would remain exactly as it was at this moment. No days, no weeks, no seasons changing. No work to do, no jobs to be finished. Harden would never move on.

She got up and went to her window. She looked out over the farmyard. The morning breeze had just begun to stir, and she drew in a deep breath. The sky in the east was barely lightening. Not only was it soundless, but the world was completely colorless, composed only of shades of gray. Even the charred, blackened scar of the burnt-out bunkhouse had softened to a deep gray.

Another deep gray shadow detached itself from the mass that had once been the bunkhouse and began to move around it. *Who was that?* Callie frowned and squinted, trying to make out the form in the dim light. It couldn't be Mr. Fielding, nosing around her place. He'd never come alone.

But then, who said he was alone? If she hadn't noticed his shadow at first, were there other figures she couldn't discern in the half-light before dawn? Where were they? How could she spot them?

She watched and wished there was some way she could call to Harden in the barn, to wake him to come to her aid without attracting anyone else's attention.

Should she get the shotgun? Would she even be able to use it?

Her frown deepened as she continued to watch the suspicious shadow. Merciful heavens! She breathed a sigh of relief. It was only Harden.

It didn't seem so strange to her that he was examining the ruins of the bunkhouse. After all, sooner or later, the two of them would have to get rid of what remained and erect a new one.

But what was he doing looking at it at this time of day?

She leaned forward until she feared she might fall out the window trying to see better. Quickly, she ducked back in. It wouldn't look very good if he caught her spying on him. Then she realized he appeared to be much too intent, searching through the pile of rubble, to notice her.

He stepped carefully onto a charred beam. Callie held her breath until she was certain he wouldn't fall. He moved cautiously over the burned wood, making his way around the sooty frames of metal bedsteads, rising like skeletons out of the ashes. Occasionally, he kicked a piece of wood out of his way. Once or twice, he bent down to examine a piece more carefully, but then he always just tossed it away again.

Then he stopped on top of a blackened heap. At first, he only kicked at a beam. Then he picked up a piece and tossed it aside. He picked up more pieces from that same pile and tossed them all back over his shoulder.

If she didn't know better, Callie would swear he looked as if he were searching for something. How could there possibly be anything left worth salvaging in that pile of rubble? There hadn't been anything in there all that important in the first place.

At last, he squatted down and began pulling away burned slats with both hands. If he'd been looking for anything special, apparently he believed he'd found it and that it was worth retrieving.

She watched with intense interest. She was grateful the morning light was increasing in brightness. Now she could see better. Colors were beginning to appear. Shadows were making the outlines of things sharper.

Finally, Harden gave a great tug. Something loosened from the pile and came out. He held it in front of him, dangling down in two tattered pieces with ragged flaps.

It appeared to be his saddlebags.

Callie could easily understand why he would want his saddlebags, although she was a little puzzled why he hadn't gone for them sooner. She'd watched him trying to shave with a sharpened sickle with never a word of complaint. On the other hand, if his razor had survived, she didn't think it was going to be of much use.

He opened one flap of the bag, drew out a single object, then tossed the rest aside.

What did he have now, that everything else in the saddlebags was so unimportant?

Oh, merciful heavens! Callie felt her heart jump and her knees grow shaky as she could see more clearly what he held.

What was Harden doing with a gun?

11

*H*ARDEN STOOD IN the ruins of the bunkhouse. The acrid smell of the ashes he'd kicked up in his search tickled his nose. He wanted to sneeze, but he rubbed his nose instead. Sneezing would only awaken people he'd rather let sleep, people to whom he'd rather not have to explain why he was looking for his gun, why he even possessed a gun.

When Callie had asked him if he had a gun, he'd told her no. He hadn't been lying. At that point in time, he truly was not in possession of a firearm—on his person or among his current, extant personal possessions, to the best of his knowledge and recollection.

Oh, my goodness, he had to laugh to himself. He was starting to sound like a bureaucrat! Maybe it was time to accept that transfer to Washington.

Now, as he examined his gun, he could truly say he'd never been lying. He'd hoped it had survived the heat and flames, but the barrel was misshapened, and the hammer and trigger were bent beyond repair. It was hardly worth calling this piece of ironmongery a gun anymore.

He'd have to get another one. He supposed he could go into town with Callie and the children whenever they planned their next shopping trip. He'd had a little money in his back pocket the night of the fire. He could only hope that would be enough to buy the quality of gun he'd need.

He wondered if he could get away from Callie and the children long enough to hide from them what he had to do.

He hoped no one in town would remark on a farmhand buying a gun. He especially hoped none of the ladies of the Society would catch him. They had never trusted him. They might try to have him thrown in jail on suspicion of being a bandit. Even if they didn't go that far, it was dead certain they'd go running back to Callie, reporting it all. Who knew what kind of distortions the tale could take on in their devious little minds?

Frugal and Refrain were barking and growling again. Callie prayed it wasn't Mr. Fielding back so soon.

She wasn't sure where Harden was, or what he'd do if he met Mr. Fielding again. Sooner or later, she knew she'd have to confront him about his strange behavior regarding the gun. She'd rather do it when the children weren't around. Right now, she just wished she could stall for a little more time to think about it.

But the dogs kept barking. It couldn't be Mr. Fielding, she tried to assure herself. He would have just walked right into her house—dogs or no—and proceeded to track her down wherever she was so he could try to bully her again into selling him her farm.

But Mr. Fielding and his crude hired hands didn't appear.

If it wasn't Mr. Fielding, who was it?

She put down the clothesbasket and went to see what was bothering the dogs. They didn't usually bark like that unless something really annoyed them. She paused for just a moment. Maybe she ought to call for Mr. Daniels or run inside for the shotgun. Even if she wasn't very good at using it, that wasn't exactly common knowledge. The gun was big, and that in itself usually made an impression on an intruder.

"Miss Jackson," she heard a call. "I just heard the dreadful news."

It was Charlie Wilson, her next-door neighbor to the east.

She should've known it was him. For some reason best known only to canines, Frugal and Refrain had both taken an immediate, profound, and unrelenting dislike to him— even worse than toward Mr. Fielding. Her human brain just couldn't figure out why. Unlike Harden, she couldn't even blame it on the man's cigar. Mr. Wilson's wife didn't allow him to smoke.

"What dreadful news is that, Mr. Wilson?"

"Why, about your bunkhouse."

He was trying to make his beady little brown eyes wide with surprise. Maybe if he had eyebrows and if his forehead didn't stop at the top of his head, he'd have succeeded better at lifting his eyebrows.

"My bunkhouse burned a couple of days ago. Don't tell me you're just getting around to finding out."

He heaved a deep sigh. It was a shame he wasn't as good at looking surprised as he was at looking sad and forlorn.

"Bob in Pieces paid us a visit yesterday. Brought us our mail."

Along with all the other town gossip, Callie silently added.

"We sure appreciated it. News pretty much takes its time getting around to way out where we live."

"You only live two miles from here, Mr. Wilson. That's the way to Salina, so people are coming and going along that road all the time."

Undaunted, he continued, "I don't get into town or out and around as much as I used to, what with trying to keep the farm going, looking after LeRoy, and nursing Betty June."

"How's she doing?"

He bobbed his head from side to side. "Some days are better than others."

"I guess that's to be expected with what ails her."

It seemed the polite thing to say, even though no one, not even Doc Hanford, had been able to find the cause for what ailed Betty June. Doc Hanford always maintained that was because no one had yet found a scale for measuring degrees of crazy.

"I suppose so," he agreed. "But she stays cheerful—usually. I just thank the Lord that Betty June was able to give birth to that big strapping son of ours—he's such a help around the farm—before she took to her sickbed, just wasting away."

Perhaps *wasting away* wasn't the most accurate term to apply to Betty June, Callie thought, but she graciously refrained from making any disparaging comment. The last time she'd seen Betty June, the woman had taken up two entire sofa cushions while she sat there and ate a dozen fried eggs, an entire side of bacon with a big bowl of grits and butter on the side, and downed it all with a gallon of buttermilk.

Perhaps *strapping* wasn't quite the right term to describe LeRoy, either. The reason he was such a help around the farm was because, with him around, Charlie didn't need to hitch two mules to the plow. He just let LeRoy haul it around.

"How old is LeRoy now?" she decided was a safer and a bit more cheerful subject to broach.

"Sixteen this September. He'll be going into the fourth grade."

"My, my, my," Callie mused, trying to sound impressed. "That's farther than anyone else in your family has gone."

"I know the preacher always tells us pride goeth before a fall, but I do tend to be right prideful of the boy." Charlie snapped his suspenders and grinned broadly. "Dang shame he ain't just a little older, or you a little younger."

"Oh, I think things worked out pretty fine just the way they are."

"But it would be so nice if you two had eyes for each other."

Callie shrugged. "I think if you try to do any matchmaking without the prior approval of the Cottonwood Methodist Ladies' Evangelical, Temperance, and Missionary Soul-Saving Spiritual Aid and Comfort Bible Society, Mildred Preston would have your head on a pike."

He stared at her, puzzled. "What would she want with my head on a fish?"

Callie just shook her head. "Never mind. She has her ways."

Charlie seemed to accept that. "Yes, sirree. Joining your aunt's farm—begging your pardon—it's your farm now. Joining your farm and mine—well, LeRoy's when I pass on—would've been a really good idea. I'd have . . . we'd have the biggest spread in this part of the county. Could've even rivaled Otis Fielding."

Oh, please! Did he have to mention that horrible man?

"Well, anyway, all I really wanted to say, Miss Jackson, was, if you're ever in need of anything, just let me know."

"Why, thank you, Mr. Wilson."

Callie was genuinely touched. Charlie had his hands full with his own farm, his lumbering oaf of a son, and a wife who'd taken one look at the boy and taken to her bed, demanding to be waited on hand and foot. Callie wondered how different things would be for the Wilsons if LeRoy had turned out to be Louella instead.

"I mean, I know you're all alone here now."

"Not quite, Mr. Wilson."

"Oh, I heard you'd managed to hire another hand and had two little orphans wished on you, but it ain't no kind of protection."

"You haven't met my orphans."

"Still, it ain't right for a pretty gal like you to be all alone out here, so far from town and any help. But I guess you figure you know what you're doing. You girls nowadays are so independent."

"I like to think my aunt raised me properly."

"Oh, yeah, sure. I didn't mean otherwise."

"I'm sure you didn't."

"It's just . . . way out here from town—"

"It's only a mile away."

Mr. Wilson was only trying to be helpful, she was sure, in warning her. But she'd already understood quite well what he was trying to tell her. Why did he have to go on and on?

"A pretty girl—and I must say, you're looking awful different. What've you been doin' for yourself? I don't ever remember you being this pretty."

"Why, thank you for saying so," Callie replied with a weak smile.

"Anyway, way out here, a pretty girl shouldn't be all alone, with strange men passing through all the time on their way out West or, like you said, we're right on the road up to Salina. Well, who knows what's in some folks' heads. I want you to know, if you need me, you just got to holler—"

"Thanks, Mr. Wilson," she interrupted forcefully. "It's really too kind of you to go to all this trouble. If I need you, I'll be sure to let you know," she assured him.

"Well, bye."

"Good-bye.

He waved. Callie waved back. He turned around and waved, sauntered a bit farther down the road, turned around and waved again.

"Bye."

"Good-bye, Mr. Wilson."

He moved along a little farther, turned and waved again.

Callie waved one more time, then turned around and headed back to her clothesline.

Harden was leaning against the tree, chewing on a piece of straw and grinning.

"Another would-be suitor?"

She laughed. "Not very likely."

She reached into the clothesbasket, pulled out a damp sheet, and threw it over the line. She began straightening it out and sticking clothespins on the line, holding it in place in the soft breeze.

He looked around the farmyard. "Where are the good ladies of the Society this time?"

"Probably in town, sticking their noses in someone else's business today."

"You mean they didn't offer that fellow for your matrimonial approval?"

"They wouldn't dare," she told him as she moved down the line, sticking clothespins as she went. "Charlie Wilson is almost old enough to be my father—"

He pushed himself off from the tree trunk and followed her as she worked her way down the clothesline. "That wouldn't stop them."

"And has a son—"

"Maybe the ladies of the Society will try to match you up with him instead."

"He's only sixteen."

He shrugged. "Some women like to marry them young. Train them right from the start."

"I don't think this one's going to be ready to train until he's out of grammar school."

"Oh, a really sharp fellow?"

Callie just groaned and stuck on another clothespin.

"Betty June Wilson has been an invalid since the day their son was born."

"Oh, I'm sorry. I wouldn't have joked about a thing like that. What is it? Dropsy? The canker? Consumption? Neurasthenia?"

"My gracious, where'd you learn such medical terms?"

He shrugged. "Same place I learned Spanish."

Callie already knew somehow that he wasn't going to tell her where that was, either.

"Well, the plain and simple truth is, Betty June suffers from consummate laziness."

"Hmm." He stroked his chin. "There's a lot of that going around. No cure, either."

Callie laughed.

"So, do you think the ladies of the Society have decided to stop pestering you about getting married, then?"

"No. Mildred invited me to dinner. A person wouldn't have to be a prophet to know what she's got planned for me."

"But she hasn't brought anyone here lately." He chuckled. "Do you think I scared the ladies away the other day?"

Callie laughed aloud. "Ha! No. And it's going to take more than you in a sheet to scare away Mildred Preston."

"How about me without a sheet?" he suggested with a mischievous grin.

She pointed a warning clothespin at him. *"That* will lose me my farm. So don't even think about it."

"Oh, I think about it, Miss Jackson. I think about it a lot."

She used a little more force than usual to stick the clothespin on the line. She thought about him a lot, too. But it wasn't something that was safe to admit. She knew exactly where such a confession would lead.

"Then maybe you don't have enough work to do around here to keep your mind occupied, Mr. Daniels."

"Oh, I've got plenty to keep my mind occupied. For instance, I do believe that I am just a shade more attractive than this Wilson fellow."

"Maybe."

"I've got all my own teeth." He gave her a grin almost as wide as Bob's.

She shrugged, unimpressed. "So does Bob in Pieces."

"I've got all my own hair and eyebrows."

"Eyebrows can be highly overrated."

"You only say that until the rain starts running down your forehead into your eyes."

Callie tried her best not to laugh.

"What about that walking scarecrow the ladies brought around the other day?" Harden asked. "Is that all those ladies can find to match you up with? You can do better than that!"

"Maybe."

"What do you mean, maybe?" he asked.

Callie knew exactly what the man was fishing for. After that incident on the porch and her reaction to him after Mr. Fielding had left, how could he believe that she wasn't madly attracted to him? How could he not understand how dangerous that attraction was for her without some sort of commitment from him?

Well, for once, let the self-assured rascal not get what he was looking for, for just a little while. He liked to tease her so much. She decided taking a little of his own medicine might not be a bad remedy for Harden Daniels. She grinned to herself as she bent down for another sheet.

"I suppose some people might consider you extremely attractive, Mr. Daniels—why, yourself, for instance."

He grumbled something incoherent.

"But some people don't set a whole lot of store by mere physical appearance. Some people don't find broad shoulders, wavy hair, and blue eyes the least bit attractive."

"Like yourself and your late aunt, for instance?" he offered.

She found his broad shoulders, wavy hair, and blue eyes unbelievably attractive, and Aunt Samuela had taught her not to lie. But not answering wasn't exactly lying, was it?

She gave a noncommittal shrug.

"Then what do you set store by, Miss Jackson?"

"Oh, kindness."

Callie knew Harden was kind. Hadn't Bob told her how he'd taken the "lost and forlorn" children under his wing and brought them all the way out to her? Hadn't she seen for herself how he'd almost gotten himself in trouble with Mr. Fielding and his henchmen just because he was worried about her?

"You must admit, it was *very* kind of Mr. Tucker to come

all the way out here to offer to rebuild the bunkhouse for me," she teased.

"But he was expecting to get paid for his work," Harden protested.

"It was still kind of him to make the trip."

"Mildred probably hounded him until he agreed."

"But it was still a kind gesture. Don't you agree?" she repeated.

After a bit, he answered, "Yeah."

"And loyalty," she continued. "I set store by loyalty."

Even though he hadn't been working for her for very long, she'd seen how Harden could be loyal—a lot more loyal than the worthless farmhands her aunt had hired.

"Yes, indeed. Loyalty. You must admit, Charlie Wilson caring for an invalid wife for sixteen years—especially when she's not really an invalid—requires a very special kind of loyalty. Don't you agree?" she asked, prodding him into making some sort of reply.

"Yeah."

His answers were getting slower, and it was taking him a longer time to agree to each question. He crossed his arms tightly over his chest.

"Steadfastness."

"What?"

"Steadfastness," she repeated a bit more slowly. "Don't tell me a man who knows about neurasthenia and Russian czarinas doesn't know what steadfastness is."

"Sounds like a church word—not medical or political."

"My, my. Maybe that's why you don't know what it means," she continued to tease.

"I _know_ what it means."

He sounded as if he was getting slightly irritated. She grinned. She'd tease him just a little more, and then they'd have a good laugh together. Her kisses would smooth his ruffled feathers caused by her bantering.

"Yes, indeed. Steadfastness. Like the Reverend Preston.

He's been the pastor at the Cottonwood Methodist Church for fifteen years now."

"Maybe that's just easier to do if a man has a different kind of job than I have."

She waited for him to make some kind of funny remark. He always had a ready, witty answer. Instead, Harden spun around on his heels and headed for the barn.

Callie dropped her clothespins and hurried after him.

"Harden, what's the matter?"

He just kept walking.

"Harden, I'm sorry if I said something to hurt you."

He just kept walking.

"Mr. Daniels! Damn it! Stop and listen to me!"

She'd actually cursed, she thought with shock. The aggravating man had actually made her forget her religion and curse!

"The least you could do is stop and turn around and listen to me!" she cried.

He kept on walking.

At last she caught up with him. She seized his arm and jerked it so hard she almost toppled over. But at least she'd halted his headlong flight into the barn.

"Harden, what's the matter?"

"Nothing. I'm doing what you respect and admire. I'm picking a job and sticking with it. I'm cleaning your dang barn."

He turned away from her and started walking again.

"For goodness sake, what's wrong? One minute we were teasing—"

He spun around and glared at her. "Is that what you call it?"

"Yes. I . . . I thought so . . ."

Why didn't he think so? What had she said that was so wrong? She'd only pointed out traits in other people that she found admirable. She'd never said Harden didn't possess them in great abundance.

She stood there, waiting for an explanation. She didn't understand what was happening at all.

"Apparently I was wrong."

"Apparently."

Callie reached out and placed her hand on his arm. It was the best she could do by way of an apology under the circumstances.

If she had it her way, if she didn't have to worry about the children, about the farm, or about the stern and ever-watchful ladies of the Society, she'd wrap him in her arms and kiss away every word she'd said that had ever caused him pain.

But that wasn't the way it was. That wasn't the way it ever could be, so she just had to settle for touching his arm.

"I'm sorry if I said anything that hurt you, Harden. I truly am. I . . . I was only trying to tease, to make a little joke the way you always do. My grandfather, Aunt Samuela . . . we never joked or teased each other. Everything around here was deadly serious. I haven't been doing it as long as you have, and I guess I'm just not as good at it."

He reached up and rubbed the back of his neck. Instead of shaking her off, he used the arm she wasn't touching.

She pressed his arm more closely. He still didn't move away.

"Should I take this as a sign that you accept my apology?" she asked, looking pleadingly up into his eyes.

He chuckled. "Yeah. Seeing as how you were raised by Aunt Samuela, I can believe every word you say."

He kicked at the ground with the heel of his boot.

"Look, I'm real sorry I got all hot under the collar, especially with you, Callie. I . . . I'm not real happy, myself, with roaming around, not really having a place to call home. But it's the only life I have right now, and I've got to live it this way. I don't have much of a choice."

He took a step back from her. She had to drop her arm to her side.

"Look, I'll be working in the barn until supper. I . . . I think maybe I ought to eat in there—"

"You most certainly will not! You can't leave me alone with those two children when, the first night here, one of them tried to eat the cat!"

"He didn't try to eat the cat," Harden told her with a weak laugh.

"I know. But he still tried to kill me, and he still swears you told him to."

She grinned at him. His smile deepened. She reached up to touch his cheek. She ran the tip of her index finger across the little crease at the corner of his mouth that only appeared when he smiled.

"That's better. I like it so much better when I can see you smile."

Harden reached up to take her hand. He pressed the back of her hand against his lips. Then he dropped her hand and backed way.

"I'd still better get my work done before supper. I wouldn't want you to lose the farm because of something I *didn't* do."

Harden kicked at the straw on the floor as he made his way into the dark coolness of the barn. Since he had boots on this time, he kicked a few bales of hay and the back of the door while he was at it.

He should have known better. He should have been able to control his temper.

Callie's awkward attempt to tease him shouldn't have set him to remembering what he didn't want to.

She'd hit a raw nerve, claiming there were other qualities besides mere handsomeness that attracted her to a man— qualities that he'd never be able to possess.

He could be kind. He actually enjoyed being with children, which was more than Callie, with all her church upbringing, could say.

He could be loyal. Even if his family had accused him of treason against the Confederate States, he knew where his true loyalties lay, and he'd worked for them. Three years spying for the Union Army, two of which had been spent in a Confederate prisoner of war camp—where he'd never given away a single secret, no matter what—sort of proved he could be loyal to his country and his cause. He'd always been grateful he hadn't just been shot on the spot when he'd been caught.

But, according to Callie, he wasn't steadfast, either. He was a federal marshal, for Pete's sake, and part of his duty included tracking fugitives. How could a man offer a wife and children a stable, loving home when he was always gone, chasing after murderers and bandits, never knowing which assignment he wasn't coming back from?

He'd never be able to offer her the stability she sought. She'd do better to marry a man like Herbert Tucker. But it galled him to think that someday she eventually might.

He was jealous! That was it, pure and simple. He was unbelievably jealous that Callie might fall in love with someone else. Why couldn't she fall in love with him? What if she did?

Maybe he should just take the advice of some of his fellow marshals. Take his pleasure with whichever lady in town seemed willing, then be on his way. But he couldn't do that to Callie. Yet she deserved a better life than he could offer her and a better man than he could ever be.

12

$\mathcal{P}$AYDAY, CALLIE THOUGHT with dread. Harden deserved to be paid.

She'd also promised the children they'd all go into town to do some much-needed and eagerly anticipated shopping.

"Aunt Samuela always took care of paying the farmhands," she muttered plaintively. "I haven't the faintest idea where she kept anything. Ledgers. Receipts. Cash box. Oh, especially the cash box! Where is it?"

She'd already ransacked the kitchen cupboard and the wardrobe in Aunt Samuela's bedroom. There wasn't that much furniture in the place. There couldn't be that many more drawers to hide things in.

There was a big chest at the foot of the bed. That was her last hope.

Callie tugged open the heavy lid and peered inside. The whole thing smelled like naphtha. *This must be it*, she thought with triumph. Every time they went to the store, Aunt Samuela's money always smelled like naphtha.

Sure enough. There was the large ledger. There was a small metal box with a lock on it, and a larger metal box with an ever larger lock on it.

"Oh, please, dear Lord, don't let this thing be locked and I have to search for the key now, too," she prayed out loud. By the time she'd found everything, it would be too late to travel into town.

She decided to start small and work her way up to bigger problems. She picked up the little box.

The lid lifted with ease, revealing a large stack of folding money and several bags that, when shaken, appeared to be full of coins.

"Oh, thank you, thank you, thank you," she said gratefully as she hugged the bills to her chest. "I swear I'll spend it carefully."

She looked with curiosity at the larger metal box. If the money was in the small box, and the records in the ledger, what was in the large box?

She lifted the lid. Papers. Nothing but a stack of papers jammed inside. Callie grimaced with disappointment and let the lid drop closed.

She'd have to clean that junk out soon. She'd have to go through Aunt Samuela's things, too, and sort out what she wanted to keep and what she knew she'd have to give away.

Callie chuckled. She knew Beatrice would insist on her giving *all* the dresses away—or, most probably, burning them.

The ladies of the Society would know of some poor woman deserving of their charity to give the dresses to.

Before she went downstairs to gather up the children for the trip and to pay Mr. Daniels, she stopped by the mirror. It was such a small mirror, but Aunt Samuela had always maintained it was just the right size: not so big as to allow one to dwell too long on personal appearance but just large enough to make sure one's hair wasn't mussed and that one's buttons were straight so that it didn't appear as if one had been doing anything that would mess up one's neatness.

Callie studied her reflection. Her buttons were straight, even on this hideous green dress. How could Mr. Daniels have thought she looked pretty in it?

What would he think of the way Beatrice had arranged her hair this morning? she wondered. She patted a curl here and a stray strand there.

Would he think she looked beautiful again? She hoped so.

Payday.

Harden had the ten dollars Callie had given him. When he'd checked the night after the fire, he couldn't believe how lucky he'd been to have another twenty in his pocket.

Well, shopping without money might work for two little children, Harden thought as he drove them and Callie into town in her buggy, but it wouldn't do for him. He couldn't buy everything needed with thirty dollars. Well, if worse came to worst, he decided, he'd just do without an extra shirt for a little while longer.

"I think you should wear blue," Beatrice advised Callie as they descended from the buggy and invaded Corrigan's General Store. The little girl spied the bolts of cloth lined up along the back wall and headed straight for them.

Walter headed straight for the candy.

Callie stood in the doorway.

"You look puzzled," Harden said. "What's the matter?"

"I can't decide."

"I'm sure Beatrice will be delighted to help you pick out some fabric."

"No, no. It's not that. I can't decide whether to pick out the cloth first and then treat myself to candy, or pick out the candy first and eat it while I'm choosing fabric."

Harden shook his head. "I don't believe even Congress is faced with those kinds of momentous decisions."

"You don't understand. I don't go into town that often. I've got to make this last."

"Why?"

"Because—"

"I'm not the only one who can come and go as I please," he reminded her. "Anytime you get the hankering for some candy, you just hitch up the buggy and drive right on into town. It's only about a mile out."

"That's right. I . . . I can do that now," she said, her eyes brightening. "I feel so silly. I don't have to worry about Aunt Samuela scolding me for being a frivolous gadabout, for spending money foolishly."

"Oh, spending money on candy ain't *never* foolish!" Walter called his assurance to her from across the store.

"As long as you don't do anything that's not prudent, upright, sober, and moral while you're here, you don't have to worry about the ladies of the Society scolding you, either."

Callie started to laugh.

"I think I'll have some candy," she announced, heading for the long counter covered with glass jars filled with so many colored sweets that they looked like a display of precious jewels.

"Hooray!" Walter cheered. With one pudgy finger, he pointed to round white-and-red peppermints, little sugary yellow lemon drops, and long strands of black licorice. "Look at this one. And this. We got to get some of this."

"Maybe we could get just a little of each," Callie suggested.

Harden leaned over her shoulder and whispered in her ear, "While you're concentrating on the candies, I think I'll take a little stroll around. I really don't think you'll be needing me when you and Beatrice start looking at fabric and, to tell you the truth, I don't think I want to be here."

"What about Walter?"

"He's still young. He'll get over it." Chuckling, Harden headed for the door.

He spotted Mr. Corrigan on the way out. Very quietly, he approached him.

"Excuse me, do you sell guns here?" Harden asked.

"Indeed, we do. But just a few, lad. Just a few."

"I need a good revolver, very accurate, small bore, small caliber—"

"Ah, then you'll be needing to see Mr. Gunther," Mr. Corrigan said.

"Where's his shop?"

"Across the street, right next door to the blacksmith."

Mr. Corrigan pointed as if Harden could see through the walls of the store to his eventual destination.

"You'll be having to listen real close to him. He's a German fellow, never quite got the hang of the English tongue. But, faith, if he doesn't make the best guns to be had hereabouts."

"Thanks. And . . . um . . . would you do me a big favor?"

"And what would that be?"

"If Miss Jackson asks where I've gone, you haven't seen me. The lady gets a mite nervous when I mention firearms."

Mr. Corrigan gave him a conspiratorial wink. "Say no more, lad. Say no more. I've got a wife and three daughters of me own, and they're all a bit skittish around the gunpowder."

Harden headed out the door and across the street. He just hoped the best German weapons in town weren't beyond his means.

Callie's arms were laden with two bolts of cloth wrapped in protective brown paper. Beatrice also juggled a bolt. Walter carried the bag of candy pressed close to his heart.

She placed the bundles in the back of the buggy, then looked around.

"My goodness, where's Mr. Daniels?" she asked.

Beatrice looked around, too. "I haven't seen him since we got here. I was too busy shopping—and actually spending money for a change, too!"

"I saw him at the candy counter," Walter offered.

"And after that?" Callie asked.

He shook his head and popped another piece of peppermint candy into his mouth.

"Oh, dear. He said he was going to wander around a little. But I thought he'd be back by now."

She hurried back into the general store.

"Mr. Corrigan, please, have you seen Mr. Daniels, my hired hand? He's about so tall . . ."

She extended her arm above her head until she figured her hand was just about the right height. She just hoped Mr. Corrigan wouldn't wonder how it was she knew precisely where Mr. Daniels would stand.

"Sure'n I haven't seen the follow since he left here while you and the little lady were perusing the bolts of cloth."

"Which way did he go?"

"I'm sorry to say, miss, I wasn't watching."

Callie slumped in disappointment as she left the store. Where was he? It was time to go home, to give the children supper, and get everyone to bed so they'd be ready to work tomorrow. She couldn't leave without Harden.

She stood on the wooden sidewalk, looking up and down Main Street.

He wasn't in the general store, that much was certain. She hoped and prayed he hadn't gotten himself into any trouble and ended up at Doc Hanford's, or worse yet, at his brother's, the undertaker. He wouldn't be in Audrey Finster's millinery shop. He certainly wouldn't be in Herbert Tucker's carpenter shop, unless he planned on driving a stake through his heart.

Maybe he'd gone to the barbershop. He hadn't had a really proper shave in a couple of days. Did she dare invade that bastion of masculinity, if only to ask if Mr. Daniels were sitting under one of those hot, steaming towels?

Perhaps he'd gone to the blacksmith's to look over some of the horses. That was another fortress of masculinity that she didn't feel comfortable assailing—alone or with two small children in tow.

She decided to pursue other, easier options first.

But the other options that presented themselves weren't any better. The Red-Eye. The Rusty Nail. The Stars and Garters. Hawkins Saloon. She read the signs with dread.

Which one was he in? Which one should she try first?

She'd already been inside Hawkins Saloon. She'd probably feel the least uncomfortable going in there. On the other hand, what if someone should recognize her? She wouldn't want to be accused of frequenting the place.

Should she take the children as protection? Or would they make so much noise they'd get her thrown out, attracting a lot of unwanted attention.

Which saloon did she stand the best chance of going into without having any of the ladies of the Society seeing her?

Oh, my goodness. She'd stood on the street worrying about this before. She felt as if she truly were going around in circles.

What would she find if she went into one of the saloons?

Harden drinking at the bar? She could handle that, she thought. She'd just haul him on home and fill him up with strong, black coffee.

Harden gambling away his hard-earned pay at the faro or keno tables? She'd scold him and drag him home again, too.

Harden upstairs, doing any number of things that made her blush even as she stood there forcing herself not to think about it?

He was just a man. Aunt Samuela had told her men just couldn't live without that sort of thing or they went blind or insane or killed people. Women, of course, being more sensitive creatures of a nobler nature, didn't have that sort of problem.

Callie drowned in a wave of guilt. She'd tempted the poor man and then never let him have the release he so desperately needed. Was he in there even now, spending his masculine passions on some . . . some *other* woman?

Callie's guilty blush turned to a flush of anger. *How dare he!*

How dare he trifle with her affections and then spend time with some other woman—some other woman who wouldn't remember him from Adam and whose name he probably didn't even know!

In a flash of surprising realization, Callie felt tears gathering in her eyes. Why on earth was she crying?

My goodness, she was jealous! She thought she only cared about Harden because he was kind and took care of her when she really needed it. She felt a deep need for him that she attributed to some perverse enjoyment of the stories Aunt Samuela had told to warn her away from men.

She found it a little difficult to believe what must be the truth: She was in love with Harden Daniels!

Now what was she going to do?

"There he is!" Walter shouted. He was pointing down Main Street toward the blacksmith's shop. Harden was walking away from the store next door: Gunther's Gun Shop.

He grinned sheepishly at her as he approached the buggy.

"You haven't been waiting for me long, have you?" he asked.

"No. Not really. It just seemed like an eternity."

He frowned. "What do you mean?"

He knew exactly what she meant, she thought. Why would he pretend otherwise?

"We didn't know where you'd gone. We were worried."

"I wasn't worried," Walter said. "I know Mr. Daniels is a big boy. He can find his way home by himself."

"*I* was worried," Callie corrected.

"I'm sorry. Everything always takes longer than you think," he said by way of apology.

"Where were you?" she asked. But she had the feeling that he knew that she knew exactly where he'd been.

"Gunther's Gun Shop."

"What in heaven's name do you want with a gun?"

Oh, my goodness! He'd been denied his release too long and was indeed about to shoot someone, Callie thought with rising panic. Aunt Samuela had been right. And it was all Callie's fault!

"Wow! Who're you gonna shoot?" Walter demanded.

"No one, I hope," Harden answered.

"Then why do you want a gun?"

"Why shouldn't I have a gun?" he countered. "Unless Aunt Samuela had yet another rule against farmhands owning guns."

"Not that I know of. Except for the shotgun for hunting, we never really had or needed anything else." She turned to Walter and Beatrice. "Why don't you two get into the buggy?"

They climbed over each other and the bolts of cloth.

Now that the children were safely in the buggy, Callie turned to Harden. Her eyes were probably still just a little red from the tears she'd come awful close to shedding, yet she tried to look as serious as possible.

"It's Mr. Fielding, isn't it?"

"Fielding?" he repeated.

"You don't have to pretend you're half-witted with me, Harden. It's because of that incident with Mr. Fielding and his horrible hired hands that you bought that gun. Isn't it?"

"No. What makes you think I have any reason to seek out Fielding with a gun?"

"Not seek out exactly. Just . . . if he comes around again . . ."

"That's right. That's the reason. It's for *if* he ever comes around again with his hired guns, threatening to hurt you or the children. It's for protection. You don't have to worry. I'm not going to go sneaking over to his farm some night and shoot him in the back of the head."

He wouldn't do that. He couldn't, Harden told himself. Not until he'd found the money. Fielding was the only one who knew where he'd hidden the stolen payroll.

Callie pressed her lips together and stood there, thinking. Everything Harden said made sense. Then why didn't she believe him?

"Don't you know by now? I'm not the kind of man who would shoot down another in cold blood. But I am a man who will do whatever I have to do to protect the people I . . . I care about. Now come along. I think it's time to take the children back home."

Before she'd even allow him to sit down for supper, Callie had made him promise to leave the gun in the barn with his things. She didn't want the children to be able to get hold of his gun.

Harden didn't want the children to be able to get hold of his gun, either. Beatrice would probably prop it up, stick a daisy in the barrel, and use it as a flower vase to decorate the living room. Walter would probably wing Callie with it—if she was lucky.

So he'd waited until after supper, until after the children were tucked in bed. Now he could sit in the barn, in peace and quiet, without having to answer dozens of questions, and examine his gun in peace.

Callie would be in bed now, too. She'd be lying there with her green eyes closed. Her auburn hair would be pulled back in a single, long braid down her back, but little wisps of hair would have worked their way loose and framed her face like some sort of magic veil.

"Stop thinking about her with a loaded gun in your hand, son," he warned himself. "You're liable not to be paying attention and end up shooting yourself in the foot."

The loud meow from the windowsill startled him.

"Prudence. Find any mice lately?"

She meowed loudly again.

"I'm sorry, girl. I don't know where your tom might be. You're lucky Aunt Samuela didn't name him Flee-Fornication."

Prudence meowed again as she jumped down from the sill, rubbed her cheek across his pants leg, then jumped up on the sill again.

"I'm sorry if you're in the mood to play right now, but I've got this swell new gun——"

Prudence meowed again. She turned, looking out the window, her tail slowly waving back and forth.

That's not playful, Harden thought. That's hunting. What's she hunting out there?

He rose quietly and made his way to the window. Someone was very clumsily approaching the house.

"Why haven't the dogs barked?" he wondered aloud.

Prudence sniffed in disdain of canine capabilities.

"I do believe this bears investigation. Thanks, Prudence," he told her, rubbing her ears one more time before he holstered his gun and set out. "I owe you a big trout," he promised.

Harden couldn't imagine why Callie or the children couldn't hear the clumsy oaf crashing through the bushes around their house. He was making so much noise, he probably couldn't have heard Harden sneaking up on him even if Harden had been deliberately making noise.

The man was peering intently into the dining room window. Was he looking to steal? The tablecloth? He tried the window, but Harden could've told him beforehand that, unless they were actually eating in there, Callie always kept the window locked.

The intruder moved around to the kitchen window. He tried that, too, without any success. Harden almost laughed. It was just this bungling burglar's luck to pick the window that always stuck.

In the yellow light that streamed out the window, Harden could now recognize the face of the intruder: Charlie Wilson.

Charlie Wilson—not a would-be suitor for Callie's hand, but trouble, nonetheless. Charlie still wanted her farm. He'd even warned her about the dangers of being alone.

Harden wasn't sure yet what the scoundrel was up to, but that didn't matter. He'd put a stop to it.

Just as he was about to come up behind Charlie and clap his hand down hard on his shoulder, he heard the sound of a buggy pulling up in front of the house.

What in the world was some idiot doing, calling at this time of night?

Harden decided curious Charlie could wait for just a moment. He made his way to the side of the house and watched.

He could see now why the dogs had been so silent. Someone—and Charlie's name sprang to the top of the list of suspects—had given each a big steak to chew on to keep them occupied.

As Harden watched the ladies descend from the buggy, the tune to the children's nursery rhyme ran through his head. "Sing a song of sixpence, a pocketful of rye. Four and twenty blackbirds baked in a pie. When the pie was opened, the birds began to sing . . ."

That's just what it looked like, except there were only two of them. Some woman all in black, her loose shawl flapping around her like wings, descended first. Another smaller version followed.

He had no idea what their names were, but from the looks of them, one thing was certain. They were ladies of the Society, and they were heading for Callie's front door.

What were they doing here without Mildred? he wondered. All Callie needed was some lady of the Society to catch her in a compromising position, and she'd lose her farm.

Mildred hadn't seemed to see anything wrong with his appearing at the door in a sheet. Had some member taken great offense at that? It was easy to see the Society was rife with internal feuding. Who would want Callie to lose her farm this badly?

Charlie, for one.

He had to warn Callie!

Harden slipped into the shadows at the side of the building. The crows were already heading for the front door. He didn't have time to run all the way around to the back door. He looked up.

Well, when you're fighting birds, you've got to learn to fly, he figured. Hand over hand, he shinnied up the drainpipe.

"Lord have mercy! I haven't done this since I was fourteen," he exclaimed.

Once on the porch roof, he headed for Callie's bedroom window. The sash lifted easily.

"Callie!" he whispered. "Callie! Wake up!"

She stretched sleepily. With her arms extended above her head, the outline of her breasts was clearly visible in the blue shadows of moonlight. He felt a surge of longing stab through him as he paused to watch her.

No time for that now, Daniels, he scolded himself. *If she gets caught with either Wilson or you in her bedroom and loses the farm, no matter how much you believe she might care about you now, she'll hate you for the rest of her life.*

She opened her eyes.

"Callie! Callie! It's just me. Don't say a word."

When she realized it was him, she sat bolt upright in bed, clutching the sheet to her chest.

"Harden!" she whispered. "Oh, my goodness. What are you doing here? We shouldn't. We mustn't. But—"

"Hush, hush!"

"The children won't hear. They're all the way across—"

"No, no, no. That's not it."

"What's wrong?"

"Be quiet. There's trouble."

"Oh, my goodness! Is it Mr. Fielding?"

"No. Charlie Wilson."

"Who? But he's harmless."

"At this very moment, Charlie Wilson is trying to break

into your house, and two ladies of the Society are heading for your front door."

"Who? Why?"

"I recognized them from your aunt's funeral, but I've never met them or learned their names. If you can add two and two, I think you know what all this means."

"Merciful heavens! If they catch us together, no matter what I say, I'll lose my farm. Oh, Harden, what'll I do?"

"Just wake the children. Grab a book, sit in their room with them, and pretend you've been reading to them all this time."

"What?"

"Just do it! It sounds crazy, but it might just work. Whatever you do, don't go back into your bedroom until I tell you it's all right. Don't leave the children. Don't let the children leave you alone. I won't be here. I have to take care of Wilson. The children are your only defense."

Before Callie could spring out of bed and wrap her robe around her, Harden was already heading down the drainpipe.

Just as his feet hit the ground, he heard the first loud, insistent rapping at the front door.

"Open up, Miss Jackson!" he heard the crotchety voice cry. "Open up! We know you've got a man in there!"

Harden continued on his way around back. Charlie was still struggling with the other window. That one stuck, too, only just a bit farther up. There was about six inches of opening that Charlie was desperately trying to fit his head through.

"No, no, no!" Harden heard him mutter. "Not yet. I'm not in yet."

Oh, it was pretty definite these three were in cahoots. But who the heck were those women? Which of the ladies of the Society would benefit from helping Wilson take Callie's farm away from her? Well, Harden figured, it was time to find out.

His hand descended heavily on Charlie's shoulder. "Say there, can I help you, friend?"

Charlie jumped, hitting his head on the bottom of the window. "Ouch!" He rubbed his head.

"Mind telling me who you are?" Harden asked. "I'd kind of like to know whose brains I was going to be blowing all over the ground."

Charlie swallowed hard. Large beads of perspiration popped out on his forehead, dripped past the place where his eyebrows should have been, and into his eyes. He started to move his arm to wipe his brow, then apparently thought better of moving at all until Harden gave him permission.

"I . . . I . . . I'm Charlie Wilson, her next-door neighbor, I . . . I was worried about Miss Jackson's safety. Yeah, that's right. So I was . . . I was checking to make sure all the windows were locked."

"Oh, is that all?" Harden replied with a chuckle. He kept his hand clamped tightly on Charlie's shoulder and gave him a little shake. "Well, aren't you just the best dang neighbor a lady ever had!"

"Who . . . are you? Why are you here?"

Charlie tried to look tough, but without eyebrows, that quality seemed to elude him.

"I'm Harden Daniels, Miss Jackson's hired hand. It's my job to make sure she's safe in her house."

Charlie relaxed just long enough to reach up and wipe his brow with the sleeve of his shirt. He grinned.

"Yeah, well . . . it . . . it looks like the windows are all secure so . . . so I think I'd better be gettin' back home, and you can be moseying on over to the barn."

"Oh, no. You can't go yet, neighbor."

The grin fell from Charlie's face.

Harden's grip tightened. He wasn't about to set this one loose until the vultures of the Society had gone on their way, too.

"If you're so worried about Miss Jackson, then I'm sure

you'll want to see the horrible accident that almost happened to her a few days ago."

"No, thanks, really. I got to be getting on home." Charlie tried to pull away.

"No, no. It's really important," Harden insisted as he held Charlie tightly and guided him toward the barn. "You see, a couple of days ago, a load of hay in the loft dumped down on top of Miss Jackson. It fairly suffocated her before Walter and I could dig her out. Now, if a terrible accident like that could happen to a lady as careful as Miss Jackson, why, it could happen to just about any one of us. Don't you think so?"

"I . . . I guess."

"So I want to show you exactly how it happened, so you can make sure that nothing like that ever happens to . . . well, to you, for instance. Do you understand what I mean?"

Charlie nodded his head and tried to swallow hard.

"Get up, get up," Callie urged the children as she lit the lamp on the table by the bed. "Grab a book—any book. I'm going to read to you."

"But we just got into bed," Beatrice complained as she propped herself up on her elbows.

"Do you really need this story now? Can't it wait until morning?" Walter asked, still lying there rubbing his eyes.

The pounding on the door grew louder as it echoed through the house.

"I said open up, Miss Jackson! We know you've got a man in there with you." Widow Marsden's voice grew more insistent.

"What's that?" Beatrice asked with a sneer.

"Widow Marsden," Callie pronounced with a shudder. Widow Marsden by herself was horrible enough. But Harden had warned her that there were two ladies of the Society descending on her house like a plague. If she only knew who else had come with the widow.

"Who's Widow Marsden?" Beatrice asked.

"A very unpleasant woman who could see to it that my farm is taken away from me."

Beatrice gasped. "Ick! Not her!" Then her eyes grew wide with fear. "How can we stop her?"

"You both have to do exactly as I say."

13

"*S*HE WON'T TAKE my farm away from me!" Callie declared with fierce determination. "Not if I have anything to say about it."

She leaned closer to the children, holding both arms out as if to draw them into a ring of conspiracy. She looked each one deeply in the eyes.

In a whisper, she invited, "Not if you'll help me."

Walter stopped rubbing his eyes and sprang to his feet on the bed. "Sure!" He bounced eagerly up and down. "Can I shoot her with Mr. Daniels's new gun?"

"No, no! Now, hush!"

Callie frantically tried to still the bouncing child. That was all she needed Widow Marsden to hear downstairs—a rhythmically creaking bed overhead!

"The gun is out in the barn, anyway. Or maybe Mr. Daniels is using it now," she added with a little shudder of dread.

If Harden was using his gun, was someone else using

their gun against him? she worried. If they were, she'd surely have heard the gunshots—but she certainly didn't want to be listening for them.

"Let's not think about that now. We've got work of our own to do. Now, Walter, stop jumping. Beatrice, grab that book. Hurry!"

She indicated the large Bible lying on top of the dresser.

"It's a Bible."

"It won't bite. Stay here and find a real good story, and look like you're actually reading it."

"I can't read," Walter protested.

"Just pretend. And stop jumping."

"But it's hard to read with all those thees and thous," Beatrice protested. "Don't you have anything else?"

"In the first place, we don't have time to go looking for another one. Thunderation! I don't even have time to explain this to you both. In the second place, Aunt Samuela never kept any other books in the house. She said reading was a frivolous waste of time."

"No . . . other . . . books?" they chorused. Both children looked completely horror-stricken. But that didn't stop Walter from bouncing.

"Stop jumping!"

"Don't worry. *I* can manage it," Beatrice reassured her as she sat on the edge of the bed and opened the Bible. "I'll keep him in line, too."

"Find something the ladies of the Society would approve of to read to children. Noah's Ark is always a good bet."

"Sodom and Gomorrah?" Beatrice suggested with a giggle. "David and Bathsheba? Song of Solomon?"

"Now you sound like Mr. Daniels."

Oh, how Callie wished he was here to help her now! No! She quickly changed her mind. It would not be a good idea to have Widow Marsden catch her upstairs in her late aunt's bedroom with the hired man, even if the children were present.

Besides, Harden had assured her he was taking care of Charlie Wilson. She had to trust that he was.

"Christmas story! Christmas story!" Walter cried, still jumping up and down.

"It's too early for that," Beatrice scolded, suddenly serious. "I can't read when you're bouncing. Now sit down and behave!"

Callie didn't stay around to find out if Walter obeyed.

"I'm coming," she tried to call in the sweetest voice she could manage as she ran down the stairs. "I'll be right there."

Under her breath, she mumbled, "Hold your horses, you pinch-faced, constipated old battle-ax!"

As she made her way down the hall, she finally heard the creaking of the bed stop. She wondered if Beatrice had sat on Walter or knocked him out with the big Bible. Either way, she sent a grateful prayer heavenward. It stopped just in time, too.

She pulled open the door.

"Why, Widow Marsden! Ruth Miller! What a completely unexpected surprise!" she exclaimed in as pleasant a tone as she could manage. "What brings you—"

"Don't bother with all that polite, namby-pamby, wishy-washy, sociable stuff," Widow Marsden growled as she pushed her way inside, her shawl flapping around her like the wings of some giant buzzard swooping down on a victim that wasn't quite dead yet. "It's about time you opened the dang door."

"It's good to see you again, too, Widow Marsden."

Widow Marsden glared at her with a squinted, rheumy eye. "You don't fool me one bit, you brazen little hussy. Flagrant Jezebel! Lascivious harlot!"

Ruth Miller flapped in behind her.

It was a little too early for Halloween, or Callie would have suspected they left their brooms out by the hitching rail.

"I beg your pardon!" Callie exclaimed. "You have no

right—you have no reason—to call me anything like that!"

"Oh, yes, I do. Your dear departed aunt ain't dead an entire week, and you've got the unmitigated gall to bring a man into your bed!" Widow Marsden declared.

"Don't be ridiculous!" Callie tried to laugh as she closed the door behind them. This whole thing wasn't very funny at all.

"We have it on a very reliable authority—"

"Who told you?" Callie demanded.

"It was an anonymous tip."

"If it was anonymous, how do you know how reliable it is?"

Widow Marsden coughed and pulled her pinched lips together more tightly. She glared at Callie through narrowed eyes and shook a gnarled finger under her nose.

"We have it on good authority that, even as we knocked on your door, you were upstairs in your bedroom, cavorting in a sinful and shameless fashion, without the benefit of clergy, with a man!"

"Would it be better if I'd been cavorting in the front yard?" she shot back.

"Carolyn Jackson! How dare you speak to me in that tone of voice!"

"No! How dare you come in here accusing me of doing horrible things, on the word of someone who doesn't even have the nerve to give his name," she countered. "This is completely preposterous! The only man around here is my hired hand, and he's sleeping in the barn."

"We'll just see about that!" Widow Marsden was already heading up the stairs, with Ruth Miller following close behind.

"What's the meaning of this? Where do you think you're going?" Callie demanded, hurrying after them.

"Where does it look like we're going? Upstairs."

"Wait just a minute. This is my house. You can't just go parading through here as if you own the place!" Callie rushed up the stairs behind them.

Widow Marsden spun around. "Why are you trying to stop us? Do you have something to hide?"

"I have nothing to hide," Callie declared. "But this is still my home."

"Not for long."

"You have no right!"

"Your aunt appointed the ladies of the Society as the sole arbiters of your behavior. Even though they've never seen fit to elect me president of the Society—"

"Yet," Ruth interposed.

Widow Marsden gave a disgruntled cough. "It still behooves me, as a member in good standing of the Society, to do my appointed duty and to monitor your behavior."

"Isn't it a little late in the evening to be doing any monitoring?"

"Sin knows no season! Lust has no timepiece!" Widow Marsden pronounced with the voice of doom.

"Wantonness has no calendar," Callie supplied. "I think we can carry that image to ridiculousness."

Widow Marsden gave a haughty sniff. "You can make light of this situation now, if you please. You'll be singing another tune when we dispossess you of this farm."

"I'm not making light of this situation. I'm making light of *you* and your ridiculous accusations," Callie told her as pointedly as possible.

"I'm still a member of the Society that has the right to turn you out into the street with only the clothes on your back, and you'll speak to me with respect. As soon as I was told of this horrendous, disrespectful, and flagrant flaunting of the rules of propriety—and of the stipulations of your aunt's will, I—"

"We," Ruth amended.

"*We* rushed right over here."

Widow Marsden puffed harder and harder as she neared the top of the stairs. Was it terribly unchristian and down-right inhuman, Callie wondered, to hope the old battle-ax suffered a massive stroke and keeled over dead before she reached the top?

She only wished she'd had the foresight to run up the stairs ahead of the old biddy and give her a shove downward.

"As I recall, this was your bedroom." Widow Marsden glanced at the appropriate door. "But since you've got two small children living here with you now—"

"And who knows what horrible sort of influence you're exerting on their young lives?" Ruth demanded.

Widow Marsden gave a grunt of agreement. "I've got it on good authority—"

"That same really reliable anonymous authority?" Callie asked.

"That you've shoved those poor little darlings into the cramped space and taken over Samuela's spacious bedroom," Widow Marsden finished. "You're probably only feeding them scraps, too, but we'll address that situation later."

Seizing the doorknob, Widow Marsden twisted it in her gnarled fingers and pushed the door inward.

"Miss Callie! Miss Callie!" Beatrice and Walter declared joyously in bright-eyed unison. The big Bible was opened reverently between them.

The lamp on the table was glowing. The sheets were smooth as glass. All the discarded clothing was somewhere out of sight. Their little shoes were stowed neatly side by side, toes pointing outward, beside the bed. It looked as if Beatrice had parted Walter's hair in the middle and combed it so smooth it was plastered down against his head. She had arranged her own hair into two perky plaits. Callie could almost suspect they'd pinched their cheeks to give them a wholesome, apple-cheeked glow.

"Have you come to finish our story?" Beatrice asked.

Widow Marsden wheeled on Callie. "What is the meaning of this?"

"Mith Callie weads us gweat stowies. Are you the wicked

witch from Hansel and Gwetel?" Walter asked, lisping sweetly. "That's one of my favowite faiwy tales."

Callie had heard him murdering English grammar, but she'd never heard this incomprehensible lisp before. The little tyke was a darned good actor. Maybe *he'd* be the one to give Edwin Booth some stiff competition.

She had a sneaking suspicion these little monsters were going to try to finagle a big favor out of her when this insane incident was all finished. If they managed to succeed, she could hardly deny them.

"I shouldn't be afwaid of you, should I, Mith Lady?" Walter continued in wide-eyed bewilderment.

Widow Marsden was not easily impressed.

"What are you children doing in here?" Widow Marsden demanded. "Why aren't you in your own room?"

"This *is* our room," Beatrice answered sweetly. "Miss Callie said she'd rather stay in the bedroom she was used to, and she let us sleep in this big, comfy bed!"

She clasped her hands at her breast and looked around the sparsely furnished room in unmistakable awe and wonder.

"Isn't this a beautiful house?" she asked in a breathless gasp. "It's so much bigger and nicer than the orphanage we came from. There aren't any roaches in the oatmeal. The rats in the barn are so much smaller than the ones we had in our dormitory. There are only two of us in this big bed—and no fleas. We even get to eat off our *own plate* with *a fork of our very own!*"

They looked at each other, beaming joyfully, and proclaimed together, "We don't have to share anymore!"

Widow Marsden fairly growled. "Well, what do you think you're doing in here, anyway?"

"We had our milk and cookies before bedtime, just like we always do, ma'am," Beatrice explained. "Then Miss Callie reads us a story. Walter's favorite is Noah's Ark, but my favorite is Jacob's Ladder. Do *you* have a favorite?"

Widow Marsden didn't bother replying to the question.

She stormed out of the children's bedroom and raged across the hall. Callie followed a bit more slowly.

"He's in there, huh?" she demanded.

Callie said nothing. She could only hope that Harden had managed to stop Charlie Wilson.

Widow Marsden pushed open the door and stared into the empty darkness.

Callie breathed yet another prayer of thanks that she'd had just enough time and foresight to pull the covers up so that it looked as if the bed hadn't been slept in and that, all this time, she'd actually been reading to the children.

Widow Marsden thundered down the hall to the next door.

"That's just the sewing room," Callie warned.

"Sewing room?" Widow Marsden repeated with a little sneer. "Isn't the kitchen good enough for you?"

She pushed open the door and gasped.

"Why, that close-mouthed old biddy! Samuela actually had a sewing machine and never breathed a word."

Callie could almost see Widow Marsden's face growing green with envy. Mixed with the red of her self-righteous anger, her face was growing more and more livid all the time. Any minute now, Callie expected the woman's head to go shooting off like a Roman candle.

"If that isn't the height of self-righteous modesty," she grumbled in her shock and awe. "How can anybody top having something to show off and *not* show it off? Damn Samuela and her holier-than-thou attitude! Nobody'll be able to beat this one."

Widow Marsden wheeled around and glared at Callie. Recovered from her surprise, she was giving free reign to her anger again.

"I don't know how you managed to get away with this," the woman threatened as she stomped down the staircase, "but when I find out, heads are going to roll!"

"I didn't manage to get away with anything," Callie said. "I didn't do anything wrong."

"She'll find out, you know," Ruth warned her as she followed Widow Marsden down the stairs.

"There's nothing to find out," Callie protested. "If I were you, I'd be more concerned with finding out who this anonymous informant is and stop believing everything he tells you!" As they stormed their way down the walk, she called after them, "He's really not reliable at all."

Callie slammed the door shut behind them. Through the window, she watched them flapping off into the night like a pair of harpies, seeking out more evil-doers. She felt sorry for whomever they had decided to target next. She hoped they would be denied their next prey just as they had this time.

Weak with nervous exhaustion, she slumped to sit at the bottom of the stairs. Beatrice and Walter came to sit beside her.

"We did good, huh?" Walter asked, leaning his head against her shoulder. He yawned.

"Did we chase them all away?" Beatrice asked, leaning her head against Callie's other shoulder.

"Well, they're gone for now," Callie replied. She wrapped both her arms around the children. "I couldn't have done it without you."

"We know."

"How'd you get the room so tidy?"

Walter started to giggle.

"We shoved everything under the bed," Beatrice confessed.

"I'd have been in a real fix if she'd decided to check for a man under the bed."

Beatrice's fingers flew to her lips. "Oops! We didn't think of that. Sorry."

Walter reached up and mussed his hair. "She combed my hair till it hurt," he complained.

Callie rubbed the top of his head, trying to make him feel better. "Walter, where did you learn to talk silly like that?"

"The rich old lady's house."

"Did *she* talk like that?"

"Course not! But sometimes a pretty lady would visit her."

"I keep telling you, it was her daughter," Beatrice insisted.

"Couldn't have been," Walter denied. "She didn't look like her."

"Yes, she did. Only without the wrinkles and gray hair."

"Anyway," Walter continued, obviously trying to ignore his sister's penchant for always being right. "She'd bring this little kid with her."

"He was older than you," Beatrice told him with a sneer.

"Was not."

"Was, too."

"The kid talked funny, like that."

"When they came visiting was the only time we were allowed downstairs," Beatrice explained.

"We were supposed to play with him." Walter grimaced.

"But every time he came over, Walter would start talking like that, and nobody ever noticed the difference." Beatrice giggled. "Except us!"

"Well, I don't know if it convinced Widow Marsden and Ruth Miller that everything I was doing here was perfectly innocent, but it threw her off my track for just a bit. Thank you again."

"Can we go into town and get candy again?" Walter asked. "Lots and lots of candy? Real soon?"

Yes, indeed. There was the favor.

"Of course," Callie replied. "How could I refuse?" She genuinely meant it.

"That's what friends are for," Beatrice said, wrapping her arm around Callie's shoulder.

"Friends?" She'd never imagined herself friends with a ten-year-old, even when she had been ten years old.

"Sure."

"You're still not like a mama," Walter told her.

"I know."

"Does it make you upset when we say that?" Beatrice asked.

"No, because I know it's true. Even though you're both very nice children and I'm glad we can be friends, I don't really *feel* like I could be your mother. I am upset because you two don't have a real place to live. I'm upset about Mr. Fielding and his nasty hired hands trying to force me into selling my farm. I'm upset about what just happened. I'm so worried it'll happen again."

"What was that all about, anyway?" Beatrice asked.

"I've got a sneaking suspicion. But I wish I knew all the details."

"Maybe we'll find out when Mr. Daniels comes back in," Beatrice suggested.

"You certainly will," Harden said as he emerged from the kitchen.

Callie sprang to her feet and began to run into his arms. Goodness gracious! She pulled to an abrupt halt. Harden was standing there, holding Charlie Wilson firmly by the collar.

"I've got just the man who can explain it all, too," Harden said. He gave the collar a little shake. "Can't you, Wilson?"

"No, I won't!" he declared nervously. "You can't make me!"

Harden examined him with distaste. "Maybe. Maybe not. Maybe you don't want to find out that I can."

Charlie gave a loud gulp.

"I'll tell you what, Wilson. I'll start, and when you find something wrong with my tale, you just jump right in and correct me. Fair enough?"

Charlie just snorted.

Harden turned to Callie. "If I were you, I wouldn't be surprised if Frugal and Refrain weren't too hungry tomorrow."

"What happened?"

"The best I can figure, Wilson here kept the dogs from

barking at him the way they usually do by giving them big steaks to keep them occupied. Isn't that right?"

Charlie said nothing.

"Well, I guess I'm right, then," Harden said.

"If Betty June finds out you wasted good meat on dogs, she'll have your head on a platter," Callie threatened.

Charlie gulped.

"Gosh, from the way you all talk about her," Harden added, "I suspect she'd have it served to her on a dinner plate."

Charlie gulped again.

Then Harden grew more serious. That was what truly worried Callie. "You were incredibly lucky tonight. If I hadn't just happened to look out the barn window—at Prudence's insistence—I'd never have seen Wilson sneaking around your property, trying to break in. Now, why would he be doing that?"

"I have a feeling it has something to do with an anonymous tip Widow Marsden said she received," Callie said. "Something about my having a man in my bedroom."

"Considering the fact that you're a highly moral lady and I sleep in the barn, there could be only one way to get a man in your room. That would be if he broke in. But why would Mr. Wilson want to break into your house and risk getting caught with you in a compromising situation? What would happen to Mr. Wilson if his wife found him fooling around?"

"She'd make his life a living hell."

"She's *already* made my life a living hell," Charlie grumbled.

"What would happen to you?" Harden asked Callie.

"Widow Marsden has already threatened to have my farm taken away from me."

"Who do you think would buy your farm if it was put up for sale?"

"Mr. Fielding."

"Maybe. Who else would want your farm?"

"Why, the man who's already mentioned how advantageous it would be to join our properties," Callie replied.

Harden turned to Charlie and gave him a little shake. "How close are we, Charlie, old boy?"

"You can't prove it!" he cried and bolted for the door. "You can't prove a thing!"

He left the door swinging in the wind. Beatrice ran over to close it.

"I just wish I knew what Widow Marsden and Ruth Miller hoped to get out of this," Callie said, shaking her head. "It isn't my farm they want. Ruth Miller's husband owns the haberdashery. He wouldn't know what to do with a plow. Widow Marsden's son is in jail now. Even if he wasn't, he wouldn't stoop to doing honest, manual labor. I can't think of any reason—"

"What does she want that she doesn't have?" Harden said.

"She's always wanted to be president of the Society. Even though she came up with the idea of calling it a society so they could sound superior, nobody has ever thought she was superior enough to be president. Nobody has ever even nominated her. I'd be surprised if they'd vote for her, anyway. Everyone knows she and her good-for-nothing son are living on any kind of charity they can beg, steal, or blackmail out of others."

"How would Wilson be able to give her the presidency?"

"He can't," Callie insisted in frustration. "His wife isn't even a member of the Society. They don't even go to the Methodist church in town. They used to go to the Baptist meetings over in Barkersville until Betty June got too big to haul around."

Harden stroked his chin. "How could *you* get her the presidency?"

"Me? I can't do anything for her," Callie denied in surprise.

"Unless she caught you doing something you shouldn't be doing," Harden said. "Then she could be the most moral of the moral, superior to the superior, worthy of being president."

"She would still be upright, sober, and very moral, even with her rotten son in jail." Callie's eyes grew wide as she realized the truth of his words. "Oh, my goodness, Harden! Do you really think so?"

"It makes as much sense as anything else."

"But Aunt Samuela was the founder of the Society. How would it look if Widow Marsden dispossessed me, her niece?"

"As if she were vindicating the reputation of the fine, upstanding woman whose wanton, profligate niece went astray."

With a groan, she sank into his strong, comforting embrace.

"Then it's not over yet."

"I'm afraid not."

She drew back slightly so she could look into his eyes. She feared the worry she saw in his blue eyes reflected the concern that clouded her own.

"Widow Marsden won't be satisfied until she's shamed me and become president of the Society."

"Wilson's not through yet, either. He's still stupid enough to think he can outsmart me. He'll keep trying until one day I won't be here."

Callie felt her knees going weak. She had already been through enough tonight. She couldn't bear the thought of Harden leaving. She felt sick to her stomach that he might still be thinking of eventually leaving her.

She clutched at him more fiercely. She feared she'd feel him pull away from her, but he held steadfast. She knew she could truly depend on him.

"There's one way I can think of to catch him before he can do any further harm."

"What's that?"

"I'll have to move back in here from the barn."

"Tonight?"

"It's pretty late, and we've had a lot of excitement. I don't think I'll be hauling all my furnishings in right now. But if you don't mind, I think I'll be spending the night in the sewing room again."

"Here's your pillow," Callie told him.

This time she handed it to him instead of tossing it at his head.

"Here's a sheet and a blanket, although I don't really think you'll need one." She placed the folded linens on the sofa.

"Yeah, it is getting warmer as the days go on."

"Haven't you noticed? It does that every summer."

Harden chuckled.

"Anyway, just in case Meddling Mildred shows up early in the morning again, or Widow Marsden chooses to make another unexpected midnight appearance, I thought it might be safer to give you something a little more opaque to wrap up in."

"Thanks."

"I feel better already with you in the house. Safer. When you're around, I know nobody will be able to hurt me."

"That's a big responsibility you're giving me credit for. I hope I can live up to it."

"I think you can. You've saved my life and my farm for me so many times."

"That's the reason I'm here, Callie."

That's partly why you're here, Daniels, he told himself. *Remember, you've got another job that takes precedence over everything.*

He didn't want to think about that tonight. Callie stood before him in a soft, white woolen robe with little pink rosebuds running down the front opening. Of course, the front was pulled tightly up to her neck, the way she'd had it when those two old harridans and that bungling charlatan Wilson had tried invading her home.

He longed to reach out and gently pull apart the two sides

of the front of the robe, exposing the delicate nightgown that he'd already seen underneath.

He cringed inwardly just thinking about what would have happened if that scoundrel Wilson had reached Callie first, or what would happen if that despicable Fielding should set his hired guns on Callie.

She was pure and innocent. He was the only one who would have respect for her that way. He didn't just care about the rightness and justice of her keeping her farm. He cared about *her*. Yes, he supposed, if he had the nerve to come right out and say it, he was in love with her.

All the while his mind was telling him how much he cared for and respected Callie, his body was telling him an entirely different story. The rest of his body was turning into some kind of drooling, slavering beast that couldn't wait to get his hands on her.

He reached out and stroked her cheek.

"I want to protect you, Callie. But I don't know if I can protect you from myself."

Her voice was soft and low as she replied, "Why would you believe I'd want to be protected from you?"

She took a step closer to him.

Harden had never considered himself a stupid man. If that single step wasn't an invitation, nothing was.

14

$\mathcal{H}$E HELD HIS arms outstretched for her.

"Come to me, my love. I'd sweep you up in my arms and carry you away. But this has to be your choice and yours alone."

Very slowly, but with a trusting boldness, she stepped toward him. "You are my choice, for now and for always."

Harden tried not to cringe with the realization that he didn't have an always. Men like him never did. But he would love her now, while he could, as much as any man had ever loved a woman.

"I will cherish you, Callie, to the end of my days."

He enveloped her in his arms, welcoming her with a steady, warm kiss on her lips. He savored the smell of her hair, the soft aroma of the soap that still clung to her nightgown, the flowered scent she always wore.

She entwined her arms about his neck, running her fingers through his hair. He shivered as she kissed his jaw and moved slowly down his neck.

He reached up to unfasten the rosebud clasps of the robe. Slowly he spread the halves apart. He relished the feel of her soft, smooth skin against his own as he slid his hands up her arms, pushing the robe off her shoulders and down to the floor.

She never stopped him. As soon as her arms were freed from the robe, she reached up and began to unbutton his shirt. He closed his eyes and moaned as her delicate fingers slid down his chest.

"Callie, I can't do this to you. Not here. Not now."

"I know," she whispered. "There's not enough room on the sofa."

He groaned. "No, I mean . . ."

He wasn't sure what he meant anymore. He only knew he needed Callie. "Are the children asleep?" he asked.

"I think so."

"Good."

He bent down and scooped her up in his arms. He managed to pull open the door with her still in his arms.

"Quiet," he warned her as he crept out into the hall.

"Don't drop me," she pleaded.

The children's door was shut fast. The only sound in the house was the ticking of the clock on the mantel downstairs, echoing up the stairwell. Outside, the crickets chirped, and a lone owl hooted.

He gave her bedroom door a push with his foot to close it. It slammed shut.

"Oh, goodness! Don't wake the children." She stared at him in wide-eyed expectancy, waiting for Beatrice or Walter to start begging for a drink of water.

They listened and waited. Now the only sound came from the crickets.

Her room was dark, as she had left it when Harden had warned her about the intruders.

"You've been here before," she said as he lowered her to her feet. "Although, as I recall, the last time you came in through the window."

He laughed softly. Then he gazed into her eyes with fiery intensity. "I didn't stay long enough last time."

"Welcome back. I . . . I want you to stay this time, Harden."

"I'll be here when you wake up," he promised. Taking her hand in his, he drew her toward her bed.

She sat and urged him down to sit beside her.

"You can't imagine how I've wanted to do this," he said as he pulled her into his embrace.

He kissed her once again, letting his lips savor the soft smoothness of her skin. He traced his kisses down her neck and onto the gentle roundness of her shoulder.

"Ever since Beatrice made me pretty?" she asked with an uncertain little laugh.

"Oh, no. I knew you were beautiful from the first moment I saw you. I just couldn't figure out why you hid your beauty."

"Maybe I was just waiting for the right man."

He only wished she were right—that he was the right man for her.

In the moonlit darkness, he leaned back against the pillows, pulling her over on top of him. She leaned over him, her hair falling like an auburn curtain around them. Her breasts hung pendulous, brushing softly against his chest.

"I've wanted you every day."

He pulled her down flattened against him, desperate to hold her, yet fearful of frightening her away.

"If I don't have you this very minute, I'm afraid I'll explode."

"I want you, too, Harden. Something about you . . . I don't know . . . something strong, male . . ."

She could barely talk, she was so breathless with holding him close. He rolled her to her side on the bed beside him. The mattress and pillows were soft beneath her. Harden lay firm and strong beside her. She pressed herself close against him. From the feel of his strong chest pressing against her breasts, down to where their hips brushed against each other, to the feel of his knees and toes down his long legs entwined with hers, she desired every inch, every part of him.

She had never felt this excitement, except when she was with him. As he leaned above her, his features highlighted by the moonlight streaming in the window, she knew she needed him more than anything else; more than light, more than air.

He kissed her again, then drew her nightgown over her head. He gave it a toss. It fluttered to the floor in the moonlight like a glimmering wraith.

Slowly pulling back from her, he slipped out of his shirt and trousers, then cradled again beside her.

"You're more beautiful than I'd ever imagined," he whispered. He reached out tentatively.

His hand was warm as he cupped her breast in his palm. She felt her nipples tighten under the gentle caress of his callused fingertips. Her thighs trembled as if she had been walking for miles. She needed to move to relieve the weakness, yet each stroke of Harden's hand made her tremble more and more.

"I need you, Callie."

"I need you, too, Harden."

"I need you now."

"Come to me, my love."

Harden's shaded body shifted and loomed above her.

"You look so wonderful up there," she told him.

"Not me. You're wonderful." He chuckled.

He lowered himself to barely an inch above her. The hair of his chest brushed lightly against her breasts. His muscular thighs rested against hers.

She needed to open, to envelop him. He was hard and searing, yet so slow and gentle she could only moan with exquisite intensity.

It seemed to her he wanted to say something, but each time he began, he only groaned hoarsely.

At last the intensity burst within her, as Harden released a deep breath and rested his head against her shoulder.

"I love you, Harden."

"Oh, sweet Callie, I love you, too. I'll remember this for the rest of my life."

"I'll keep reminding you," she promised with a little laugh.

He groaned again with pleasure and placed a kiss on her shoulder.

As he slipped off to lay beside her, she placed her hand against his arm. She just wanted to keep touching him. She never wanted to be apart from him ever again.

He covered his eyes.

"Oh, sweet heavens! I never meant . . . Oh, Callie, can you forgive me?"

She cradled her head in the hollow of his arm and listened to his heartbeat slow to normal. She sighed in deep contentment.

"What should I forgive you for? You've made me so happy."

"But suppose I . . . suppose you get . . . you know . . . with child."

"Now you sound like one of the ladies of the Society," she teased.

He laughed, but Callie could tell his heart wasn't truly in it.

"Callie, I have other things to do, other commitments—"

"Oh, my heavens! You're not already married, are you?"

Her hand flew to cover her heart, which had suddenly stopped beating. She felt sick to her stomach. She was so sure she was going to die, she figured she'd better jump up and get dressed with what little strength she still had left so the ladies of the Society wouldn't find her naked corpse in bed, and have yet another item to gossip about.

Then that wretched Widow Marsden wouldn't be able to point at her lying in her coffin and say, "I told you so," and all the other ladies would say, "You're absolutely right, Madame President."

"No, no," Harden protested. "What kind of man do you think I am?"

With a breath of relief, Callie declared, "No, you're wonderful!"

"Of course, some of the men tease that I've been married to my work for years."

"What is your work, Harden? I mean your *real* work?"

"What do you mean, my *real* work? I'm just your farmhand." He studied her, his face completely devoid of any expression.

"I'll admit you fooled me at first," she told him. "But after everything you've said and the things you've done, I can't believe you're just a simple wandering farmhand, looking desperately for any work that will come along."

"I can't lie to you, Callie. Not now. But I can't tell you the truth, either."

"You're a spy!" she declared with a giggle. She couldn't think of any more ridiculous accusation to prompt him to tell her the truth.

"Not anymore."

"You *were* a spy!" she exclaimed. "My goodness, I was only joking, but I . . . I never imagined . . . never would have believed it was true!"

"During the war," he admitted.

"Which side?"

"Does it matter now?"

"I . . . I guess not."

"I served with the Union," he told her anyway. "Does it make a difference? Will you never speak to me again?"

"Don't be silly. I will, but some of the people in town probably won't. If Ruth Miller finds out, she'll spit in your direction every time she sees you. If Widow Marsden catches you in here, she'll see we're both shot."

Harden shrugged. "I've been through worse."

"You served with the Union. But, you're from . . . or at least you said you were from Virginia."

"That's the truth. I really am from Virginia. My parents were . . . not exactly pleased with my choice of service. I haven't seen them in five years."

"I'm sorry." She drew her hand through the dark strand of hair that brushed across his forehead.

"So am I, yet in a way, I'm not. I knew my duty and I did it. I regret that they couldn't understand. I have a job to do now, too, Callie. I can't tell you—I *won't* tell you what it is, so don't ask me about it."

"It's Mr. Fielding, isn't it?" she declared excitedly, propping herself up on one elbow.

"Don't ask."

"It must be," she insisted. "Why else would you have been eavesdropping on that conversation?"

"I *told* you. I was afraid he'd hurt you."

"How else would you know he was dangerous?" she continued to demand.

"He kept insisting you sell him your farm," he replied, his voice growing louder with frustration at her refusal to drop the subject. "I'd suspect any man of trying to harm you. Would you have suspected Charlie Wilson?"

"No."

"Well, aren't you glad I did?"

Callie pressed her lips together and lay there, silently considering his words. He did have a good point.

"Come now," he said, drawing her down into the bed again and cuddling her closer into his arms. "It's time to sleep. I have to get up early."

"The cows get milked at five."

"At four-thirty, before the children are awake, I have to move back into the sewing room."

Callie smiled and stretched, and reached out for Harden.

She opened her eyes with a start. She was alone in bed.

"Oh, my goodness! Where is he?" she demanded in panic as she frantically looked around the room.

He was gone. His clothes were gone. Where could he be? How long was he intending to stay there? Was he ever coming back?

"He promised he'd be here in the morning."

Panic was drawing tears into her eyes. With the edge of the sheet, she wiped away her tears, so she could better see to do what she had to do.

He'd brought her robe into her room from the sewing room and laid it at the foot of her bed.

She pulled on her nightgown and robe and ran down the stairs. Everything else looked the same. She rushed into the kitchen.

Propped up between two ripe tomatoes sat an ominous-looking piece of paper.

"My gracious! I've done this before. It's worse this time. I don't want to do this again." Callie stretched out her hand in dread. "At least he, too, had the courtesy to leave me a note."

She picked up the note anyway and examined it.

"At least the paper is cleaner, and the note is more neatly written."

She began to read:

"My darling Callie, you looked so peaceful sleeping I didn't have the heart to wake you. So I placed a kiss on your cheek and came downstairs to leave you this note. I'm sorry to leave you so early. I've gone to check the fence along the southern property line. It's going to take me all day, so don't wait supper. I won't go hungry. My apologies to Walter for taking the last of the apple pie. I love you more than you'll ever know."

Callie's breath released in a shudder of relief as she held the note to her breast. He hadn't left her. He wouldn't leave her. He loved her.

Someday, when she was very, very old, she would read this letter once more and realize all over again how very much Harden loved her and how very silly she had been ever to doubt his love.

He'd be safe riding the southern fence, she assured herself. Mr. Fielding's holdings were to the west, and Mr. Wilson's were to the north. They'd have to go too far out of their way to bother Harden where he was working. Harden would be safe.

"You look fine," Beatrice assured her. "I don't know what you're so nervous about."

"I shouldn't be going to dinner at the Prestons'."

"Who?" Walter asked.

"Mildred's house, with her husband, the minister."

"Don't worry. You look just fine. Even if we haven't had time yet to make you a new dress, that green one improved a lot when we added that lace collar."

Callie glanced down at her dress. She smoothed her hands over the skirt. Yes, it did look a lot better than anything else in her closet. She didn't give a hang about Mildred or the reverend and especially not about the man they had invited as a would-be suitor. Would *Harden* like it?

"I fixed your hair real nice, too," Beatrice said.

Thank goodness the child wasn't overburdened with useless character traits like modesty.

"It looks so good, they won't even notice if your dress is new or not," she assured Callie.

"But I really didn't want to look *too* good tonight."

"Why not?" Beatrice demanded. "Why didn't you tell me sooner? I wouldn't have gone to so much trouble."

"Yes, you would have. You know you enjoy arranging hair, and you know you're good at it."

Beatrice giggled.

"But I don't want to look too appealing," Callie explained. "I don't want Mildred to think I approve of the man she's decided would be my perfect life's companion."

"Another one?" Mildred said scornfully.

"Who is he?" Walter asked.

"Andrew Nesbitt. He smells very bad."

"Why?" Walter asked. "Is he a pig farmer or does he clean outhouses or something?"

"He's the blacksmith's assistant," Callie explained.

"Which isn't ordinarily a particularly smelly job," Beatrice added.

"Except if you sweat a lot," Callie said.

"But a good bath and a little toilet water should take care of that. Does he eat a lot of onions and garlic?"

"I don't know. I don't want to know. I don't know how to explain it. He just smells. Oh, I'm really not looking forward to sitting across the dinner table from him," she wailed.

"If you didn't want to go, why didn't you just tell her no?" Beatrice demanded.

"Because nobody ever tells Mildred no."

Again, Callie glanced nervously at the clock on the mantel. There must be something wrong with the silly thing. The hands had only moved two minutes since she'd last looked at it, even though she knew perfectly well she'd been waiting an eternity.

"Where could that man be?" she demanded.

"Chasing bad guys," Walter offered.

Callie certainly hoped not.

"How could he be this irresponsible and inconsiderate?" Callie demanded.

"Does he know you're waiting for him to come home so you can leave?"

"I . . . I think so."

"Did you remember to tell him you'd been invited to the Prestons'?"

"I . . . I think . . . I don't remember. Considering all the excitement and confusion of the past few days, I'm afraid now that the thought completely slipped my mind."

She looked at Beatrice in alarm, as if the child could give her some solution to her predicament.

"Oh, now what am I going to do? I really have to be

leaving," Callie said. "But I can't just leave you two alone here."

"Yes, you can."

"No, I shouldn't."

"Miss Callie, we traveled all the way from New York to Cottonwood by ourselves," Beatrice said. "I think we can spend one evening alone in the house."

"But you weren't on the train alone," Callie pointed out. "There were conductors, and engineers to drive the train. There were porters to help you with your baggage."

"We didn't have any baggage," Beatrice reminded her.

"There were people to cook the food and serve it to you at the stops."

"I cook better things than the hog slop they served us!" Beatrice protested.

"I know. I've tasted your cooking. But this isn't an entire train with a staff of people. It's just my house, and I can't leave you all alone here."

"Walter won't break anything."

Callie believed for a moment that Beatrice could read her mind.

"We'll eat cold meat and vegetables for supper, so you won't have to worry about him setting anything on fire."

"You can't sleep right with only a cold meal in your little stomachs for supper," Callie protested. "Besides, that's not the problem. I just don't want anything to hurt *you*. If Mr. Daniels were around, I'd feel you children were safe," Callie told them with a worried sigh. "But he's not."

"Mr. Fielding and Mr. Wilson aren't after Walter and me. Widow Marsden can't blame us for anything. We'll be all right."

"I don't think they'd hurt you if they knew, but I wouldn't put it past Mr. Fielding to do something very dangerous, like setting the house or barn on fire. I don't think he'd care much one way or the other if you children were inside."

Beatrice gave an audible gulp. Even Walter stopped his usual squirming and watched Callie with wide, worried eyes. The memory of the bunkhouse burning to the ground was still very vivid in their minds.

She knew she was breaking down their resistance.

"Besides," she told them. "You'll be *my* protection."

"I'll protect you, Miss Callie," Walter declared. "Just lemme use Mr. Daniels's gun."

"No, no!" What was it about men and guns? she wondered.

"You can keep me busy so I won't have to pay much attention to Mr. Smelly," she offered.

Walter laughed.

"And when we all get tired and bored, you two will give me a very valid reason for leaving early."

"Leave where?" Walter asked.

"The Prestons'." Maybe she hadn't explained her plan quite as clearly as she had supposed. "I can't leave you home alone, so I'm taking you with me."

"Oh, no!"

"Not to Meddling Mildred's!"

"But I'll die!" Walter howled.

"She's a *very* good cook."

"She'll make me say grace."

"You can say grace. They taught you at the orphanage. You say it here."

"No, not in front of *people!*"

"Then you can hide behind me, and maybe she won't notice you until after she serves dessert."

"Dessert?" Walter breathed a little easier. "What kind of dessert?"

"Probably pecan pie. Mildred is famous for her pecan pie."

"Not apple, huh?" Walter looked a bit disappointed.

Maybe she ought to try another form of bribery, Callie decided. "She has a cat."

"Not in the pie!" he exclaimed.

"No, no. I think her name is Kitty."

He eyed her expectantly.

"Would you like to visit her?"

He nodded.

"I still don't think this is a very good idea." Beatrice shook her head in a dire warning.

"Neither do I," Callie replied.

15

$\mathcal{C}$ALLIE SAT AT the long, mahogany dining room table, to the Reverend Preston's right, on the same side of the table as Andrew Nesbitt. The children sat beside each other across the table from her.

"Thank you so much for inviting me, Mildred, Reverend Preston," Callie said in one shallow breath. She wished she didn't have to draw in another one until it was time to leave.

She couldn't believe any person could look as clean and scrubbed as Andrew did, and still smell so bad.

"Thank you for having us, Reverend and Mrs. Preston," Beatrice said politely.

To anyone else, the little girl might appear to be sitting quite normally at the table beside the Reverend Preston, with her hands folded primly in her lap. But Callie, who was sitting directly across from her, could see her leaning away from Andrew Nesbitt and trying to breathe out of only one side of her nose.

Callie tried not to laugh.

Linda Shertzer

"Thank you for being so understanding about my having to bring the children along, too," she added.

Mildred smiled at the children.

"Oh, I just love children."

Then she smiled knowingly at Callie. "When one has children, one has to be prepared to sacrifice one's own independence and devote oneself entirely to the welfare of the children."

"I understand."

Mildred shook her head. "I suppose you think you do, but I don't think you've had the experience to cope with the unpredictable incidents a child or two can bring to one's life."

Callie couldn't resist laughing at Mildred's remark. Her life had been so full of unexpected incidents lately, she hardly knew what day it was.

"He stinks!" Walter declared, pointing at Andrew Nesbitt.

"What?" Mildred asked.

"I said he stinks!" Walter repeated with every bit as much distaste. "Don't tell me you can't smell him. He's sitting right next to you."

Callie rummaged through her mind for something polite to say to put this embarrassing comment out of their minds. At last she hit upon something.

"The creamed corn is very good, Mildred," she said.

"I like creamed corn." Andrew shoveled a spoonful into his mouth. Several globs landed on his belly.

Callie figured Andrew used a spoon so he wouldn't stab his tongue with his fork.

She was glad Andrew had let everyone know he liked the corn. It was the first thing he had said all evening.

Who could bother with food at a time like this? What if Mr. Fielding's horrible farmhands had waylaid Harden and goaded him into a fight? What if Harden had deliberately sought out those men and started the fight himself? No, he couldn't possibly be that stupid.

"How do you like the chicken and dumplings?" Mildred asked the children.

"It's delicious, ma'am," Beatrice answered.

Who cared about the chicken? Callie silently protested. What if Charlie Wilson's grudge caused him to sneak up on Harden while he was working? At this very moment, was Harden lying dead or wounded in someone's field while Callie sat there trying to eat?

She couldn't swallow. She couldn't even manage a bite.

"I can't cut my chicken," Walter complained.

"Well, my goodness, it's a good thing they sat you next to me, then, isn't it?" Mildred asked, picking up her knife.

Had Widow Marsden's anonymous source informed her that Harden was the one who had foiled her despicable plan? Had she lain in wait in the darkness for him and stabbed him with a knife she kept concealed under the flaps of that black shawl of hers? Was Harden lying dead at Widow Marsden's feet while she, with bloodied knife still in hand, tallied up the votes she would get at the next regular election of officers of the Cottonwood Methodist Ladies' Evangelical, Temperance, and Missionary Soul-Saving Spiritual Aid and Comfort Bible Society?

"Walter," Mildred continued, "I'm just about the best chicken cutter in Cottonwood." She reached over and began sawing away at the contents of Walter's plate.

Without anything to do, Walter started pressing down on the bowl of his spoon, watching it flip on the table.

"Stop playing with your utensils, dear," Mildred told him as she handed him back his plate.

Walter pushed his chicken onto his plate with his other hand, then shoved the food into his mouth.

"Walter!" Mildred exclaimed. She picked up a roll and placed it in his hand. "This is the proper way to get the food off of your plate and onto your fork."

"You sound like a mama." Walter shoveled in a few more mouthfuls. Then he belched loudly.

"Oh, Walter!" Callie exclaimed.

"Oh, Walter!" Beatrice exclaimed. "That was a good one."

"That was horrible!" Mildred exclaimed in horror. "Polite people do not make those kinds of noises at the table."

She glared at Callie. "They were such polite, adorable children when I first met them at your house. Honestly, what have you been teaching these children?"

"Nothing," Callie replied.

"It would appear not."

"They just sort of came to me this way."

Callie didn't care what they'd done for her in outwitting Widow Marsden the previous evening. They were only supposed to have provided her with an excuse to leave early by claiming they were tired. They weren't supposed to get her thrown out.

This kind of behavior, especially in front of the minister and the president of the Cottonwood Methodist Ladies' Evangelical, Temperance, and Missionary Soul-Saving Spiritual Aid and Comfort Bible Society, canceled all debts.

"Well, now," Mildred said, rising from the table. "You all just wait here while I clear the table. Then we can have dessert."

"I'll help you," Beatrice offered, gathering up a handful of messy knives and forks.

"No, no, no. The china is fragile. You have to be very careful not to break it."

"Oh, my goodness. My mama taught me to be very careful with nice things. You should've seen all the pretty things in the house we used to live in before our mama died and we had to go to the orphanage."

"Nice things?" Mildred repeated, her curiosity obviously piqued.

"Our mama worked for a rich old lady who had lots of crystal goblets and fancy china. We lived there for three years and never broke a thing. Not even Walter," she declared proudly. "Now do you believe it's safe to have me help you?"

"Well, yes . . . yes, of course. Aren't you just the nicest, most helpful little girl!" Mildred exclaimed as she carried a pile of dirty plates into the kitchen.

"My mama taught me to be helpful," Beatrice replied, following her. "She taught Walter to be polite, too, but it seems to take boys longer to learn that lesson."

Mildred sighed. "I know what you mean."

Beatrice deposited the dirty dishes carefully in the sink without even making a loud clinking noise.

"Why, thank you so much, Beatrice. This is the dear girl I remember meeting at the Jacksons'."

"You mean that day you saw Mr. Daniels in the sheet?"

"Well, yes, dear. Although I hardly think that's something an innocent little girl should dwell upon." Mildred paused for just a moment. "Tell me something, dear. Does Mr. Daniels do that often?"

"Heck, no!" Beatrice declared. "He's not even around that much."

"He's not?"

"No. He's always off somewhere on the farm or out in the barn."

"What's he doing all this time?"

Beatrice shrugged. "I don't know. Working, fixing things, sleeping in the barn."

"Really?"

"Sure."

"Not . . . not sleeping . . . in the house?"

"Heck, no. There's no place else to sleep in the house. There's only two beds, and Walter and I got one of them."

"Couldn't he share Callie's bed?" Mildred asked.

Beatrice could tell she was trying to sound as frivolously carefree as possible, and all the while it was so easy to see the lady was dying of curiosity.

She really liked Mrs. Preston, but so far, Callie was the one who had taken her and her brother in, fed them, washed their clothes, fixed their baths. She wasn't about to turn traitor on Callie.

"Heck, no! Just before we left home this evening, she called him inconsiderate and irresponsible."

"She did?"

Beatrice watched Mildred nod with satisfaction. "I always did think Callie was a sensible girl."

"Reverend Preston is real quiet, isn't he?" Beatrice asked.

Mildred looked at her with surprise. "You noticed."

"At least he's still around. I hardly remember my papa."

"I don't, either," Mildred answered quietly. "My aunt raised my sister and me, too."

"Don't you have any children?"

"No, we don't, dear. I had my little niece Patsy, my sister, and her husband living with us for a little while, but they've moved into a nice house of their own."

Beatrice looked around. "You should have kids. This is a really nice house. I'll bet you've got some neat bedrooms upstairs."

"Well, maybe someday, during the day, you can come visit me."

"Really?"

"Really."

"Would Reverend Preston mind?"

Mildred decided she wasn't even going to bother to ask him. "Of course not!" she declared. "I'll make very sure he doesn't mind."

Mildred picked up the pecan pie sitting on the kitchen table. "I hope everyone saved room for dessert," she announced as she entered the dining room.

"Oh, boy!" Walter exclaimed. "It sure smells a lot better than this fellow." He jerked his thumb in Andrew Nesbitt's direction.

Callie glared at Walter.

"Ow! Beatrice kicked me under the table," Walter complained.

"It's just your imagination," Beatrice told him through clenched teeth. "Now, eat your pie before you're wearing it."

Walter didn't say another word until after dessert.

"The pie is delicious, as always," the Reverend Preston said.

Mildred looked at him, completely surprised. He rarely said this much at any meal.

"As a matter of fact, I look on Mrs. Preston's pecan pie as the triumph of our sixteen years of wedded bliss."

"Sixteen years, and my best accomplishment is a pie?" Mildred muttered.

"I have never tasted anyone else's pie—and mind you, as a minister of the gospel, I attend a lot of church suppers— that is anywhere near as good as Mrs. Preston's."

"How very kind of you to say so, dear. Well, now," Mildred declared, rising from the table, "why don't I tidy up the dining room and kitchen a bit while you two"—she shot Callie and Andrew a beaming smile—"take yourselves off to the parlor for a little chat?"

"No, no," Callie insisted. "Let me help you, Mildred."

"Nonsense. What are children for?" She picked up her own plate, then gestured for the children to gather the others.

Beatrice quickly complied.

Walter sat there. "I think I'm tired. I'm ready to go home."

"Not until we get cleaned up," Beatrice warned him.

Walter reluctantly picked up his plate and headed for the kitchen.

The Reverend Preston didn't say a word, but he picked up his own plate and followed them into the kitchen.

"Hey, this is a big place, with big windows!" Walter exclaimed, craning his neck to look every which way. "Wow! Look at all the cupboards."

He ran from one to the other, pulling them open, then slamming them shut.

"This one smells like breakfast," he said.

"That's where I store the apples."

"It smells like that fat lady who came to our house with you that day."

"Mrs. Luckhardt?"

Walter couldn't care less what she was called. He was too busy exploring.

"Look at everything in them! The orphanage never had this much food." He turned around and stared at Mildred. "Are you sure there's only two of you here?"

"Yes, dear, I'm afraid so."

He pulled open the cupboard under the sink and dove inside. He emerged with a tall bottle.

"Wow! Look at this funny-shaped bottle with the long neck." He shook it. The amber liquid inside sloshed from side to side. "What's this?"

"Oh, nothing, nothing," Mildred claimed, trying frantically to get it out of his hands.

He pulled out the cork in the top and sniffed. "Phew! It smells like the rich old lady! Lotsa her friends used to smell like this, too, 'specially when she had a big party."

The Reverend Preston strode over to Walter and held out his hand for the bottle. Reluctantly, Walter surrendered it. Mildred's face wore an expression of ultimate doom. The Reverend Preston took a sniff.

"It's bourbon! Bourbon in my house? In the parsonage?"

Mildred cringed.

"What will the Board of Trustees say?" the Reverend Preston demanded. "What will the bishop say? What will the Cottonwood Methodist Ladies' Evangelical, Temperance—oh, I can say no more!"

He sniffed at the bottle again. "It's mighty fine bourbon." He looked at Mildred. "What's this doing in our kitchen?"

"Abner, I can explain."

"Please do. I've never heard of bourbon having particularly medicinal purposes."

"I don't use it for medicine," she confessed, her head hanging low.

"Mildred! You don't actually drink the stuff straight, do you?"

"Heavens, no!"

"Then why is it here?"

"It's in the kitchen because . . . because I cook with it."

"Cook—?"

"Just a few things—just one, actually."

"Which is?"

"The pecan pie."

The Reverend Preston's eyes popped open wide.

"The pie that's my favorite? The pie that won first prize at the county fair three years in a row? The pie that you've been bringing to every church supper for the past sixteen years?"

She nodded. "The pie that everyone always finishes first."

The Reverend Preston sniffed at the bottle again. "Well, I can certainly see why."

"Are you angry?"

"Just a bit . . . disappointed."

"No more so than I."

"What? How can you be disappointed?"

Mildred suddenly lifted her head and glared at him. She glanced about, right and left, at the children. "I don't think you really want to know right now."

The Reverend Preston gave a little gulp. He corked the bottle and handed it back to Mildred. "Very well, my dear. We'll discuss this later. In my study."

Walter ran to a side door and pushed it open. "Wow, Bea! Look at this!"

Beatrice circled around the Prestons and joined Walter at the door.

"Oh, my goodness!" she murmured looking right and left, up and down at shelves and shelves packed with books. "Books!"

"Yeah, great!" Walter ran to the back door. "But, wow! Look at this! There's even a big door that goes right outside to the grass. No steps. No sidewalk. Look! A river! Hey, who broke the bridge over it?"

"Just a little accident when we had that big rainstorm," Mildred explained.

"Yeah, there were a lot of accidents during that storm," Beatrice said.

"Wouldn't you like to take a little walk outside while it's still light?" Mildred asked him. "I think it would be a very good idea for a little boy who's as active as you to be outside."

"Can I go see the broken bridge?"

"I suppose so."

Mildred headed for the kitchen door. As they stepped outside, Walter slipped his hand in hers.

"Hey, that smells like my mama's closet!" he exclaimed.

"I thought _I_ smelled like your mother's closet," Mildred corrected with a grimace.

"You do. But so does that." He pointed to the plant growing beside the back step, low and greenish gray with long stalks of tiny purple flowers.

"That's my lavender," Mildred said.

"Yeah! Yeah! That's what my mama always smelled like. You smell like my mama."

"Why, Walter, I'm . . . I'm so touched."

"You have a study," Beatrice murmured, still standing in the doorway, staring in awe and wonder at the dark wooden bookcases climbing to the ceiling.

"Yes," the Reverend Preston said cautiously. "But no one's allowed in there without me."

Beatrice supposed he was waiting for her to go tearing through it like Walter had torn through the kitchen. Well, he could just keep waiting, she decided. She was much more grown-up than that.

"May I go in?"

He looked at her, obviously surprised.

"Did you think I wouldn't ask?"

"Frankly, yes. I . . . I baptize them, but I don't really have a lot of experience with children," he confessed.

Beatrice nodded. "I sort of figured."

"Do you have a lot of experience with books?" he countered.

"Not as much as I'd like."

The Reverend Preston stood there for a moment, his lips pursed. Beatrice thought he looked as if he was thinking so hard it hurt.

At last, he placed his hand on her shoulder and took a step into his precious study, bringing her with him.

"In that case, young lady, I believe you and I have a lot in common."

"The corn was good," Callie offered.

"The corn was good," Andrew agreed, nodding.

"The chicken was good, too," Callie offered.

"The chicken was good," Andrew agreed, nodding again.

"I thought the pie was particularly good," Callie offered.

"The pie was good," Andrew agreed, still nodding.

Apparently, Andrew couldn't handle sentences of more than four words.

That was about all the conversation she had left, Callie thought with dismay. Andrew had none of his own. Even Herbert Tucker, with his condescending manners, had been able to carry on a conversation and not just parrot everything she said.

"I wonder where the children are?" she asked.

"The children were good," Andrew said. "I like children."

The little devils were supposed to have been her excuse for leaving early. Now it was past nine o'clock, and she still hadn't left. Tarnation, she hadn't even seen them since seven-thirty. She'd been sitting here smelling Andrew and trying to devise something to say besides, "Why don't you take a bath?"

The children had probably tied up the reverend and his wife and were, even now, rifling through the house looking for money and silverware. She wouldn't even bother with trying to find them a good home in Cottonwood. How soon could she send them back to New York?

"I hope the children aren't bothering Mildred and the Reverend Preston too much."

"I like Reverend Preston. I like Mrs. Preston."

I was right, she thought as she rose in exasperation from the sofa. *He can only handle sentences of four words.* She bore no grudge against Andrew, but if Mildred ever tried to invite her to dinner for the sole purpose of meeting an eligible bachelor ever again, Callie decided she'd bake her in her own oven.

"I've got to find the children and take them home. Good night, Mr. Nesbitt. Thank you for a very . . . very . . . well, thank you for the evening."

She headed toward the kitchen. Mildred and Walter were sitting at the table, finishing off the last of the pie.

"Where's Beatrice?"

Walter, his mouth full, just pointed at the doorway.

Callie found Beatrice installed in a large, red leather chair in the reverend's study, a large, very expensive-looking book opened on her lap.

"What are you doing in here?" Callie demanded.

Beatrice placed her index finger over her lips. "I'm reading," she replied in a whisper.

"I don't think you're supposed to be in here without the reverend."

"I'm not."

She pointed to another large, red leather chair at the other end of the room. The Reverend Preston's head lolled against the back. He was blissfully sleeping off Mildred's good meal.

"It's time to go home," Callie announced as she went back into the kitchen.

"Do we have to?" Walter whined.

"It's just for tonight, dear," Mildred told him. Then she turned to Callie. "If it's all right with you, we'd very much like to take the children on a little picnic tomorrow—if the weather holds."

"You would?"

"Yes," Mildred replied in a tone of voice that made Callie think Mildred was surprised that Callie would be surprised.

"Both of you?"

"Of course, the reverend and I. Who else would drive the buggy and carry the picnic basket?"

"Please, please, please." Walter was fairly on his knees, begging. "We won't even pester you for candy anymore."

"My goodness," Callie replied with a laugh. "How can I say no?"

Harden swallowed the last of the pie and downed it with some water from his canteen. It was just about time.

The sun would almost be down by the time he reached Fielding's property line. He'd find a safe place to tie his horse. Then, in the twilight, he'd be able to slip through the fields undetected until he made it close enough to Fielding's house.

The dinner hour was always a good time to sneak up on a place. Even the men who'd been set to stand guard were too busy grumbling about having to eat while standing watch, or about how cold the food was, or how bad the food was, to pay a whole lot of attention.

Maybe it was a bad move, Harden debated, but he'd leave his gun on the saddle. He'd gotten this far without it. If he got caught any closer, he could always revert to his act and pretend he'd just gotten lost on the way to the outhouse.

Fielding wouldn't be expecting anyone, anyway, he figured. The man was too arrogant and self-assured to even consider for one moment that someone might be planning trouble for him.

Harden crept past the bunkhouse. He figured it could hold about ten men. Most of these men were probably just ordinary, honest, hardworking hired hands—except maybe the four low-down varmints who'd deserted Callie to come here to work. He'd have to be pretty careful not to actually kill any of the ordinary farmhands.

The hired guns probably slept in the house. Those were the men he would have to be most on the watch for. Two of them were standing on the front porch, taking a smoke. He recognized them—the two oafs who'd been to Callie's house. A third joined them and lit up. As long as they were busy out front, Harden decided to do a little reconnoitering around back.

He drew closer. Some of the windows showed in the darkness as rectangles of yellow light. Most of the windows were dark.

He avoided the lit windows. He could easily see which opened from the kitchen and which from the parlor.

He was interested in the darkened rooms. Dark rooms could hide things, and that was what he was looking for.

The payroll shipment from Saint Louis to Fort Laramie had never arrived. With his dying breath, the conductor in the baggage car had identified Otis Fielding. They could have convicted Fielding then and there, but the gold hadn't been recovered, so the federal authorities had decided to bide their time.

His sources had had their eyes on Fielding for some time. The money he'd spent, even on his lavish way of life, had come from the income of his own farm. He hadn't spent any of the gold, and if he hadn't spent it, that meant it was still somewhere around. That meant it could still be recovered.

That was Harden's job.

One of these rooms had to be Fielding's office. He raised his head to peer over the windowsill. The bold gold lettering on a large, black, cast-iron safe glimmered in the dark. Harden duly noted it. But that was too easy and too small. There had to be another safe, another room, another hiding place.

"Hey, you there!"

16

"*H*EY, HEY," HARDEN demanded indignantly. "Can't a man have some privacy while he's answering Nature's call?" He pretended to button his fly, and shook his leg.

"Mr. Fielding catches you pissin' on his petunias, he'll add your danglin' jewels to his watch fob," the man warned. "Now, move along. Move along. We got outhouses and enough trees for that sort o' thing."

Harden turned to go.

"Wait a minute. Who the hell are you, anyway?"

"Ben. They just hired me."

"Oh, okay."

Harden continued walking away from the house. Slowly, slowly, he told himself. Just kind of sauntering along. He stuck his hands in his pockets and started to whistle and kick a stone along the path.

"Hey, wait a minute! We ain't got no Ben here!"

Harden heard the man's boots in the dirt. He didn't turn back to see him coming after him. All he heard was the man yelling for the others. There were three of them, just waiting on the porch, with nothing to do but whale the tar out of him.

Harden pounded harder away from the house.

The bunkhouse loomed before him. Awakened by the alarm, some of the men were already pulling on boots and trousers as they headed out the door.

He couldn't risk cutting in front of the bunkhouse. To the men there, he was just another intruder. They were waiting for him and they were rested. Even if only one of them could actually catch him, the rest would be upon him soon enough to hold him down. They'd beat him up, then haul him off to Fielding for explanations.

For Fielding, there wouldn't be any explanations.

Should he risk cutting around in back of the bunkhouse? Harden debated as he ran. He didn't know what was behind it. He could be running into a blind alley. He'd better decide quickly.

He dodged around the back.

Damn! A solid wall of hay bales loomed in front of him. If it hadn't been dark, he'd have spotted it easily. As it was, now his problem was how to get around it.

There was no way around it. The pile extended right to the barn wall. The only way was over it.

Harden jammed the toes of his boots into the hay. His fingers grabbed at the twine as he hauled himself up.

Already, he could hear men shouting as they came around the other side of the bunkhouse to head him off. He wouldn't have time to climb down.

Harden jumped. Instead of landing on his feet and driving his hipbones up to his ears, he landed on the fleshy part of his shoulder and rolled to standing. He took off at a run and didn't look back.

Damn! He'd failed. All this and, for the first time in a long, long time, he'd failed. He hadn't found where Fielding had hidden the gold. He hadn't even been able to get a good idea of the layout of the house and grounds.

He'd never be able to go back, either. Even if they sent a new marshal, Fielding and his men would be on the lookout for any intruder. He'd failed at his job, and he'd ruined the assignment for anyone else. Maybe he ought to just find another line of work. Maybe Mr. Miller had an opening for a salesman in that haberdashery of his.

By the time he reached his horse, he knew no one was following him—at least on foot, but they wouldn't let him get away. They were saddling horses, gathering guns, and riding out after him even as he urged his horse into a gallop for home.

Home, he thought with a pang of regret. For six years, he hadn't thought of anyplace as home. Now he knew Callie's was where he belonged. If he lived long enough.

Harden was dripping with sweat and dust as he burst into the kitchen. His face was hard and intense. He didn't even smile when he saw her.

"Harden!" Callie rushed up to him. "You look awful!"

"Thanks. I feel awful." He didn't kiss her. He didn't even touch her. He barely glanced in her direction as he headed for the sink.

"Do you know what time it is?"

"Just in time, if I'm lucky."

"At first I thought you were still out riding the south fence, but not at eleven o'clock at night. I've been so worried. Where have you been?" Callie demanded.

"I've been *here*," Harden told her sternly as he stripped off his filthy shirt. "I've been here all the time."

"No, you haven't."

"*Yes*, I have. Where are the children?"

"Upstairs, sleeping."

"Good."

He started pumping water into a basin and splashing the dust from his head and face.

"I've been here with you all evening, do you understand?"

"But *I* haven't been here," she protested as she ran to get him a towel. "The children and I had dinner at Mildred's."

"That . . . that wouldn't be common knowledge."

"People saw us riding through town."

"No. I mean, common knowledge to . . . your neighbors."

"Mr. Fielding!" Callie cried. "You haven't gotten into some sort of trouble with Mr. Fielding, have you? Have you killed him?"

"Not yet," he said as he dried himself on the towel. "But I don't think some of his farmhands are too fond of me right now. As a matter of fact, I've got a bad feeling some of them are going to be showing up in just a little while."

He stood directly in front of her, peering into her eyes. She could feel the intensity of his drive emanating from his body. What on earth had he been doing? She wanted to reach out and touch his bare chest, feel him against her own skin once again, but she was afraid she'd get burned.

"I've been here with you all evening, do you understand?"

"I understand better than you think I do, Harden." She laid her hand on his bare shoulder. His body was still hot from exertion. "Why won't you let me help you?"

"You *are* helping me by telling them exactly what I tell you to say, and then staying out of this."

The barking of the dogs and the pounding on the door made Callie jump.

He pointed at her. "Remember," he whispered. "Or I'm dead, and you'll be wishing you could say the same thing."

Harden headed up the stairs.

The pounding on the door grew louder. Callie opened the door.

"Mr. Fielding!"

Callie was used to seeing the man come to her house with two or three of his personal bodyguards around him. She'd never seen him standing there backed up with a dozen.

He started to enter her house, but she refused to move out

of the way. Only one time in her life, when she was just a very little girl, she'd dug in her heels and refused to obey Aunt Samuela. She'd gotten quite a spanking for disobedience, as she recalled. But she also recalled, after all these years, how to dig her heels in stubbornly and not budge an inch.

Mr. Fielding and his men stayed on the porch.

"What are you doing here, bothering honest, hardworking citizens at this time of night?" she demanded.

"I'm looking for that worthless farmhand of yours." He tried peering over her shoulder. "Where is he?"

"He's here."

She figured that was part of what Harden had told her to say.

"Where is he?" Fielding repeated.

"What business is it of yours?" she countered.

"Who is it, Miss Jackson?" Harden called from the top of the stairs.

Callie almost slipped through the cracks between the floorboards. Harden stood there without his shirt on. The top two buttons of his trousers were unfastened. Did he have to overdo it? Wouldn't just one button have sufficed?

"It's Mr. Fielding," she replied. "And I think he's brought some of his little friends with him."

Mr. Fielding turned to a man standing behind him and pointed his cigar at Harden. "Is that him?" he demanded.

The man squinted. "Hard to tell in this light. Too bright."

Fielding grabbed the man by the front of his shirt and shook him. "Is that him?" he shouted.

"I . . . I think so. Yeah. Yeah, that's him."

"Miss Jackson, your farmhand has been trespassing on my property—"

"Ridiculous!" she declared, staring him directly in the eye. "He's been here with me all evening."

"He can't have been. My foreman saw him—"

"Are you calling me a liar, Mr. Fielding?" she demanded in the haughtiest of tones she had heard Aunt Samuela use.

This time, she thought she was doing a pretty good imitation.

"My foreman saw him."

"Are you going to believe the word of an illiterate workman, or are you going to take the word of the niece of the founder of the Cottonwood Methodist Ladies' Evangelical, Temperance, and—"

"But he saw him," Mr. Fielding insisted.

"Impossible!" she declared. "Need I remind you of my dear late aunt's strict rules? I intend to maintain the same standards of behavior for my workmen, too. No farmhand is allowed to leave the property after dark. They are also not allowed to leave the property without my permission. I certainly would never have given him permission to leave, much less to travel to *your* property."

She tried to say it with as much disdain as if she'd been denying her farmhand permission to visit a dung heap.

"But I saw him!" the foreman insisted.

"Where?" Callie turned to the foreman, glaring at him as if daring him to reply. "Tell me exactly where you saw him."

"Right outside the house, taking a . . . begging your pardon, ma'am . . . in the bushes."

The hired hands standing behind him chuckled.

"In the bushes?"

"Yeah."

"In the dark?"

"Yeah, well, it was dark. The sun's down. It's usually dark."

The hired hands chuckled again.

"And you were standing directly in front of him?"

"Well, no, not exactly face-to-face. I was behind him 'cause I wasn't about to get my boots . . . wet on."

The hired hands snickered.

"He stood still long enough for you to get a really good look at him."

"Well, no. He was kinda runnin'."

"So, you only saw this man from the back, only in the dark, in the bushes, moving very quickly, and yet you're so absolutely certain that it was my farmhand."

"Yes—no—well . . ."

"You lout!" Mr. Fielding cried, slapping the foreman on the back of the head. "You told me you saw him!"

"Well, I did. I guess I just didn't see him too good."

"Clod!" Mr. Fielding slapped him again. Then he turned to Callie. "By the way, little lady, speaking of your late aunt's rules, I happen to know one of her rules was about not allowing farmhands in the house. So what's this farmhand doing in your house?"

"We had an intruder the other night. Mr. Daniels is here to protect me. And therefore, he stays at night—all night."

"But what's he doing upstairs?" Mr. Fielding leered at her.

"I'm certainly not about to let him sleep on the *good* sofa downstairs. On the other hand, that's none of your business."

"Oh, but it's the business of them busybodies of the Society of crying, whining do-gooders. I wonder what they'd have to say if I told them I found you with your farmhand upstairs."

"Not being a mind reader, I have absolutely no idea." She glared at him boldly. "We could always go ask them. But I think they would look slightly askance at any information given them by anyone who stands to benefit from my losing my farm, especially after that intruder last night. They'd also tend to be a bit doubtful if the only other witness was a man in your employ."

She refrained from smiling at the thought of her triumph. As a matter of fact, she wasn't quite sure she'd talked her way out of this one yet. But she kept her chin lifted defiantly.

"I'd say you would probably be the person who could benefit most, Mr. Fielding. I know for certain you're not one of Mrs. Preston's favorite people, so I'd say they'd probably believe you the least."

She stood there and glared at him. "Good night, Mr. Fielding."

She slammed the door in his face.

Walter helped Mildred spread out the big old quilt under the elm tree. Abner set the picnic basket on the quilt.

"Why don't you unpack the basket for us, Beatrice?" Mildred suggested.

Beatrice lifted the lid. "Books!" she exclaimed with surprise.

"Didn't you pack any food?" Walter complained.

"Of course," Mildred said, patting his hand in assurance. "I've made lots of things that I know little boys just love."

Beatrice was lifting out a book at a time.

"*Pride and Prejudice. Romeo and Juliet. Oliver Twist.*" She recited the titles one by one, reverently, as if reading a roster of the angels in heaven.

Mildred watched Beatrice as she thumbed through the stack of books that Abner had chosen from his library for her to carefully pack.

Mildred glanced at Abner. He was grinning.

"It appears you chose well, Abner," she whispered to him. "I had no idea you knew so much about what children like to read."

For the first time in many years, she actually laid her hand on his. She was startled when Abner turned to her and winked.

Beatrice looked up in awe and wonder.

"Have you read any of them?" Abner asked.

"I got to read parts of them. There was a room in the rich old lady's house that nobody ever went in. Walter and I watched once for a whole week, and no one went in and no one came out."

"That sort of makes sense."

"So we decided we had to see what was in there. Oh,

Reverend Preston, it was a whole room just full of books! Floor to ceiling, wall to wall, three whole sides. Of course, there weren't any shelves on the wall with the windows, and there was a little place in the one wall for the door, otherwise how could you get in or out? But can you imagine three whole walls full of books?"

"Yes, I can. As a matter of fact, maybe someday I'll get to show you a whole building full of books."

"Oh, thank you!"

"So what did you and Walter do with this room full of books?" Abner asked.

"Well, we figured, since the rich old lady had probably forgotten all about this room, it would be safe if we went in, 'cause nobody would catch us. Then we decided it would be all right to borrow just one book and take it upstairs to read, 'cause if nobody went into the room, nobody would notice if one was missing, and anyway, there were so many books in there, no one would notice just one out of place."

"Which one did you borrow?"

"I don't remember the name, but it had lots of pictures of flowers with Latin names. Next we picked one that had lots of animals with Latin names."

"Did you ever find a book in English?" he asked.

"We finally found one with lots of maps, and Walter and I pretended we were going to all those places. I wish we'd had time to look at more, but our mama got sick and died. They didn't have any books at the orphanage."

Abner looked thoughtful as he stroked his chin.

"I believe I shall have to investigate remedying that situation."

Mildred smiled. He might not say much, but when Abner set his mind to something, it generally got done. That was one of the things that had attracted her to him so many years ago, she recalled. In her mind, she could see him as he was then: a fiery-haired, intense young divinity student. No wonder she had fallen in love with him.

Funny how, over the years, things like that kind of faded

from memory. He became so interested in his good works and without much to keep her busy at home, she took up her own projects. Without children to draw them home again, there hadn't been much else between them.

Funny, too, how just a little thing could bring back a flood of memories.

"But, Reverend Preston, these are too wonderful to risk having anything happen to them," Beatrice protested. "We shouldn't be bringing these on a picnic."

"Oh, indeed, we must," he insisted. "There are few better moments spent than those under a tree with a book in your lap and one of Mrs. Preston's famous huckleberry turnovers in your hand."

"Do you put that funny stuff in the huckleberries?" Walter asked.

"Indeed not!" Mildred disclaimed.

Abner shot her a mischievous glance. "Maybe you should."

"Oh, Abner!" she exclaimed. For the first time in sixteen years, Mildred felt her cheeks flush.

"Maybe there are a lot of things we should be doing that we haven't."

"What do you have in mind?"

"I believe this was your idea, dear," Abner said. "I am now firmly convinced that Callie Jackson has absolutely no idea how to raise these children. I think we do."

"Oh, Abner!" She clutched at his arm, at her heart, at his arm again. "Are you serious?"

"Of course, I'm serious. But I believe we need to ask the children first if they would like to live with us."

"Walter thinks I smell like a mama."

Abner shrugged. "You couldn't find a finer endorsement than that."

With Harden working in the field and the children gone on a picnic with the Prestons, the house was silent and, for the first time in many weeks, unbelievably peaceful.

"The perfect time to get some cleaning done with no one underfoot!" Callie decided.

She'd been dreading this task, but, like everything else, it was one that, sooner or later, had to be done. She needed to send Aunt Samuela's old things to charity. Her aunt would never have any more use for them. Beatrice would shoot her before she would let her set foot outside the house in one of those old monstrosities. But someone might be able to use them, Callie reasoned.

When she entered Aunt Samuela's room to clear out the wardrobe, the chest at the foot of the bed was the first thing that caught her eye. "Well, there is that box," she reasoned.

She knew exactly what every one of her aunt's old dresses looked like. She knew all her shoes, hairpins, and underclothes. She knew she would be getting rid of everything. But she had no idea what was in that box. With no one to bother her, today was the perfect day.

She took the box into the kitchen where the light was much better, and she set it on the long kitchen table. There was a lot more room to sort the papers into piles that way.

"Hello, Miss Callie," Bob called from the kitchen door.

"Hello, Bob. Come in and join the fun."

Bob never needed a second invitation.

"What kind o' mess you got there, Miss Callie?" he asked as he poured two cups of coffee. He placed one in front of her, then sat down across the table from her.

"I've been cleaning out some of my aunt's old things. I found this in a big trunk at the foot of her bed."

"What? With the ledger and the cash box?"

Callie stared at him in surprise. "I looked all over for those things. How did you know where they were?"

"I didn't." Bob shrugged. "Just sort o' stands to reason. She didn't have a study like the reverend or a real office like Mr. Fielding. So it figures she'd keep close to her what she valued most."

Callie nodded in agreement. "She kept me at the other end of the hall."

Bob just chuckled. "Land o' Goshen! Make sure Walter doesn't wet the bed before you check the mattress for bills!"

"It's a little late for that, but thanks for the warning, anyway."

"Hey, do we get to share whatever you find?"

She already knew the box was full of nothing but old papers. But she couldn't resist the temptation to tease Bob just a little.

"Sure. Why not?"

Her hand hovered over the lid of the box.

"Ready for the grand opening?"

"Go ahead." He clenched his coffee cup. "I'm ready for anythin', provided Samuela don't come poppin' outta there."

She opened the lid.

"Papers?" Bob said with disappointment.

"Old papers."

Callie decided to start in the front and work her way back. She pulled out the first one.

"A receipt from Rupert's Feed and Grain Store for chicken feed." She offered it to him. "Do you want that one, Bob?"

"No, upon further consideration, I think I've changed my mind. You can have them all."

She put it aside. "Are you sure you won't change your mind? You never know. There might be some stock to a valuable gold mine or something in here."

"I think I'll pass."

"Suit yourself." She pulled out the next paper. "Hmm. A newspaper clipping. The Cottonwood *Crier,* dated October 24, 1864. It's the obituary of Martha Stansbury."

"How interestin'," he commented without much enthusiasm.

"No, that is interesting," she insisted. "I didn't think those two ever got along after that argument about adding the word *abolitionist* to the Society's name."

"Maybe Samuela kept it just to gloat."

"You're horrible."

"Well, ain't no sense in keepin' it now. They've either gone on to their reward and mended their fences, or are still battlin' it out in Hell."

Callie put it aside.

"Another old receipt for a hammer from Corrigan's."

She put it aside.

"I swear, Bob. Aunt Samuela was so . . . so parsimonious and unsentimental about—"

"Face it, she was downright mean and stingy."

"I can't deny she was, at times. That's why it's so hard to understand why she kept a lot of this useless stuff. She kept it all in chronological order, too. How rigid and methodical could one person be?"

In spite of her good intentions to work her way methodically through the pile from front to back, Callie started rummaging through the stack haphazardly.

She pulled out a handful and quickly rifled through them. "I mean, look at this. There must be half a dozen receipts right here for feed and grain that has been eaten, turned into cow or chicken—"

"And then manure," Bob commented.

"They're still manure. Out they go," she said.

As she started to lay them aside, she decided to flip through them one more time.

"Oh, my goodness. It's my grandfather's obituary."

She stopped to look at it just a minute. Then she laid it in another pile.

"I believe this is something I'll want to keep."

"I always thought you and the old man didn't get along too well."

"I was eight years old," she pointed out. "I didn't have much say in the matter."

"Why you keepin' it?"

"Well, someday we'll either make our amends or battle it out in Hell. I figure I ought to know who I'm arguing with."

She dipped into the box for more papers.

"My grandmother's obituary," she murmured. "I didn't realize the newspaper had been printing that long."

"Sure. This wasn't such a backwater little town."

"A train ticket. From Cleveland, Ohio. This must be from the year Aunt Samuela went back to help my mother—"

She started digging more furiously through the old papers, tossing away receipts, bills, broadsides, and more old clippings from newspapers.

"Bob!" Callie shot to her feet, holding in front of her a small piece of paper, folded in half. She started laughing and crying at the same time. "It's the bill from the doctor—Ernest P. Walford, M.D.—for delivering a baby girl! It's dated June 12, 1844. That's my birthday. This is me!"

She was so excited, she fairly danced around the kitchen, giggling and sobbing, wiping at her eyes with the back of her hand.

"It's made out to Samuela Jackson."

She stopped dancing. The broad smile on her face began to fade. She blinked to keep the tears out of her way so she could still read it.

"Well . . . well, maybe my father was so angry at me for thinking I caused my mother's death that he even refused to pay the doctor. That's what it is."

"Maybe."

"Yes, that's what it is. That's what it's got to be," she kept telling herself.

Slowly she unfolded the paper.

"Cleveland, Ohio. Twelfth day of June, 1844 anno domini. 4:30 ante meridian. Baby girl Jackson," Callie read at the top of the page.

She waved it in front of Bob.

"See, it *is* the doctor's record of my birth. Now I know who delivered me."

She searched the page for more information, but the ink had faded and the writing was hard to read.

"I swear, Bob, the man wrote worse than Pete, my former farmhand! If doctors are supposed to be so darned smart, and supposed to be working for the good of humanity, why can't they learn to write better?"

Bob shrugged.

"If I could just make out this scrawl," she lamented, peering closely at the paper.

"You don't read with your nose, Miss Callie," he reminded her.

"This is important, Bob. Maybe I'll find out my father's name. I'll know if he's dead or still alive. If he's still alive, maybe I'll try to write to him. Maybe he remarried. Maybe I have half-brothers or half-sisters. Maybe I still have a family somewhere."

"Maybe."

She examined the paper.

"There it is. Father: Chester Farnsworth."

Bob started choking on his coffee.

"Are you all right?"

"Just went down the wrong pipe, that's all." He wiped his mouth on his sleeve.

"Imagine, my real name is Carolyn Farnsworth. My father was Chester Farnsworth."

Bob grunted.

"That means my mother was Paulina Farnsworth. Now, why couldn't Aunt Samuela ever tell me a simple thing like that?"

Bob just grunted.

Callie looked at the paper again, just to see the name of her real father actually written down on a doctor's bill for all the world to see, for posterity—just for her. Callie sighed and smiled with satisfaction.

What did her mother's name look like? Again, she searched the scribbling on the paper.

"Mother—"

Her knees buckled under her. Without any realization of

the time between, one second she was standing up and the next she was sitting in a heap on the kitchen floor, still holding the paper, still staring at the words written on it: "Mother: Samuela Jackson, unmarried."

17

"*I*'M A BASTARD."

"Oh, don't worry about it, Miss Callie," Bob said, rushing over to help her up. "People are callin' me that all the time, and I don't pay 'em no heed."

"No, no, really—"

"Come now. Sit on up here." He managed to lift her into the chair. "Give me that silly piece o' paper."

He held out his hand, but she refused to hand him the paper.

"Come now, Miss Callie. Don't be stubborn."

He tried to pry it gently from her rigid fingers.

She clutched it more tightly, and cried, "No, no! Mine!"

Afraid of tearing it, he released the paper and concentrated instead on how he could help and comfort Callie.

"Let's get a nice fresh cup o' coffee into you."

Making certain that she was propped up securely so she wouldn't go tipping over onto the floor again, Bob poured more coffee into her cup.

"Just a dang shame there ain't somethin' a bit more bracin' around here."

He held the cup to her lips.

"Come now, drink this," he urged. "It'll do you a world o' good."

She shook her head and waved away the cup until the coffee splashed out over the tabletop.

"Aunt Samuela was really my *mother*."

"'Twould appear to be the case. Come now, take just a sip o' this. It'll make you feel better, right as rain."

He tried again, with no more success.

"Bob, what happened?"

Harden stood in the doorway. Callie was sitting at the kitchen table, staring off into space, mumbling incoherently to herself and clutching a yellowed piece of paper to her chest. Bob appeared to be trying desperately to get her to take a sip of coffee.

"Harden, am I glad to see you!" Bob exclaimed, placing the cup on the table. "Maybe you can get her to come 'round."

"What happened? Fielding? Wilson? Was either of them here? If they hurt her, I'll kill them. I swear!"

"No, no. Nothin' like that."

"Then what happened?"

"Why is she my mother?" Callie asked no one in particular. "She's my aunt."

"Don't try to think about it now, Miss Callie," Bob said, trying to comfort her.

Harden pulled the chair out from the table, with Callie still in it, so that he could stand directly in front of her. With both hands, he took her by the shoulders. He peered intently into her eyes.

"Callie. Callie, look at me," he commanded.

She shrugged awkwardly. Her arms flailed about as she tried to get him to release her. All the while, she still clutched the piece of paper. She wouldn't look at him. She wasn't quite aware of what she was doing.

He wasn't about to let her go. He kept moving her shoulders, trying to maneuver her so that she had to look him in the eyes. Finally, he grasped her chin in one hand and forced her to look at him.

"Callie. Callie! What happened?"

"Why didn't she tell me so herself?" she asked. "Why didn't she ever tell anybody? Didn't she love me enough?"

"Get her to show you the paper," Bob suggested.

"Callie, give me the paper." He held out his hand.

Callie dropped it in his hand but didn't look at him again.

Harden studied the paper for a moment, then turned to Bob.

"It's pretty obvious I'm not going to get anything out of Callie right now. Do you know anything about this, Bob?"

Bob shook his head. "I don't know any more than you do. But I've been around this town long enough to be able to make certain surmises."

"Such as?"

"Chester Farnsworth—"

"The man whose name is down there as Callie's father?" He pointed at the paper.

"Yeah. He was a drifter, come through town back in . . . oh, I guess it was 1843." He chuckled weakly. "From the looks o' things, it would've had to have been 1843, wouldn't it? Anyway, I didn't think much of him, myself, but heck, I didn't have to. Ol' Man Jackson hired him, anyway. Right before Christmas, Farnsworth took off for parts unknown. Ain't nobody ever seen hide nor hair of him since. Knowin' what we know now, a body could pretty much figure out why."

"So you think he and Samuela were . . . friendly."

"Oh, a lot more'n that, don't you think?"

Harden nodded. "It does sound a bit suspicious."

"Right around that time, Samuela's mother suffered some kind o' nervous prostration that nobody could ever figure out," Bob continued. "Just up and took to her bed like Betty

June Wilson done. But instead o' eatin' herself to an early grave, she just plain withered away."

"I suppose that could've been brought on by the shock of finding her daughter in a family way with no husband in sight."

"Nobody thought much of it then. The town wasn't as big back then. Sometimes the loneliness out on them farms just drove a woman plum crazy. Then, long about mid-January o' the followin' year, Samuela departed for Ohio, tellin' everybody she had to go take care of her sister, who was always in delicate health, who's now in a family way, and has been bedridden."

Harden shrugged. "No one would think amiss of that."

"Course not. No one thought nothin' of it, either, when, 'long about June, Samuela comes back with a newborn and tells folks the heart-wrenchin' tale about her sister's death, and the father's grief over the loss of his wife, and how he don't want to set eyes on the child ever again."

"A bit melodramatic, but understandable."

"Ol' Man Jackson turned into a reclusive, taciturn, parsimonious old curmudgeon. He used to be a pillar o' the church, but he never set foot in church again after that. Lookin' back, I guess he figured he couldn't face 'em again, seein' as how his daughter hadn't quite turned out the way he'd planned."

"I would've thought he'd turn her out for good."

"Guess that's happened to lots o' girls in that situation, but with Ol' Lady Jackson gone, I guess the ol' man figured he needed someone to take care of him in his old age—flesh and blood and all that, I guess. On the other hand, he'd have had to pay a housekeeper, but Samuela he could get to work for free. But I never saw him smile again, never heard him say a kind word to anyone after that—especially not to Samuela. Heck, I never even heard him talk to Callie."

"I guess forgiveness wasn't in his vocabulary."

"Now, mind you, I don't know none o' this as gospel. I

can only make my surmises and suppositions based on what little I can piece together."

"I guess some of these things we'll never know for a certainty, Bob." Harden reached out and clapped him on the shoulder. "But, well, you know how gossip can travel in these parts. For Callie's sake—"

"Shoot and thunderation, man!" Bob exclaimed. "You know you don't have to go tellin' me to keep my big mouth shut."

"Thanks, Bob." He glanced back over his shoulder at Callie. She was still sitting in a daze at the table. "I'm sure if she were in a proper state right now, Callie'd thank you, too."

"I'm goin' back into town. You want me to send Doc Hanford out?"

"Not right now. Let me get her tucked safely into bed. Maybe a good night's sleep will help clear her head."

"If she ain't no better in the mornin' . . ."

"I'll be sending for the doc," Harden assured him.

"She really needs you, Harden. Take good care of her."

"I will."

As Bob closed the door behind him, Harden came to stand beside Callie.

"She was my mother," she was still babbling. "Why didn't she want anyone to know she was my mother? Was I too ugly to claim as her own? Was I a bad baby, crying all the time so that she couldn't stand me?"

He picked her up in his arms.

Suddenly, Callie looked at him. Her eyes seemed to focus better. She blinked as if actually seeing him for the first time.

"Oh, Harden. I'm so glad you're back. I've just had the most horrible news."

"It's very late. Why don't you tell me about it while you get ready for bed?" he suggested as he began to carry her through the vestibule and up the stairs.

She looked into his eyes with great seriousness. "Aunt

Samuela . . ." she began. She stopped, took a deep breath, then began again. "Mother . . . Samuela . . ." She stopped again and tried to start again. "No, wait. I'm confused."

She closed her eyes and swallowed hard. She opened her eyes again and drew in a deep breath.

"I'm all right now."

"Are you sure?"

"Yes. You can put me down now," she told him as he brought her to her bedroom door. "I can stand. I can walk. I was a little shocked at first, but I'm going to be all right now."

"Do you mind if I come in with you?" he asked, nodding toward the door. "Just to make sure you're all right."

She smiled at him. "You know I'll always want you, Harden."

He lowered her to stand, but her legs buckled under her, nevertheless.

"It looks as if you're not quite as steady yet as you thought you were."

He carried her to her bed and laid her upon it. Then he sat beside her, still holding her hand.

"Aunt Samuela was really my mother. Chester Farnsworth—whoever he may be—is my father. I can understand why an unmarried lady would choose to hide from the entire town the fact that she'd had a child out of wedlock. Why couldn't she have at least told *me* the truth? Why didn't she lie to everyone else and say she'd married this Chester Farnsworth—or *somebody*—while she was back in Cleveland? Why couldn't she have lied and said she was a widow and I was her daughter? Why couldn't she own up to me somehow? Why didn't she want anyone to know I was her daughter?"

Harden gathered Callie up in his arms and held her close. He reached into his pocket and loaned her his handkerchief to wipe her nose.

"I suppose I should be consoled by the fact that she

actually chose to keep me, instead of putting me out for adoption or just abandoning me on someone's doorstep."

"She must have truly loved you, after all."

"Then why didn't she ever *say* so?" she demanded. "Why didn't she *ever, ever* say so?"

Harden had no answer to that question.

"Why didn't she ever hug me or give me a little kiss on the cheek? Why didn't she tease and joke with me? Why didn't she ever tell me I was pretty?" Suddenly, very angrily, Callie demanded, "Why did she *deliberately* make me look *ugly?*"

Very slowly, Harden answered, "I think she was trying to protect you."

"Protect me? From a mother's love?"

"From any kind of love."

Callie shook her head. "I don't understand."

"Suppose—just suppose—Aunt Samuela fell in love with this Chester Farnsworth, but he didn't love her. He just . . . used her and left her. What kind of impression of love would that leave in your mother's mind?"

"Not a very good one, I guess."

"She'd want to protect her daughter from doing something that she looked on as foolish and irresponsible—and sinful."

"Yes. I guess I can understand that now, but—"

"Let's suppose, on the other hand, that she wasn't really in love with this Chester Farnsworth. She just had a mad, passionate fling!"

Callie giggled. "Not Aunt Samuela!"

"I know." Harden couldn't help but chuckle, too. "It's hard to imagine, isn't it? But, for the sake of argument, let's just suppose."

Callie nodded and wiped her nose.

"She paid for her fling in ways that cost her her own mother and the love and respect of her own father. If anyone had discovered the truth, it could have lost her—in her eyes—the respect of her entire town. Wouldn't you want to protect your own daughter from making that same kind of mistake?"

"You're right both ways. It even makes a lot of things about my growing up finally make sense. But it's still so hard to bear."

She shook her head and began to cry again.

"My father probably stayed around just until he found out he'd gotten my mother in a family way. He didn't even love me enough to stay around. My own father didn't love me," she wailed.

"But—"

"My own mother didn't love me enough to claim me as her own. For all those years . . . I wasn't good enough for her to love."

"No! No, you mustn't ever think that! So many people love you, Callie. You can't count the hard hearts of two careless, selfish people. Beatrice and Walter love you. Bob would bend over backwards and turn himself inside out if you asked him. More than anything else, *I* love you, Callie. I love you more than my own life."

"I love you, too, Harden. But am I doing the same thing my aunt—my *mother* did? In loving you, am I doing exactly what she tried to keep me from doing for so many years?"

Harden turned her to face him. He held her chin between his fingers and held her eyes with his own. He wanted her to hear and to understand every word he was about to tell her.

"There's one big, important difference here that you're neglecting to take into consideration."

"What's that?"

"You're not Aunt Samuela, and I'm certainly not Chester Farnsworth. I've fallen in love with you, Callie. I will *never* leave you, my darling. Never!"

He swept her up in his arms and held her tightly to him.

"This isn't just a mad, passionate fling, I promise you. I want to hold you like this and make love to you every night.

I want to wake up every morning to see you sleeping on the pillow beside me. I will love you for as long as I live."

"Love me now, Harden," she asked, pulling him down closer to her. She offered her lips to kiss.

"How could I ever refuse you anything, my love? Or how could I deny myself the pleasure of loving you?"

"Make love to me now so that I know somewhere in this world someone does love me."

"Not somewhere in the world, Callie," he told her. "Right here by your side for as long as we both shall live."

He kissed her. She had been so shy and timid the first time they'd made love. Now she approached him with a passion to equal his own. She wrapped her arms around his chest and pulled his body tightly against her. He could feel her pressing against his erection.

"You're driving me insane!" he murmured hoarsely.

"You're all I've ever wanted."

In his eagerness to love her, he fumbled with the buttons of her dress. It was so hard to think clearly when her fingers traced lazy circles over his chest and down his stomach. Her hands pressed flat against his chest. She began to stroke his body with her palms, stirring him to passion. He could hear his own heart pounding furiously in his ears as his blood coursed more rapidly through his veins.

He moaned softly in her ear. "I need you, my love."

"Harden, you make me want to live forever—only if I can spend my life with you."

He slid her farther down the mattress so she lay flat. He gently pulled her dress from her, exposing her white body, with its pink-tipped breasts and small triangle of curling hair.

"You're so beautiful. You're perfect."

He wrestled himself out of his own clothing, growing clumsy with his desire. It took so long, she was afraid he'd die before he ever had the chance to truly live.

At last, he lay beside her, warm and throbbing with desire

for her. His hands slid over her body, his fingers tingling with the intoxicating sensations every part of her gave him.

She was warm and welcoming as he loved her. She breathed deep sighs of pleasure as he throbbed within her. He closed his eyes to savor the intense quiver of heat coursing through him.

He relaxed against her, slowly and gently kissing her cheek as his breathing returned to normal.

He drew her to his side.

"The first thing tomorrow morning," he told her sleepily, "you and I are going to pay a visit to Reverend Preston so he can marry us. First thing tomorrow morning."

Callie stretched and reached for him, but Harden wasn't there. She sat up, searching for a note. There wasn't one.

"He's left it downstairs," she assured herself. She went down to look.

Harden hadn't left a note on the kitchen table or on the dining room table or on the little round table in the middle of the parlor. She ran through the house, frantically searching.

"I'm being silly," she finally told herself. "He's only gone to the outhouse. Nobody leaves a note if they're just going to the outhouse."

But she waited and waited, and Harden still didn't return.

"Nobody takes that long in the outhouse!"

Maybe he was out doing his chores, she hoped.

But the farmyard was as silent as the day her other farmhands had all left her. She began to worry.

Callie sat in the middle of the sofa, waiting for Harden. The longer she sat there, the more certain she became that she was never going to see him again.

For all his sugary-sounding protestations of undying love and admiration, he'd been no better than the faithless, disloyal farmhands who had left her helpless. For all his noble-sounding claims of morality and steadfastness, he was no better than her worthless father, who'd made love to her mother and then left her on her own and doomed her to a lifetime without love.

At least she could take some comfort in the fact that no one could prove she and Harden had had anything in common beside his need for a job and her need for a farmhand.

She'd be able to keep her farm. She'd be able to live here until she, too, was a bitter old woman who never made a joke, who never teased, who never smiled. But at least she'd keep her farm. Right now, though, she just couldn't figure out why.

Mildred sat on the sofa across from Callie, smiling at her. When Aunt Samuela had passed away, Mildred had smiled down on her understandingly, comfortingly, benevolently. Today she sat there smiling at her, her eyebrows raised in a tentative, pleading expression. She'd never seen Mildred look at *anyone* that way.

The Reverend Preston sat beside her with his fingertips steepled in front of him. Callie wondered if there was a particular course that divinity students took to learn how to do that, or if it was something a man was born knowing how to do, something that sort of proved he had the calling.

"Callie," Mildred said, pronouncing her name as if she were calling on the Almighty for favors, "we know that, as nice as Beatrice and Walter may be, you didn't send for them to come live with you. We also know that, as nice as you may be, you have absolutely no idea how to raise children properly."

Callie nodded. There wasn't a thing Mildred was saying that she could find anything to argue with.

"I believe you're also aware that Mr. Preston and I have so longed for children, and for so many years have been denied." With the edge of her handkerchief, she dabbed at the corner of her eye.

"We've enjoyed the time we've spent with Beatrice and

Walter," the Reverend Preston continued. "We believe they've enjoyed being with us."

"We have! We have!" they exclaimed.

Mildred clasped her hands in front of her anxiously and looked at Callie with deeply pleading eyes. Callie almost could have laughed at the situation. Imagine! The high and mighty Meddling Mildred Preston actually begging someone else for their benevolence.

"We'd like to make the arrangement permanent, if you have no objections."

Callie glanced from Beatrice to Walter, and back to Mildred. She looked at the Reverend Preston. The look in his eyes was as anxious as the look in his wife's.

"I have no objections at all."

Mildred drew in a deep gasp and clutched at her husband's sleeve.

"Of course, I'm going to miss them," Callie continued, "but I don't think they could have found a better home than with you two."

Beatrice and Walter ran to her and wrapped their arms tightly around her neck. "You have to come visit us."

"You're only moving across town, not across the country. I'll probably see you every Sunday in church, anyway."

The Reverend Preston coughed. "I certainly hope so."

I might as well be going to church, Callie thought as she closed the door behind them. *I'm not going to have anything else to do with the rest of my life.*

"How're the new farmhands workin' out?" Bob asked.

"About as well as you predicted the first time," Callie answered, listlessly stirring her coffee.

"Zack Keegan?"

"If he moved any slower, he'd be going backwards."

"Oscar Barrett?"

"He even has to be reminded how to milk a cow."

"Eugene Redmond?"

"He worked real hard. Got all his own chores done and

went looking for more, and did everything just perfect—for the first two weeks. Then he got paid. I haven't seen him since."

."I have. He was doing real fine over at the Red-Eye."

"I'm sure they named the place after him."

Bob was quiet for a few moments. Then he cleared his throat, as if that could help him gather up enough courage to ask, "Have you heard from—"

"No!" Callie snapped. Then, a bit more calmly, she repeated, "No, I haven't. For the first week, I kept telling myself he'd write to me, letting me know where he was, explaining to me why he'd gone away and left me all alone. I blamed the slowness of the post for my not getting his letter. Another two weeks passed, and I thought maybe he was waiting until he'd found another job."

"It's been six weeks now, Miss Callie," Bob said.

"I've given up ever hearing from him again. I know he's never coming back."

"You shouldn't let that man bother you so much," Bob scolded. "You look just awful, Miss Callie, like you're losin' weight. You're not worryin' about him so much you're not eatin', are you? You can't let that man ruin your life and your health."

"I don't feel so well in the mornings, Bob."

"Oh, Miss Callie! You ain't losin' your breakfast, are you?"

"Just sometimes. It's nothing serious. I think I just caught some kind of—"

"I ain't no doctor, but I don't need no Harvard degree to know who you caught it from," he said, wagging a finger under her nose. "You shouldn't, either."

"I don't," Callie replied with a grimace. "I don't even have a sister I can go blaming this on. Well, at least I can take some consolation in the fact that I won't be alone here much longer."

She just kept moving the spoon around and around in her cup.

"Yeah, and you won't be here for long, either. You know what this means, don't you?"

Callie nodded sadly. "I'm going to lose my farm," she pronounced with a feeling of inescapable doom. "My baby and I will be penniless, wandering around somewhere, looking for someone to have pity on us and give us a handout. But at least I can keep my farm until it's impossible to hide any more the fact that I'm . . . I'm in a family way."

"I'll stick with you, Miss Callie," Bob promised.

"If you do, you'll be the first person who ever has."

"I have reluctantly called this general meeting of the entire membership of the Cottonwood Methodist Ladies' Evangelical, Temperance, and Missionary Soul-Saving Spiritual Aid and Comfort Society, for the sole purpose of examining the worthiness of one Miss Carolyn Jackson, and determining her right to keep the farm left to her by her aunt, Samuela Lucretia Jackson."

Mildred Preston rapped her gavel on the tabletop.

"I'm really sorry to have to be doing this, Callie," Mildred said.

Several murmurs arose from the assembled membership.

"Rules are rules," Widow Marsden insisted, springing to her feet. "Your aunt made certain stipulations in her will, and we made a promise to her that we have to fulfill."

"I have always believed it was a good idea to temper justice with mercy," Mildred said.

"There is no justice for the wicked!" Widow Marsden declared. "There is no mercy for evil-doers."

"Yes, yes, Naomi," Mildred said, exasperation clear in her voice. "Why don't you just sit down and let us get on with this meeting? I'm sure we're all eager to get these unpleasant proceedings over with as soon as possible— except you, Naomi, as it seems you actually enjoy them."

"I rejoice in seeing goodness triumph and evil defeated," Widow Marsden asserted.

"Fine. Now sit down, Naomi, and stay quiet so we can get this over with."

Mildred looked from Callie out over the faces of the ladies of the Society.

"Carolyn Jackson, you've been accused of failing to lead the sober, moral, prudent, and upright life that, according to the stipulations of the last will and testament of your late aunt Samuela, you were required to lead in order to retain possession of your farm. Do you have anything to say on your behalf?"

No sense in trying to hide it anymore, Callie thought with a sigh of resignation. She rested her hand atop the growing bulge at her waistline and looked Mildred in the eye.

"No, Mrs. Preston, not a word. I think everything is pretty clear."

Widow Marsden stood up and faced the group again.

"There is certain evidence, which I personally have been collecting, that needs to be presented to the membership."

Mildred groaned. "Now, Naomi, you know we've got to take these things one at a time."

Widow Marsden coughed with exaggerated importance. "Very well. We'll do it one at a time. Sober."

Mildred rapped her gavel. *"I'm* the president, Naomi," she reminded her. "I'll take care of this. Sober. Callie, have you been sober?" she demanded.

"Yes, I'm sober. I've always been sober."

"Naomi—or anybody else—can you offer any evidence to the contrary?"

No one answered.

"Has *anyone* seen her under the influence of Demon Rum?" Mildred asked.

No one came forward to claim they had.

"Charge dismissed." Mildred rapped her gavel. "Prudent. Callie, have you been prudent?"

"I've been very careful with my money since Aunt Samuela died," Callie claimed.

"Does anyone have any evidence to the contrary?" Mildred asked.

Mrs. Corrigan raised her hand.

"Noreen," Mildred recognized her.

Mrs. Corrigan opened the huge ledger balanced on her lap. She ran her bony finger down the page.

"Callie came into our store and bought three bolts of cloth and a bag of candy four months ago. I wouldn't say three bolts of cloth in one trip was being prudent."

"Has she bought anything since?"

As she ran her finger down the column, Mrs. Corrigan grimaced. "Nothing except a little coffee two weeks ago."

"Can you remember the last time she bought any bolts of cloth?"

Mrs. Corrigan flipped through several pages. At last she stopped, ran her finger down the page until it was almost to the bottom. Then she looked up at Mildred and said, "The third of June, 1864. One bolt of dark green calico."

"Four bolts of cloth in two years? I guess that's about as prudent as a person can get." Mildred rapped her gavel again. "Charge dismissed."

"That still leaves one very big problem unresolved," Widow Marsden insisted. "Callie, you've never been married, have you?"

"No. Everyone in town knows that."

A rustle of murmurs arose from the membership.

"Yet, even as we speak, you admit you're bearing the child of your farmhand?" Widow Marsden accused.

Callie lifted her head proudly and stared Widow Marsden in the eye.

"Yes."

She had never breathed a word to a soul about what she'd discovered about the true relationship between herself and her supposed aunt. She never would. She couldn't shame the memory of her own mother by exposing her for the hypocrite she was. On the other hand, she was determined never to be so concerned, as her mother had been, with what everyone else would say that she would deny her own child. She would *never* deny her baby!

"This man disappeared from your ranch four months ago, isn't that right?" Widow Marsden continued.

"Yes."

"You haven't heard from him since, have you?"

"No."

"Is there any possibility that this man will return to make an honest woman of you?"

Callie swallowed hard. She had been taught to tell the truth. She wouldn't stop now.

"I very seriously doubt that I'll ever see him again."

She tried not to let her throat catch with the pain she still felt. Day after day, for the past four months, she'd forced herself to face the fact that Harden had used her and abandoned her. She would have thought by now she'd have hardened her heart, but she hadn't.

Widow Marsden turned to face the membership of the Society. "Ladies," she declared. "We were appointed by Samuela Jackson to oversee the behavior of her niece. It's pretty evident the girl has broken—nay, blatantly flaunted—every good behavior her aunt had ever intended for her. It's also pretty clear that we would be as remiss in our duty as Callie has been in hers if we did not carry out Samuela's wishes."

A murmur of mixed responses arose from the membership.

"We've got to sell the farm and distribute the proceeds to a worthy missionary charity. We've *got* to!"

Widow Marsden slammed her fist on the table for emphasis, then glared at Mildred.

"If *you*, as president of the Society, do not insist that the statutes of the will be complied with, you'll be remiss in your duties, and if you're remiss in your duties, you can be expelled from office!"

Mildred glared back at Widow Marsden. But the sinking

feeling in the pit of Callie's stomach told her she wouldn't be owning her farm much longer.

"Callie," Mildred said with a heavy sigh, "as difficult as it is for me to do this, I must agree, the evidence—not to mention your own admission—is overwhelmingly against you keeping your farm."

"I understand, Mildred," Callie told her. "I don't hold any grudge against . . . well, against most of you."

"Very well, then. I suppose the time has come to put this to a vote. All those in favor of . . . dispossessing Carolyn Jackson from the farm bequeathed to her by her late aunt, Samuela Jackson, raise your hand."

18

"*Y*OU CAN'T VOTE yet!" Harden's voice rang through the hallowed sanctuary of the ladies of the Society.

The ladies gave a collective gasp as he strode boldly up the aisle between them, to stand directly in front of Callie.

She was glad she was already sitting down or she'd have fallen. Her heart pounded at the very sight of him—in spite of the fact that she hadn't seen him in four months, in spite of the fact that she hated the very sight of him for leaving her the way he did.

If he'd left her, why had he come back? Was he as bad as Eugene Redmond, thinking, even after he'd messed up so badly at a job, that he could come back to the same job again and again?

Mildred pounded the gavel on the tabletop until Callie thought for certain one of them would have to break. At least the membership quieted down.

"Why, what a surprise, seeing you again, Mr. . . . Daniels,

isn't it?" Mildred commented sarcastically. She glared venomously at him.

You can't hate him any more than I do, Callie silently told Mildred.

"Will you please enlighten us as to why we can't vote at a meeting of our own Society?" Mildred demanded.

"You can't vote on this item because all the evidence hasn't been presented."

"What makes you think there's more evidence?"

The membership of the Society leaned forward in their chairs and strained to hear what Harden had to say.

"Because nobody's asked me for any, and I'm the one with the evidence."

"Evidence!" Callie demanded, rising as quickly as her changed form would allow her. "How dare you come here today, telling people you have evidence to present against me so I'll lose my farm! Haven't you done enough already?"

"More than I'd realized."

Harden glanced boldly at her rounded figure. He smiled at her with as much love, admiration, and devotion in his eyes as she'd ever seen. She was puzzled. How could a man claim to love her so, yet leave her in such a predicament?

But she couldn't let herself be taken in by that clever, charming charlatan ever again.

"Who said I was against you, Callie?"

She glared at him angrily. "You certainly haven't gone out of your way to do anything *for* me!"

"I'm not done yet," he warned her with a mischievous twinkle in his eyes.

She turned away. She couldn't be fooled by him again.

Harden turned to Mildred. "May I ask a question of the ladies of the Society?"

"I suppose so." Mildred turned to Olive. "There isn't anything in the by-laws that states that a man can't attend one of these meetings, is there?"

Olive flipped through her book for the proper protocol. "I don't think so."

"There isn't any rule that a man can't have his say at a meeting, is there?"

Olive flipped a few more pages. "I don't find any. He just can't run for any office or chair any committees."

Mildred nodded. "Then I suppose you can go ahead, Mr. Daniels. As much as I wish there was a by-law stating we could string you up by your . . . er, thumbs, or shoot you on sight, I suppose we'll just have to allow you to have your say—and then get out."

"I appreciate your indulgence, ma'am—I think. I'll be brief."

He turned to the membership.

"If a lady falls in love with a man, and he falls in love with her, would anyone consider that immoral?"

The membership voiced a unanimous nay.

"If that lady finds herself in a family way, and the fellow responsible for that family way marries her, is that immoral?"

The membership voiced a mixture of yea and nay. Several of the ladies who voiced the most audible nays exhibited quite a few guilty blushes.

Harden turned to Callie.

"If a lady in a family way would accept the proposal of the man who loves her, would she still lose her farm?"

He held his arms outstretched to her.

Callie jammed both fists onto her hips and lifted her chin defiantly at him.

"Thunderation! I wouldn't even marry Herbert Tucker to save my farm. What makes you think I'd want to marry you now—even to save my farm?" she demanded. "I hired you before. I took you into my home—like Cleopatra nursed a viper in her bosom—to work my farm and save my farm for me, and you've made me lose it! Do you really believe I could ever trust you again?"

"Again?" he repeated. His hands dropped to his sides. "I would have hoped you'd never lost your trust in me."

"Trust you?" she repeated angrily. "You've been the most untrustworthy, dishonest, traitorous, faithless, perfidious—"

He tried to step closer to her, but Callie held out a warning hand, holding him back.

"I was never faithless to you, Callie," he said very quietly. "You knew I loved you. You also knew I had an important job to do. You also knew I was the kind of man who would do what he'd been assigned to do."

Callie stood there, twisting her mouth into a wry grimace.

"Even if I had to go away, didn't you trust me enough to know I'd come back?"

"It took you four months to come back!" she cried. "You couldn't even leave me a note letting me know where you'd gone."

"I couldn't risk having you know. I only did it to protect you."

Callie crossed her arms tightly over her breasts. "A likely story!"

"I'd been sent to spy on Fielding," Harden explained.

The ladies of the Society murmured amongst themselves. "I never did trust that man!" several maintained.

"He was suspected of masterminding a plot to rob the Army payroll," Harden explained. "The men who had helped him all ended up dead under rather suspicious circumstances, until he was the only one left who knew where the gold was hidden. He was responsible for the deaths of so many people, he had to be stopped."

"That just goes to show," one lady maintained. "You just never know who your neighbors are or what they're really up to."

"No one realized Fielding wasn't the real mastermind until *his* boss, a former Confederate captain named Delaney Forsythe, sent orders to dig up the gold and deliver it to him in Denver."

"Oh, don't you just hate it when a good Southern boy goes wrong?" one of the ladies wailed.

"I guess this means he's a Union boy." The lady gave a sigh. "Well, I suppose if Callie can stand him . . ."

"He left in the middle of the night," Harden continued. "I had to follow him, but he already had a head start. That made it all the more difficult to catch up with him. I chased him all the way out to Denver. I finally caught him, recovered the gold, and brought him to the Fort Leavenworth Prison. He's going to be spending a little time there as a guest of our government."

"Well, good for you!" Callie declared. Her voice held a little more sarcasm and less of the intense hatred it held earlier. "I'm glad you've turned out to be such a success. But you've still left me in a horribly difficult position."

"It was good for me, Callie. It could be good for you, too."

"I don't see how."

"I did my job so well, I've been given a promotion, but I haven't accepted it yet."

"Why not?"

"Because I'm not sure if I'll go back to my old profession or not." He reached up and scratched the back of his head. "Lately, I've been giving a lot of consideration to becoming a farmer. I've come back to marry you, my love, if you'll still have me."

"You really want to marry me?" *It couldn't be true,* she decided. He couldn't possibly want to marry her.

"More than anything else in the world."

"I want to marry you. You know I've always wanted to. But—"

"Don't be afraid, Callie," he urged. He took a step closer to her. This time she didn't move back or hold her hand out to keep him away.

"I'm afraid you'll leave me," she admitted. "No one has ever wanted me enough to stay around."

"Just because I'm not with you twenty-four hours a day doesn't mean I'd ever leave you. Just because my body isn't right there with you doesn't mean I'm not still with you in my heart."

"But you left me!"

"Just because you weren't in my arms doesn't mean you were ever out of my thoughts—not for one moment."

He reached out to touch her arm. She didn't pull away. She had missed him so much. She wanted to feel his warm hands against her flesh again. She wanted to feel the thrilling rush of passion when he touched her.

"Did you ever forget about me while I was gone?"

"No, Harden," she easily admitted. "From the time I got up in the morning and threw up, until the time I collapsed into bed exhausted every evening, you were always in my heart."

"Just because I was gone, did you neglect to milk the cows or feed the chickens?"

She looked at him in surprise. "Of course not!"

"Why not?"

"That's a stupid question. Of course not, because that's my job."

"I had a job to do, too, Callie. I did it. I did it well. But that doesn't mean you weren't on my mind every minute of the day."

She was silent as she considered his words.

"Every minute of the day, I thought about how much I wanted to hold you in my arms, to kiss you. I thought about returning to you, and asking you to forgive me and to marry me."

The membership of the Society released a gasp of delight, mixed with a few romantic sighs.

"Will you marry me, Callie?" he asked. Once again he held out his arms in a welcoming embrace. He waited.

Callie knew she needed to make a decision, one that would affect not just her life, but Harden's and the life of their child.

What would she do with a man who might go running off

chasing bad men at the drop of a hat? What would she do without him?

She looked at him, standing there before her. His eyes were every bit as luminous blue as the first time she'd seen him. His shoulders were still set proudly, but his eyes were watching her with a deep pleading and a desperate worry that she'd deny his supplication.

"Oh, say yes!" someone in the crowd cried.

"If she don't want him, I'll take him," someone else volunteered.

"She's a dang fool if she don't!"

Mildred rapped the gavel. "Ladies, I do not recall putting this matter to a vote!"

The membership fell silent.

"Now, be quiet so we can all hear what she decides."

In the deafening silence that followed, Harden murmured, "I love you, Callie, with all my heart. Please say you'll marry me."

She stepped into his outstretched arms and allowed him to envelop her in his warm, strong embrace.

"Yes, Harden. I love you, too."

The membership began to clap and cheer. Several ladies pulled frothy, lace-edged handkerchiefs out of their sleeves and began dabbing at the corners of their eyes.

Mildred rapped the gavel repeatedly until she had everyone's attention.

"I proclaim that, being as Callie Jackson is soon to be married to Mr. Daniels, which makes her an invaluable bulwark to the community as an example of the wedded bliss that promotes the common good and prosperity of society in general and the American way of life in general, and being as Callie Jackson soon-to-be Daniels is also soon to be a mother, which makes her an invaluable asset to the community as an excellent example of those gentler and nobler instincts that only a mother can provide, that she is indeed a most moral, sober, and upright lady, and that she be granted complete rights to determine the future of her own property, under the wise and watchful guidance of her loving husband—"

The ladies of the Society began to cheer.

"Just a minute! Just a minute!" Widow Marsden jumped up and declared. "You can't do this. Callie has behaved in a completely improper fashion—"

Trying to ignore her outburst, Mildred continued, "All those in favor of approving of Callie Jackson's marriage, say yea."

"You can't do this!"

The ladies declared, "Yea."

"All those in favor of approving of Callie's ability to dispose of her own property at her own discretion, say yea."

The ladies declared, "Yea."

"You can't do this!" Widow Marsden continued to protest.

"Olive?"

"Yes, Mildred?"

"As parliamentarian of the Society, what do you have to add to this discussion?"

"Well," said Olive, leafing through her little book, "According to Article LIV, Section A, Item 3 of the Society by-laws, anyone adamantly differing in opinion from the majority of the members, and creating unwarranted friction within the group thereby, can be expelled from the Society."

"All those in favor of declaring Widow Marsden's opinion as differing adamantly from that of the majority of the members, say yea."

The ladies declared, "Yea."

"All those in favor of declaring Widow Marsden's behavior as creating unwarranted friction within the group . . ."

"Stop!" Widow Marsden cried. She humphed and snorted. She readjusted her flapping black shawl. "I see the way things are going. Well, never you mind. I'll recall my motion—this time. But this isn't the end of this. I'll be back."

"Oh, hush, Naomi, and sit down. Now, where was I? Oh, yes." Mildred turned to Callie. "Carolyn Jackson, as the duly appointed arbiters of your behavior, we require you to marry Mr. Daniels forthwith. Can you comply with that requirement?"

"Oh, yes!" Callie replied.

"We require you to marry at your earliest convenience— and I do mean earliest!"

"Yes, we will."

"I believe Mr. Preston will be waiting at the close of this meeting, more than happy to marry you in his parlor." She added quietly, "He'd just have a conniption fit if you went over to those Lutherans."

Suddenly, Harden leaned over and placed a resounding kiss on Callie's cheek. Then he bent down and swept her up into his arms.

"Before another minute passes, I intend to call you my lawfully wedded wife."

She wrapped her arms about his neck and laid her head on his shoulder. "I can't think of anything I'd rather do than spend the rest of my life with you and our child."

"Children," Harden corrected.

Our Town ...where love is always right around the corner!

● ●

__*Harbor Lights* by Linda Kreisel	0-515-11899-0/$5.99	
__*Humble Pie* by Deborah Lawrence	0-515-11900-8/$5.99	
__*Candy Kiss* by Ginny Aiken	0-515-11941-5/$5.99	
__*Cedar Creek* by Willa Hix	0-515-11958-X/$5.99	
__*Sugar and Spice* by DeWanna Pace	0-515-11970-9/$5.99	
__*Cross Roads* by Carol Card Otten	0-515-11985-7/$5.99	
__*Blue Ribbon* by Jessie Gray	0-515-12003-0/$5.99	
__*The Lighthouse* by Linda Eberhardt	0-515-12020-0/$5.99	
__*The Hat Box* by Deborah Lawrence	0-515-12033-2/$5.99	
__*Country Comforts* by Virginia Lee	0-515-12064-2/$5.99	
__*Grand River* by Kathryn Kent	0-515-12067-7/$5.99	
__*Beckoning Shore* by DeWanna Pace	0-515-12101-0/$5.99	
__*Whistle Stop* by Lisa Higdon	0-515-12085-5/$5.99	
__*Still Sweet* by Debra Marshall (8/97)	0-515-12130-4/$5.99	

Payable in U.S. funds. No cash accepted. Postage & handling: $1.75 for one book, 75¢ for each additional. Maximum postage $5.50. Prices, postage and handling charges may change without notice. Visa, Amex, MasterCard call 1-800-788-6262, ext. 1, or fax 1-201-933-2316; refer to ad # 637b

Or, check above books   Bill my: ☐ Visa ☐ MasterCard ☐ Amex _____ (expires)
and send this order form to:
The Berkley Publishing Group   Card#_____

P.O. Box 12289, Dept. B   Daytime Phone #_____ ($10 minimum)
Newark, NJ 07101-5289   Signature_____
Please allow 4-6 weeks for delivery.   Or enclosed is my: ☐ check ☐ money order
Foreign and Canadian delivery 8-12 weeks.

Ship to:

Name_____	Book Total	$_____
Address_____	Applicable Sales Tax (NY, NJ, PA, CA, GST Can.)	$_____
City_____	Postage & Handling	$_____
State/ZIP_____	Total Amount Due	$_____

Bill to: Name_____
Address_____City_____
State/ZIP_____